DEADLY INTENT

ALSO BY BRENT TOWNS

DEADLY INTENT
A TEAM REAPER THRILLER
BOOK 2

BRENT TOWNS

**ROUGH
EDGES
PRESS**

Deadly Intent
Paperback Edition
Copyright © 2025 (As Revised) by Brent Towns

Rough Edges Press
An Imprint of Wolfpack Publishing
1707 E. Diana Street
Tampa, FL 33610

roughedgespress.com

Paperback ISBN 978-1-68549-623-4
Ebook ISBN 978-1-68549-622-7

According to a 2012 UN report, there are 2.4 million people around the world who are victims of human trafficking at any given time. In this annual US$32 billion industry, 80% of victims are sexually exploited.

From the Central Intelligence Agency World Fact Book:

Ecuador: *Significant transit country for cocaine originating in Colombia and Peru, with much of the US-bound cocaine passing through Ecuadorian Pacific waters.*

DEADLY INTENT

CHAPTER 1

"SHIT! RPG!" Kane screamed as he saw the tell-tale sign of a white smoke trail, just before the black SUV in front of them was blown sky high in an orange ball of flame. "Cara, back up!"

Cara instinctively locked the tires and skidded to a halt, then slammed the shift into reverse, and their SUV started backward with a squeal of tires.

From the back seat, Kane heard Axe say, "One wrong move, motherfucker, and I'll put a bullet in your head."

"Reaper One, report," the earpiece demanded.

Almost immediately, there was a loud drumming on the outside of their armored vehicle as though they were being smashed by a severe hail storm. But in this instance, the hailstones were made of lead, bullets ricocheting off the windscreen, their scars a reminder of the predicament the team found themselves in.

"Come on, Cara, move!" Kane snapped. He brought his HK416 up and held it across his chest.

"RPG!" the shout from the backseat was heavily-accented Spanish. "On the right!"

"Cara!"

Cara Billings spun the wheel, and the SUV slid sideways, the RPG round barely missing them as it seemed to pass in front of them just above the hood, and blew up when it hit the building on the other side of the road.

The voice in Kane's ear shouted at him again, "Reaper One, report."

"We're taking fire! I say again, we're taking fire!" he paused and then said, "The two DEA officers are dead. RPG hit their SUV."

A muffled curse in his earpiece made Kane turn to the right where he spotted the traffic jam behind them. The third SUV in their convoy, containing Traynor and the new man Craig Spencer, ex-CIA and new operations commander of Team Reaper, was stationary. Kane watched on as multiple rounds ricocheted off their vehicle as it took heavy fire.

Beyond that, the *Federale* armored technical with its fifty-caliber machine gun on the back was spraying a wide swathe of rooftops to their right with fire. Abruptly the feed of belted ammunition was cut off as the vehicle disappeared in a ball of flame from an RPG strike.

The *Federale* escort was now taking heavy casualties from both sides of the street. "Talk to me, people," Kane snapped.

From the rear seat, Axe said, "I've got fucking tangos on the rooftops and on the street, Reaper. We need to shift our asses out of here, now."

The big ex-recon marine sniper cursed again as more bullets peppered the side of their vehicle.

"Same this side," Arenas put in. Former Mexican Special Forces, Arenas was used to coming under fire, but the weight of the firepower being brought down by the Ciudad Cartel had even him worried.

"Fuck!" Kane snapped. "Defend the package!"

"Now you're talking," Axe growled. "About fucking time."

The doors on their SUV flew open as the team alighted and rapidly brought their weapons into play. Like Kane, all were armed with HK416s. They also wore ballistic vests loaded down with extra ammunition for their carbines and smaller sidearms.

In his earpiece, Kane heard Spencer bark, "Damn it, Reaper One, get back in your vehicle."

Ignoring the order, Kane picked out a target through the HK's sights and put a tattooed cartel soldier down.

"This is more like it, Reaper!" Axe shouted, the whiteness of his teeth shining in stark contrast against the darkness of his thick beard when he gave a mirthless smile.

A constant staccato of bullets peppered the SUV. A cry of alarm from the other side of the vehicle was followed by Cara's voice. "Reaper, Arenas is down! He's hit."

"Christ!" Kane swore. "Check him out, Cara. Axe, give her cover."

"I'm fine," came the semi-muffled voice over the comms. "Everyone hold."

"Reaper One? Zero. Give me a God damned sitrep, over!"

"Not now, Zero."

"Is the package OK, Reaper One? Over."

Kane shook his head. "Axe, is Gallo still alive?"

There was a moment of radio silence, and a gruff voice said, "He's fucked, Reaper."

"Did you get that, Zero?"

"Copy. The package is dead."

Another RPG shot across their position and exploded beyond their SUV. A shower of dirt and debris rained down on top of them. It was only a matter of time before one found its mark.

Kane said, "Teller, find us a way out of here before we all end up KIA."

"On it, Reaper One."

"Drop a Hellfire on the bastards, Master Sergeant."

"Sorry, Reaper Four, our current rules of engagement..."

"Oh, shut up and get us out of here!" Axe snapped.

"Copy."

Tucked in behind the door on the passenger side, Kane toggled his radio. "Cara, how you doing?"

There was sarcasm in her voice when it came back. "We're just peachy."

"Hang in there."

"Carlos?"

"I hurt like a *puta*."

Kane glanced back and saw that Traynor and Spencer were no longer inside their own vehicle and had opened fire at the attackers.

The following events seemed to happen in slow motion. A cartel soldier appeared from within a half-demolished building on the left of the stalled SUV. He lifted an RPG to his shoulder and sighted on Traynor's vehicle.

As Kane brought up his HK, he shouted into his mic. "Traynor! RPG!"

Before Reaper could fire, the cartel soldier loosed the Rocket Propelled Grenade. It blasted across the short distance and impacted the black SUV with catastrophic force.

Without so much as a thought for his own safety, Kane was up and moving. "Cara! On me."

His six-foot-four frame stood out like a beacon which attracted bullets like moths to a flame. He reached Traynor just as the orange ball of fire from the exploding SUV subsided. Kneeling beside the prone figure, he looked for signs of life.

"Pete? Pete? Can you hear me, buddy?"

Checking him over, he discovered that by some miracle Traynor seemed to be no worse for wear. A couple of abrasions but that was about it. Kane slapped him, hard.

Traynor sat up and gasped for air. He blinked a few times and focussed on Kane. "What?"

"Are you good?"

"Yeah."

"Then get back in the fight."

Traynor scooped up his 416 and inspected it for damage.

"Cara," Kane said. "How's Spencer?"

"He'll live."

The heat from the burning SUV was becoming unbearable. Reaper glanced about and saw the few remaining *Federales* making their last stand. Their commanding officer, a sub-officer named Perez was issuing orders while another of his men dragged a wounded comrade to relative safety behind one of their vehicles.

Kane toggled his talk button and said, "Axe? Time for plan B."

Up ahead near the black SUV, he saw the big man turn to stare in his direction. "What the fuck is plan B?"

———

TEAM REAPER HQ, EL PASO, TEXAS

"What the fuck is plan B?" echoed Assistant Attorney General, Mike Turner.

Team Reaper leader, Luis Ferrero turned and stared at his middle-aged boss from Washington and shrugged his broad shoulders. "No idea."

Turner shook his head. "Christ, what a screw-up. The Mexican government should have allowed a Black Hawk extraction like we asked for. Now we'll be lucky if we don't lose them all."

TEAM REAPER HQ, EL PASO, TEXAS—SIX HOURS EARLIER

"The Mexican government has turned down our request for a Black Hawk extraction of the package," Ferrero stated. "So, it means you'll do it by vehicle."

"Rolling fucking death traps, don't you mean?" Axel 'Axe' Burton growled.

"I'm with Axe," John 'Reaper' Kane agreed. He rose from his seat and walked up to the recon photo. It marked their route from the Federale holding facility in Ciudad Juárez where they were to collect their package, to the border. "This part here with all the double and triple story buildings is a killing zone."

"It's all we've got, I'm afraid," Mike Turner said. "It's the quickest way out of Mexico. The Mexicans have assured me you'll also have a Federale escort."

Carlos Arenas, Ex-Mexican special forces commander, snorted and shook his head.

"You have something to add, Carlos?" a tall, thin man asked from where he stood beside Ferrero.

Craig Spencer was the new team operations commander. EX-CIA, he had been brought in after the team's initial mission against the Montoya Cartel. He had a square jaw and an irritating demeanor, and when any of the team questioned his point of view on anything operational, he took it personally. As now.

"I would not trust the Federales," he said. "Some of them are in the cartel's pockets. And as you Americans say, it only takes one bad apple."

"Didn't you hear the assistant attorney general? We have assurances. If you don't like it, stay behind."

"Easy, Spencer," Kane cautioned him. "He's only saying what we all know. Besides, it's all of our asses on the line out there."

Spencer glared at Kane through pale blue eyes. "How about you worry about your team, and I'll worry about the operation."

Kane was about to fire back a retort when Cara interrupted, "Has there been any chatter from the cartels?"

Ferrero shook his head. "They're totally silent, which means they're definitely up to something."

Cara Billings was a former marine lieutenant and deputy sheriff. She had short dark hair, a slim physique, tanned face, and was Team Reaper's armorer. For anything fire-power related, Cara was their first port of call.

"Can it be postponed until we are able to work out a better extraction for the package?"

The 'Package' was Juan-Carlos Gallo, head of the Ciudad Cartel. Wanted in the US for drug trafficking, murder, extortion, human trafficking, and arms dealing, to name a few. When the Mexican government had reached out to American law officials, saying that he was in their *possession and did they want to come and get him, there was no hesitation.*

Ferrero shook his head. "The Federales want Gallo gone. It wouldn't be the first time the cartels have attacked a Federale building to free one of their own."

"It's still fucked," Axe growled once more. "But I want to know what the DEA guys think. After all, their asses are in the wind as much as ours."

All eyes gravitated to the two DEA agents who were to take official possession of Gallo and handle any paperwork that needed to be signed on his handover. They were both men of considerable experience.

Ben Nash, the older of the two, had served in Colombia, while Tim Gregory had served in Afghanistan.

"It is what it is," Nash said noncommittally. Gregory nodded his agreement.

"All right then," Axe said, his voice dripping with sarcasm. "They're ready to die, let's do it."

———

FEDERALE HQ, CIUDAD JUÁREZ

While the two DEA agents signed release papers for the package under the watchful eye of Spencer, Ramon Perez, the commander of the Federale escort sought out Kane. He found him giving last minute instructions to his team.

"Carlos, you and Axe secure the package in the back of our SUV. Cara will drive, and I'll ride shotgun. Whatever happens, we protect the package. There are a lot of people waiting for him back on US soil."

"What about me?" Traynor asked.

"You get to babysit our illustrious leader."

"I hate you."

Kane and the others smiled. The team leader punched him lightly on one of his tattooed arms. "Just remember, the team loves you, Pete."

The tall, ex-undercover DEA agent in his thirties, screwed up his unshaven face. "Fuck you."

This brought forth laughter which helped ease some of the tension in the air.

Perez cleared his throat to get Kane's attention. The Team Reaper leader turned to face the stocky man. Dressed in dark blue, Perez was armed with, as were most of his men, an FX-05 Xiuhcoatl Carbine.

"Something I can do for you, Suboficial Perez?"

Suboficial was the equivalent of a warrant officer in the British and US armed forces. Perez set his square jaw firm and said, "I get the feeling that your team does not think much of us, Sargento."

Kane said, "Let's just put it down to bad experiences."

Perez nodded at Arenas. "Yet you have an ex-capitán primero of Fuerzas Especiales Mexicanas with you."

"He's earned his stripes. Carlos is one of us now."

"Just so you know, Sargento, none of my men are cartel. They will fight alongside you and die if need be."

Kane stared into the man's eyes and held out a hand. "Good to have you on board, Suboficial Perez."

Perez took it in a firm grip. "You can count on us."

Spencer emerged from inside the building and called out, "Mount up!"

Behind him, the two DEA agents appeared with Gallo between them. Kane signaled to Axe and Arenas, and they stepped forward and relieved Nash and Gregory of their package.

"What's going on?" Spencer demanded.

"He's riding with us," Kane told him.

"Let me remind you, Kane, I'm operations commander," he hissed.

"You may be operations commander," Kane conceded, "but I'm the field commander. He comes with us. You and Traynor will follow in the third SUV."

"This isn't over."

Kane ignored the threat. "Let's get the hell out of here."

———

Bouncing across the intersection, Cara let her foot off the throttle of the SUV slightly. Then once again, she depressed it and brought the vehicle back up to speed. The convoy had sat on fifty-miles-per-hour for most of the journey so far. They were all very aware that once they reached the bottleneck, it would slow them down considerably.

Kane toggled his mic. "Everyone keep your eyes open up here."

"Copy."

"Bravo Three, do you read? Over."

"Copy, Reaper One."

"You got anything?"

"Roger. I'm seeing lots of activity on the rooftops."

"Copy."

"Nash, Gregory, you copy that last?"

"Roger."

Kane stared out the window to his right. The dusty sidewalk seemed to be almost totally deserted; a sure sign there was going to be trouble. He flicked the selector switch on the HK416 to fire a burst. Out of habit, he dropped out the box magazine, checked it, then reinserted it.

It wasn't long after that when the lead SUV blew up.

———

TEAM REAPER HQ, EL PASO, TEXAS

Ferrero massaged his temples, the greying hairline moving with the circular motion. "Teller, have you got an alternative route yet?"

The Airforce UAV tech shook his head without taking his eyes from the screen in front of him. "Working on it, sir."

"Work faster. Swift, get onto our friends across the border and ask them to get some help out there ASAP."

"Zero?" UAV pilot Brooke Reynolds called to Ferrero. "It looks like Reaper has his team on the move, sir."

Reynolds, like Cara, was tall and athletic, however, her hair was long and black and tied back in a ponytail. Ferrero looked at the larger screen in front of him. She was right; the team was moving towards an alley across from the burning SUV.

"Christ," Ferrero muttered. "They're headed into the lion's den."

"I count ten friendlies in all, sir," Reynolds reported.

"Damnit!" Ferrero cursed. "They were almost to the border. Do you have any idea where they're headed, Bravo Three?"

"No, sir. Nothing over that way but warehouses. Unless..."

"Unless, what?" Turner asked.

"They're three blocks from the warehouse the DEA are sitting on."

Ferrero nodded. "Reaper One? Zero. Do you read? Over."

"Copy, Zero."

"Are you figuring on slipping out the back door? Over."

"Zero? Reaper One. That's affirmative. Over."

"Good luck. Zero out."

Turner stepped in beside Ferrero and muttered, "The DEA is going to love this."

TEAM REAPER, CIUDAD JUÁREZ

"Axe! On your left," Kane snapped as they made their way along the narrow alley.

Axe brought his weapon around and fired a burst at a figure leaning out of a second-floor window to get a better shot. The bullets stitched the cartel soldier across the chest, and he fell forward from the opening and landed with a soggy thump at the big man's feet.

"Bet that hurt," he hissed.

Behind him, Kane fired his own burst at another shooter higher up. Following him was Cara. She had her HK up to her shoulder, her finger along the side plate not far from the trigger.

At the rear of the small column came Arenas who watched their six. He'd already shot two tattooed figures down.

In all, they'd managed to escape the buzzsaw with ten souls. Six from Team Reaper and four *Federales*, one of whom was Perez.

They continued to make their way warily along the alley.

"Lookout!" Axe snapped and dived behind a pile of wooden crates.

At the far end of the alley, a figure appeared with an RPG. He raised it to his shoulder and fired. Nine of the ten survivors dived onto the rubbish-strewn asphalt. Only Cara remained on her feet. She raised her HK with an uncanny calmness and dropped the sights onto the cartel soldier who'd fired the RPG. She stroked her trigger just as the rocket-propelled grenade streaked low over her head and exploded in a ball of fire further along the alley near its mouth. She didn't flinch, and the 5.56 NATO round punched into the would-be killer's head, blowing his brains out across the lumpy pavement.

"Tango down," Cara's voice was steady.

"Fuck," Axe swore. "I think I landed in dog shit."

If the situation hadn't been so dire, the remarks would have been funny. Instead, Kane said, "Cara, take point. Axe, you take over from Carlos."

"Where the hell are we going?" Spencer demanded.

"The warehouse."

"What warehouse?"

Kane grew testy. "The one the DEA is sitting on."

"We can't go there. We'll ruin their operation."

"We don't have time for this shit, Spencer. Come or stay, it's your choice."

"Reaper One? Bravo Three. We have eyes on hostiles converging on your position. Suggest you keep moving."

"Copy, Bravo Three. We're moving now."

The street at the end of the alley was deserted. No civilians could be seen in either direction, only parked cars. Cara stopped to sweep both right and left with her HK and found no targets. She toggled her mic. "Bravo Three? Reaper Two. Do you still have eyes on the tangos? Over."

"Negative, Reaper Two," Teller's calm voice came back. "They've gone to ground. But they're there."

Kane reached her shoulder. "What is it?"

"See for yourself."

Reaper eased out and scanned the street. "Looks mighty empty."

"But where the hell are they?"

"The alley on the other side looks clear. Think you can make it?"

Cara shrugged. "I guess there is only one way to find out."

"Wait," Kane said and toggled his mic. "Bravo Three? Reaper One. Is there anything on the rooftops at this moment?"

"Negative, Reaper One."

Kane turned and waved Arenas and Axe forward. "Traynor, watch our six."

"Roger."

"What's up, boss?" Axe growled.

Kane screwed up his nose as his olfactory system was overwhelmed by the stench of dog shit. "Man, you stink."

"Is that it?"

"No. I'm sending Cara across the street to the alley. I want you to keep an eye on the windows over that way. Carlos, you take the right of the street, and I'll take the left. Consider everything you see as hostile." He turned to Cara. "We've got you."

Cara nodded, took a deep breath, and then ran.

Into a hailstorm of lead.

"Window, one o'clock," Axe said calmly and squeezed off a shot. "Tango down."

Kane saw another cartel soldier rise from behind a parked car. He shifted his aim and nailed the man right in the tattooed face.

More appeared and the three shooters kept up a steady rate of fire at their targets. Cara ran, head down with her weapon across her chest. Bullets kicked up from the asphalt around her feet. Then Kane heard a weapon open fire from almost directly above him and to his left. Fist-sized chunks of the road started to lift behind Cara as the shooter followed her track. Then at the last moment, when it seemed that she would be cut down, she dived behind a parked car.

"Motherfucker!" Axe shouted. "Where the hell did the fifty-cal come from?"

"We've gotta take it out!" Kane shouted back.

Across the road, Cara hid behind the safety of the car's engine block as more rounds from the .50 caliber machine gun thundered into the vehicle.

In her earpiece, she heard Kane's voice. "Reaper Two, are you OK?"

"You want to shut this prick down sometime soon?"

"Copy. We're working on it."

"We need a rabbit," Axe pointed out.

"What is a rabbit?" Arenas asked as he put down another cartel soldier.

"Someone to draw his fire so we can take him out."

"OK. Don't miss."

Arenas broke cover and started across the street. Immediately, the shooter shifted his aim and concentrated his fire on the darting figure.

"Ballsy," Axe grumbled.

Both Kane and Axe stepped out and turned. They raised their carbines and found their target. The barrel poked from a window and spewed fire at the fleeing Mexican.

"I can't get a shot at it!" Kane shouted to Axe.

"I've got it covered," the big ex-sniper bellowed, reaching into his pocket and retrieving something.

Before Reaper realized what it was, the pin on the grenade had been pulled, and the thing was hurtling through the air and into the open window. He looked at Kane and said, "You might want to duck."

The grenade detonated with an immense roar,

blowing debris out onto the street below. Kane and Axe retreated into the alley out of the way.

The machine gun fell silent, and Kane stared at the big man. "Where the fuck did you get a grenade from?"

Axe gave him a broad grin. "Never leave home without one."

Reaper turned back and called to Perez. "Get your men across the street. Now!"

Perez barked some orders to his remaining men, and they pushed forward to the mouth of the alley.

"Reaper One? Bravo Three, copy?"

Kane paused and toggled his mic. "Copy, Bravo Three."

"There is a crowd of around twelve armed hostiles coming along the street from your right, over."

"What the hell is this? Fucking Syria?"

"Say again, Reaper One?"

"I said copy, Bravo Three."

Perez moved in beside Kane. "Is everything OK?"

"You need to get your guys across the street. Don't stop for anything. You'll have cartel assholes coming at you from the right."

"This day just gets better, *Amigo*."

"Keep your head down."

The four *Federales* broke cover and started across the street. Once again, the fire from the cartel soldiers intensified, and bullets pinged off the asphalt all around them. The second man in line suddenly cried out and fell hard. He tried to rise, but a second bullet slammed into his head, and he slumped flat. The man directly behind him stopped to check on his fallen comrade.

"Keep going!" Kane shouted at him. "Keep going!"

The man didn't heed their warning shouts and paid the ultimate price. Two bullet strikes put him down beside his friend on the asphalt, and blood began to pool around them.

"Your plan seems to be working just fine, Kane," Spencer said with an overabundance of sarcasm.

"You're next. You and Traynor."

"If you think I'm going out there, you've got another thing coming," Spencer said defiantly.

"Pete, you ready?"

Traynor gave him a grim look. "I guess."

"Movement on our six," Axe snapped and fired a burst at two cartel men who'd entered the alley. "Get your ass out there, Pete."

When the former DEA agent started across, Kane came out with him. Only for a few steps, but enough to draw some of the fire away from his man and to give himself line of sight along the street at the approaching crowd. He fired two bursts, and they dispersed behind the cover of parked cars. However, they left two of their own on the street.

"Get your ass back in here, Reaper, you crazy bastard!" Axe called out.

Kane almost casually re-entered the alley mouth and leaned against the wall. Meanwhile, Traynor had made it across and dived behind a battered Ford pickup.

"Reaper One? Zero, Over."

"Copy, Zero."

"The Mexicans have a helicopter up, and it should be overhead in one minute. Over."

"Copy, Zero."

"Reaper, they'll provide you with overwatch. Zero out."

"Reaper One to Reaper Team. Everyone sit tight. There's a helo inbound to provide us with support."

Through the gunfire, Kane could suddenly make out

the whop-whop of the helicopter. It grew steadily louder and then swept overhead with an immense roar. It was a UH-60 Black Hawk. Kane could see a door gunner as it banked to come around. It bled off airspeed as it did so and slowed right down.

The door gunner opened fire at targets of opportunity along the street. Suddenly the helo came to a hover almost above their position.

Alarm registered on Axe's face, and it didn't go unnoticed. Kane cursed. The pilot had just made himself a stationary target. Before Reaper could try to make radio contact with the bird, an RPG was fired from somewhere along the street. Its ordnance streaked through the air at three-hundred meters per second.

The rocket-propelled grenade slammed into the Black Hawk and detonated with terrible efficiency.

"Move! Move!" Kane shouted, and the three remaining members of Team Reaper bolted from the alley.

Above their position, the UH-60 dropped from the sky. The flaming wreck hit the top of the left side building and teetered on the edge before toppling over the precipice and crashing onto the asphalt below.

The narrow alley was shaken by a secondary explosion when the aviation fuel ignited, and a giant fireball rose into the sky above Ciudad Juárez.

The ensuing heat and concussive blast buffetted Kane and thrust him forward. He landed heavily, and all the air was expelled from his lungs with an audible whoosh. In the distance, he could hear shouting, and his earpiece was filled with traffic as the radio came to life in earnest.

"Zero, the Black Hawk is down..."

"Reaper is hit..."

"Reaper One, report..."

Kane felt someone grab his vest. An urgent voice said, "Come on, Reaper, get up."

He opened his eyes, and Cara's face swam around in front of him. He groaned. "Fuck."

"Tell me about it later."

With Cara's assistance, Reaper climbed to his feet and stumbled towards the cover of a parked vehicle. He slumped down against it then looked up at her. "Take over."

CHAPTER 2

"CHRIST ALMIGHTY, DID YOU SEE THAT?" Turner gasped. "They shot that helicopter down."

"Reaper One? Zero. Report?" Ferrero said into his mic.

Dead air.

"Reaper One, report, over."

"Zero? Reaper Two, over."

"Sitrep, Reaper Two."

"The *Federales* lost two more men back there, Zero. Plus, the helicopter and whoever was on board that thing. The blast knocked the wind from Reaper's sails, but we're up and moving again. Objective still the same."

"Copy, Reaper Two. Keep me informed."

Ferrero turned to face Teller and Reynolds. "Keep an eye on them."

"There's a phone call for you, sir," Swift called out.

"Who is it?"

"The Attorney General."

"Christ. Put him through."

Ferrero picked up a phone from the nearest desk and said, "Hello?"

"What the fuck is going on down there, Luis?" Attorney General William Bell snarled down the phone.

"It seems that the cartel has come out to play, sir," he answered.

"They just shot down a fucking helicopter!"

"They did, sir."

"Get our people out of there, Luis," Bell snarled from the other end of the line. "The president doesn't want this turning into a catastrophic fuckup."

"We're working on it," Ferrero snapped.

"And keep them away from that warehouse."

Christ, Ferrero fumed inside. "And what do you suggest I do...sir?"

"Figure it out, Luis," Bell snapped and hung up.

Ferrero slammed down the phone, his face the color of Swift's fiery red hair, and turned his irate glare on the computer tech. Stalking across to the console, he sat and in an icy tone said, "Cut the feed."

"What?"

"I said cut the fucking feed. What the hell were you thinking?"

Swift's fingers danced across the keyboard. "I was just following orders, boss."

"Whose? Because they sure as shit weren't mine."

"They were mine."

Ferrero turned to face the assistant attorney-general. "Why the hell would you do that?"

"Washington wanted in on the feed. They wanted it real-time."

"Well, thanks to you, I have to find another way out for my people. The warehouse is off limits."

"I'm sorry, Luis, I too was just following orders."

"Yeah? Well, those orders are about to get my people killed."

Swift cleared his throat. "Excuse me, sir."

"What?" Ferrero snarled.

"You have another call."

"Tell them to f—"

Swift cut the tirade short. "It's General Jones, sir."

General Hank Jones was the chairman of the joint chiefs. He was also a good man to have in your corner.

"Ferrero here, sir."

"I see you've cut the feed, Luis," Jones' deep voice said.

"Yes, sir."

"Can't say as I blame you. Can you patch me through to your team on the ground?"

"Yes, sir."

"Good, do it. I only want to say this once so you can have me on open comms if you wish."

"Yes, sir," Ferrero nodded and spoke into his mic, "Reaper One? Zero. Do you read? Over."

———

TEAM REAPER, CIUDAD JUÁREZ

"Reaper One? Zero. Do you read? Over."

The voice echoed through Kane's head as he brought up the rear of the small column. There was no open sign of pursuit behind them, however, it didn't mean that there was no one about.

Ferrero's voice came over the radio again. Kane depressed his mic button. "Cara, hold up."

At the front, Cara brought them to a stop. She turned to Axe and said, "Keep an eye out, I'll see what's up."

Axe nodded. "Yes, ma'am."

She walked back to find Kane, and as she passed Spencer, he asked, "What's going on?"

"No idea."

When she reached Kane, he was already communicating with Ferrero. "Yes, sir, patch him through."

Cara gave Kane a questioning frown.

"General Jones," he said.

Cara frowned. "What does he want?"

Kane shrugged.

"How are you feeling?"

"Head hurts, but I'm fine."

"Reaper? This is Jones. Can you hear me, son?"

"I can hear you, sir."

"I don't know if Luis has told you yet, but you and your people have been ordered to stay away from that warehouse."

Kane bit back a curse. "Just how are we meant to get home, sir? If it's all the same to you, I'll take them on anyway and deal with the fallout later."

"Damn it, Reaper, you grow on me some every time I speak to you. That won't be necessary. I've just been on the horn to Admiral Joseph. He's got two helos airborne, and they're headed your way."

Rear-Admiral Alexander Joseph was commander of The United States Naval Special Warfare Command (NAVSPECWARCOM).

"Thank you, sir."

"Didn't think I'd leave you out there, did you?"

"Not you, sir."

"Not anybody. However, the two birds won't be overhead for at least another hour. You'll have to find a place to fort up and wait it out."

"What about the *Federales*, sir? Can we expect some support from them?"

"Nope. After that bird fell out of the sky, they've been told to stand down. You'll need something that's got an open area so we can put one of the helos down. Copy?"

"Copy, sir."

"Good luck."

"Thank you, sir. Reaper One, out."

Ferrero came over the comms. "Reaper One? Zero."

"Copy, Zero."

"I've got Reynolds and Teller looking for an ideal location as we speak. Hang in there, and I'll get back to you. Keep moving in your current direction. Zero, out."

"Copy. Reaper One, out."

Kane called them all in. "Listen up. We need to find a place to fort up. We've got a couple of helos inbound about an hour out."

"We need to get out of here, that's what we need to do," Spencer snapped.

Not for the first time, Kane ignored him. "Axe, move out. Arenas, watch our six. Move."

"Where to?" Axe asked.

"Same direction until I tell you when to stop."

"Roger."

The team kept moving along the alley. Past some old, flattened cardboard boxes and a small pile of fly-ridden garbage bags, one of which spewed its maggoty contents onto the pavement. When Axe reached the next street, he stopped and checked both directions. All seemed deserted except for a set of traffic lights, light poles, and cars parked in the gutter. Across the street was a row of small convenience shops.

Further along the street, Axe sighted a three-level parking garage. "Hey, Reaper, take a look."

Kane peered around the corner of the brick building and saw what Axe was pointing at. He pressed his mic button, "Bravo Three? Reaper One. Copy? Over."

"Read you, Reaper One."

"Have you found anything for us as yet, Bravo Three?"

"Negative."

"I'm looking at a parking structure down to our right. Can you get eyes on it?"

"Wait one."

A minute later Teller came back to him. "I see your structure, Reaper One. It looks clear, over."

"Is it big enough to put a helo down on it?"

"Affirmative."

"Then that's where we'll be."

"Copy, I'll let the helos know. Bravo Three, out."

"Lead out, Axe."

The big man took point and moved along the sidewalk. It was an eerie feeling walking down a street which would normally be bustling with pedestrians on both sides. Other than them, there was no evidence of another living soul about. Not even any traffic. Then an armed figure appeared fifty yards in front of him, and the 416 snapped into line, and he stroked the trigger.

"Contact front."

No sooner had the words passed his lips when the cartel soldier dropped to the sidewalk, and another appeared. He was armed with an AK and fired a long burst in their direction.

Bullets snapped loudly through the air and ricocheted off cars. Firing again, the bullet slammed into the shooter's chest, and Axe heard the man cry out in pain.

"Across the street!" Kane snapped. "Move!"

They all ran to the other side of the street and ducked behind the cover of some parked cars. When no one else emerged, Kane directed them to keep going. The street remained clear long enough for them to reach the parking garage.

It was empty. Not one bay had a vehicle in it. Almost all of the gray concrete pillars had some form of graffiti on them, and most of the signage was broken.

Traynor said, "It's abandoned."

"*Sí*," said Arenas. "It once served a large shopping precinct. But there was a fire, and it burned down. It was never rebuilt. Instead, the land was sold, and other smaller shops replaced it."

Once at the top, they started to spread out. The structure had a waist-high concrete barrier all the way around it which would provide them with sufficient cover should it be required.

"Set up a perimeter," Reaper ordered. He glanced at his watch. They still had forty-five minutes until the scheduled pick up. "If you see anything, call it."

"Where would you like my men?" Perez asked.

Kane said, "Just tell them to pick a spot. There's plenty to go around."

"Reaper, did you see that?" Arenas asked as he pointed to a building two blocks further over.

Kane turned to look at it. It was the only structure in the vicinity taller than their own. He understood what the Mexican was getting at and nodded. "Keep an eye on it. If they put a shooter in there, he could cause us some problems."

He turned to Cara and said, "Let Zero know we've reached our destination."

"Copy."

He looked about to assess their position. It wasn't perfect but was better than being on the street. All they had to do now was wait.

"Nice job, Reaper," Spencer said as he stopped beside Kane. "You've got us treed."

————

CIUDAD JUÁREZ

"They are on the roof of the parking garage, *Jefe*," the slim, tattoo-covered cartel man said. "We could attack them there."

Raphael Sandoval shook his head. "Not yet. Where is the *Gringo*?"

"I'm here."

Sandoval turned and saw the tall American standing beside the armored Tahoe. He said, "It is time to prove that you are worth your money."

The 'Gringo' as he was known, was in his early thirties, solid, dark-haired, and wore wrap-around sunglasses to hide his blue eyes. "What about that other thing I was brought on for?"

"What about it?"

"It was what you hired me and my guys for," the *gringo* reminded him.

"I hired you to do whatever I want you to. And at this time, I want you to kill those Americans."

The mercenary stared at Sandoval for a moment and thought fleetingly about putting a bullet between his dark eyes. Instead, "I'll need to see a map."

The cartel man clicked his fingers, and within a couple of minutes, a map appeared. The *gringo* studied it and pointed to a spot on the map. "What is this?"

"It is abandoned. From there, you would be able to see where they are."

"All right." He turned and waved to the Tahoe. Its doors opened, and four men climbed out. All were mercenaries; all were American. "Get your gear. We've got a job to do."

———

TEAM REAPER, CIUDAD JUÁREZ

For the fifth time in five minutes, Kane looked at his watch. The helos were still thirty minutes out. Not that it worried him because it was reasonably quiet. From each of the vantage points, not a soul could be seen. In fact, it was almost like a foreign country war zone when they were waiting for the next wave of attacks. Not just over the border in Mexico.

"Bravo Three? Reaper One. You got anything? Over."

"Negative, Reaper One. Looks all quiet."

"They're up to something. They have to be."

Kane walked over to the edge of the building where Cara was positioned. He looked left and right along the street and said, "It's too quiet."

She nodded. "I agree. It makes me feel like I'm back in Afghanistan when shit was about to go down."

"Exactly."

The shot when it came, seemed to come from nowhere. Just a whistle of displaced air and then the thwack of the bullet strike. A heartbeat later, the sound of the shot arrived. Behind them, one of the *Federales* crashed onto his back.

"Sniper!" Axe shouted.

Everyone on the carpark roof dived for cover.

However, Perez was too slow and took the next incoming round. It blew him off his feet, and he skidded on his back a few feet before stopping. One look told Kane that the man was dead.

"The son of a bitch is in that damned building, Reaper," Axe cursed. "Maybe the fifth floor."

Axe was looking through his field glasses when a third round spanged off the concrete ledge beside him.

"Get the hell down, Axe," Reaper snapped and ran across to where his friend was crouched. He slumped down and placed his back against the short wall. "He can't stay there. We'll never get the helos down if they're taking fire."

"What do you propose, *Ke-mo sah-bee*?" Axe asked. "My thinking is that this fucker is a pro. The distance was around two-hundred meters. Not that far but far enough. Two shots, two kills."

"He missed the third."

"Thank Christ he did," Axe said. "So, who's going after him?"

Kane looked across the roof. "Cara, Spencer, Carlos, on me!"

They joined him against the wall. "We can't afford to have that sniper up there when the helos come in. I'm going up there after him. Carlos, you're with me."

"*Sí.*"

"Spencer, you and Cara keep everyone else alive while I'm gone. If we ain't back by the time the helos arrive, get the hell out of here."

"We aren't leaving you, Reaper," Axe growled.

"Do as I say. It's not a debate. OK, Carlos, let's move."

———

KANE—CIUDAD JUÁREZ

"Reaper One? Midnight One-One, do you read? Over." Kane's radio crackled to life as the pilot of the lead Black Hawk radioed in.

Kane and Arenas stopped in the doorway of a closed shop. "Copy, Midnight One-One. You're early. Over."

"Better than late, Reaper One. We're about five mikes out from your position and could use a sitrep, over."

"You need to hold, Midnight One-One. We have a sniper overlooking the LZ and need to clear him out. Copy?"

"Copy, Reaper One. Will fly a holding pattern until told otherwise or we fall out of the sky. Midnight One-One, out."

"Reaper One? Scimitar, over."

Scimitar was Chief Borden Hunt, a SEAL team leader they'd worked with before. "Go ahead, Scimitar."

"You all want some company down there?"

Kane glanced at Arenas. The former Mexican Special Forces commander nodded. "It can't hurt, *amigo*."

"Copy, Scimitar. An extra couple of shooters would be much-appreciated seeing as we're going in blind, over."

"Give me your location, and I'll be there directly."

Kane did as Hunt asked, and the chief said, "See you soon, Reaper. Scimitar out."

"I can not believe how quiet it is," Arenas commented.

Kane sighed. "Give me the jungle any day, my friend."

Suddenly the sound of an automatic weapon cut across the stillness. It was followed by a loud boom from just above and along from where they were situated. Kane depressed his TRANSMIT button and said, "Reaper Two? Reaper One. Copy?"

"Copy, Reaper One."

"Everything OK over there?"

"Just peachy. Axe decided to wake our friend up across the way. I think he's bored, over."

"Roger. Reaper One, out."

After twenty minutes of remaining in-situ, Arenas said, "Reaper, we have movement to our front."

Kane leaned out from the doorway and saw two men approaching along the sidewalk. Scimitar and another man. He was armed with a Knight's Armament Company M110 semi-automatic sniper rifle.

"Good to see you, Chief," Kane said and stuck out his hand.

Hunt took it in a firm grip. "You too, Reaper." He indicated to his man. "This is Pop-Eye."

"You got yourself in some shit here, Gunny," Pop-Eye observed.

"And then some. This is *Capitán Primero* Carlos Arenas."

"Sir."

The former Mexican special forces commander smiled. "Call me Arenas. We are all friends here."

"What have we got, Reaper?" Hunt asked.

Kane filled him in on the shooter, and a grim expression settled upon his face. "Pro?"

"Could be. Maybe ex-Mexican armed forces. Could even be *ex-Federale*. Definitely not normal cartel assholes."

"Let's go and find out."

———

When they entered the foyer of the building, the first thing that assailed them was the smell. Rotten carpet, mildew, piss, shit, all mixed into one gut-churning stench.

A large gang tag painted in red on one of the walls was all streaky where the paint had begun to flake away.

Kane raised his HK to his shoulder and started up the stairs. The building seemed to reek worse in the enclosed space of the stairwell, the combined stink funneling into it like a chimney. The four moved on in silence.

They passed doors leading to the first four floors. When they reached the fifth, Kane stopped on the landing and tried the door. The latch snicked as it gave and the door moved.

He looked back at Hunt and nodded. Holding up his left hand, he counted down with his fingers. He got as far as two when the door all but exploded outwards from having half a magazine of 5.56 rounds emptied into it from the other side.

"Christ!" Kane exclaimed and dropped to his haunches as razor-sharp splinters scythed through the air. He scrambled back down the stairs toward the small landing between levels.

"That wasn't no sniper," Hunt gasped as he gathered himself.

"Which means more than one shooter."

"It sounded like an M4, Chief," Pop-Eye commented.

"How the hell do you know that?" Kane queried.

"Trust me," Hunt said, "he knows."

Another burst of automatic fire rattled the door and made the holes in it bigger. One was a good deal larger than a human fist. Kane stared at it and then looked at Hunt. "You got anything that goes bang?"

Hunt reached behind his back with his left hand. When it reappeared, he held an M84 stun grenade. "This do?"

Kane took it and swiftly started back up the stairs. He hugged the wall when he reached the top step and paused.

Pulling the pin, he threw the stun grenade through the large hole. He counted the seconds off in his head, and when he heard the crump from the other side, Reaper kicked out at the door.

His heel hit it just below the handle, and the shattered door crashed back. Kane moved through with his HK held to his shoulder and his eye on the red dot sight. Apart from the blue-grey smoke from the M84, the hallway was empty.

Kane started along the hall. There were doors on either side to vacated apartments; one of which held the sniper and possibly the second shooter. Moving past the first doorway, he stopped. Using hand signals, he directed Hunt and Arenas to check the apartment.

With a crash, the door to the first apartment flew back, and the two men cleared the room. When they emerged, Kane moved on. The next three had the same outcome as the first. The fifth, however, was not vacant.

This time, when the door flew back under the force of Reaper's boot, a hail of bullets spewed forth, chewing holes in the wall across the hall. Hunt dived for cover, cursing his near miss when one of the slugs ripped through the sleeve of his upper arm, scoring the flesh.

Arenas poked his HK around the corner of the doorway and sprayed a full magazine of 5.56 NATO rounds into the room. Once it ran dry, Kane filled the doorway and waited. Inside the room, the shooter immediately rose from behind a sofa.

Reaper stroked the trigger, and a bullet burned its way into the man's brain. He flopped backward, and Kane swept the room with his carbine. It was clear. He took another step forward when an explosion from one of the bedrooms shook the whole apartment, bringing dust cascading from the ceiling and rattling the windows.

Gathering himself, Kane headed towards the room from which it had emanated. He burst through the door. On the far side of the room was a large hole in the wall. Through a haze of plaster dust, he saw three men exiting their makeshift doorway.

"Squirters in the next room!" he shouted and let loose a long burst with his carbine.

Bullets slammed into the wall around the hole. Dust and chunks of plaster fell away, dislodged by the hammering rounds.

The shooters disappeared, and Kane cursed. He whirled to Arenas. "Take the hallway! I'll follow them this way."

He moved forward and climbed through the gaping breach. Rubble crunched under his boots, and he came out in the main living area of the next apartment. The rattle of gunfire erupted from the hallway. Reaper pulled up short of running out into a storm of lead. He depressed the TRANSMISSION button on his mic. "Reaper Three, report."

"They're escaping along the hall to another stairwell, Reaper."

"Copy."

He eased himself past the door jamb in time to see the last shooter disappear around the corner at the end of the hallway. With the HK raised to his shoulder, Kane started after them, the others falling in behind him. "Is everyone OK?"

"All good," Hunt replied.

"Reaper One? Bravo Four. Do you read me? Over."

Kane raised his hand. "Hold up. Copy, Bravo Four."

"Reaper, I picked up some radio traffic a moment ago. A call went out for reinforcements to converge on your position."

"Copy. Bravo Three, you got anything?"

Teller came over the net. "Roger, Reaper One. There is a bunch of hostiles tracking in your direction."

"Copy. Reaper One, out," Kane turned to the others. "We've gotta go. But first I want to check something out. Carlos, keep an eye on the stairwell. Chief, with me."

Reaper and Hunt re-entered the apartment and crossed to the fallen man behind the sofa. They stared down at him, and Hunt said, "He definitely ain't a Mex."

Kane nodded and dug into his pocket for his cell phone. He raised it and took a picture. The hole in the forehead stood out like dog's balls. With that done he knelt beside him and riffled through the pockets. "My guess is he's some kind of merc. Most likely he's American."

Hunt agreed. "There's been a lot of ex-servicemen getting around here south of the border."

The dead man had nothing in his pockets, so Kane came erect. He hit his TRANSMIT button and said, "Midnight One-One? Reaper One, copy? Over."

"Roger, Reaper One, we read you."

"We'd like to take you up on your offer about now. The sniper threat has been neutralized."

"Copy, Reaper One. Midnight One-One is inbound. Out."

"Let's move, Chief."

They started down the stairwell and were almost at the bottom when Teller came over the net with emergency traffic. "Break! Break! Break! Reaper One, hold your position. I say again, hold your position. There are hostiles outside on the street, about to breach, over."

"How many?"

"Ten to fifteen tangos."

"OK, everyone hold. Bravo Three, is the roof big enough for a helo extraction?"

"Roger. But I doubt it would take the weight."

"It doesn't have to. Get hold of Midnight One-One and give him a sitrep. We'll start climbing."

"Copy, Reaper One. Bravo Three, out."

They made their way back up the stairs. Behind them, they could hear the cartel soldiers start their own rowdy ascent. At the top of the stairs, a sealed door blocked their exit. Kane put his shoulder to it, but it was stuck fast.

"Shit, this is all we need."

Hunt turned around to his man. "Pop-Eye, slow them bastards down."

"Copy."

The SEAL started back down the stairs, and within thirty seconds, the first crack of the M110 was heard. Meanwhile, Kane rammed the door with his shoulder once more. It still refused to budge.

Arenas came up a couple of steps and asked, "Do you mind if I try?"

Kane shrugged. "Be my guest."

Arenas pointed his 416 at the door and unloaded a full mag into it. Chips and splinters flew off with every bullet strike. Spent shell casings jingled on the concrete steps as they landed in a torrent. Once the deafening roar ceased, the ex-special forces commander reached out with his left hand and pushed the door. It swung free, and he walked through it.

Hunt leaned over the rail. "Pop-Eye, on me."

The team exited onto the roof just as one of the UH-60 Black Hawks swept overhead, the whop-whop of its rotor beating loudly at the air.

Pop-Eye took up a position behind an old airconditioning tower to watch the doorway. Arenas did the same.

Kane and Hunt walked to the edge of the building and looked across at the parking garage. The second Black Hawk had touched down on top of it and was picking up all who were there.

"Midnight One-One? Reaper one, over."

"Copy, Reaper One."

"We're in position for extraction, over."

"Roger, Reaper One. As soon as Midnight One-Two finishes we'll be right with you. Out."

"Contact!" Pop-Eye's voice snapped right before he squeezed the trigger on the M110. Suddenly, the rooftop was filled with the noise of automatic fire, the sound of the AKs standing out above the rest. Hunt and Kane took cover behind the cooling towers and set about returning fire.

One of the cartel soldiers was down in the doorway while others leaned through the gap, and sprayed bullets with wild abandon across the roof, hoping to be lucky enough to take down a target. Two more of them tried to break free of the confined space of the stairwell only to be cut down before they'd traveled ten feet.

"These guys are fucking fanatical," Hunt shouted.

"We've probably got a bounty on our heads," Kane called back.

"Reaper One, Midnight One-One is inbound. Copy?"

"Roger, Midnight One-One. Come in from the east to stay out of the line of fire, over."

"Are you calling a hot LZ, Reaper One, over?"

"Affirmative."

"Copy. Midnight One-One out."

Kane watched as the Black Hawk swept around and approached from the east. It flared, and the pilot came in and placed one wheel on the roof while the rest hung in midair. Reaper pressed the TRANSMIT button on his mic and said, "Carlos, you're up. Hunt follow him, and then Pop-Eye. I'll cover your six."

One after the other the three men fell back and boarded the helo. While they did so, Kane kept up a steady rate of fire on the doorway to keep the cartel men occupied. Hunt's voice filled his ear, "You're up, Reaper. We'll cover you."

After he fired a final burst, Kane turned and ran towards the Black Hawk. He'd made it halfway when he heard Arenas shout over the radio, "RPG! Left side!"

No sooner had the words escaped the ex-commander's lips when the Black Hawk lurched violently up and away as the pilot worked the cyclic and the collective with experienced hands. The rocket-propelled grenade slid past its tail rotor and into the distance. Kane dropped to the dirt and collection of grime on the rooftop.

The cartel soldiers!

He quickly rolled onto his back in time to see them pouring through the doorway. AKs opened fire and bullets spanged off the rooftop around him. Kane squeezed the trigger on the HK, and his attackers dived for cover. One of them cried out and clutched at a bloody leg.

Reaper scrambled across the rooftop and found himself back at his starting point behind the airconditioning tower.

The Black Hawk had pulled off station and was circling back about a mile out. Kane's radio crackled to life, and the pilot's voice came to him. "Reaper One? Midnight One-One, Copy?"

"Copy, One-One."

"We're coming back around, Reaper One. We'll not be touching down, and you'll only get one shot at this."

"Copy. What do you propose? Over."

"You'll know it when you see it. Keep an eye on us. Midnight One-One inbound. Out."

Bullets beat a loud staccato on the metal of the cooling tower and made Kane duck automatically. He leaned out and fired another burst.

He looked back at the Black Hawk and saw it start its approach. It was coming in low and fast. Kane leaned back out to fire again and managed one shot before the magazine went dry. He tossed the HK416 aside and pulled his Sig Sauer M17 handgun. He blew off four fast shots at a target then glanced back at the inbound helo.

Kane frowned. "What the...?"

There was something dangling from the Black Hawk, and it took a moment to work out what it was. A Fast Rope! Something designed for insertion, not extraction. Then he remembered how the pilot told him that he wasn't putting down. "Shit."

The sound of the Black Hawk rotor grew steadily louder above the shooting. Kane leaned out and fired twice more before checking the helo again.

"This is going to be wild," he murmured and rammed the M17 into its holster as he realized that the Black Hawk wasn't actually going to pass over the building. It couldn't for fear of getting the rope hooked on something, thus killing everyone on board.

Then he was up and running towards the edge of the building. His arms and legs pumped furiously. Bullets filled the air all around him. Kane felt one tear at a flap on his tactical vest.

Twenty feet!

Kane reached the precipice.

Ten feet!

He jumped out into the abyss!

TEAM REAPER HQ, EL PASO, TEXAS

"What kind of fucking Indiana Jones bullshit was that, huh?" Ferrero seethed at Kane.

Axe slapped him on the back as he walked past and said, "That was way cool shit, Reaper. You can fly, man. Awesome."

Ferrero glared at him. "Frig off, Axe, or you'll be next."

Kane fixed his stare on his boss and said, "Are you pissed at me, or the fact we lost an HVT because of others' incompetence?"

"What do you mean by that?" Turner asked.

"Where would you like me to start, sir? The fact that we were driving out of a hostile area when we should have been extracted by air in the first place? Or how the cartel managed to shut down whole city blocks to set up their little ambush? Or even how they keep getting enough firepower to supply a fucking army?"

"We can't do anything about that," Turner growled at the tone of Kane's voice.

"Yes, we can. It's what we do. It was what we were formed for. Attack the bastards on their home turf. Grab their drugs, their money, disrupt their operations. We're a covert operations group. Deniable operators. The problems start when you involve others. Especially those who are in the pockets of the fucking cartels."

Turner's voice softened. "I can't do anything about that. The team is still on a short leash. The people above us still aren't sure about what we do."

"And if we were CIA, they wouldn't give two shits about it."

They turned to face Cara. She continued, "We need to be able to make calls on the ground. If it hadn't been for the general today, we'd have all been killed. Just because some asshole behind a desk interferes. I thought that was what Reaper was supposed to do. He's in charge on the ground; he makes the calls."

"It doesn't work like that, I'm afraid," Turner said.

"Well, it damned well should."

Turner shrugged.

"Luis," Kane said, "You know that it's right. There are too many links in the chain."

"My hands are tied, Reaper."

Kane turned to the one person who'd said nothing the whole time since the discussion had started. Spencer sat in a chair off to the side. "What about you?"

"Me? I follow orders, just as you should."

Kane nodded and turned back to Ferrero. "All right. I'm due a couple of days off. I want to take it now."

"Why?"

"Something I need to take care of."

"All right. The whole team can have the week. After what happened today, I dare say you could all use it."

Cara caught up with him in the shower room. He'd just taken his vest and shirt off. She stared at the scar on his chest, courtesy of a sniper in the Philippines. She said, "You were lucky today."

"We all were. I like the SIG by the way. That was a good pickup. Better than the USP."

"Let's hope the rest of the team think that way."

He turned away to hang up his vest. On Kane's back was a large tattoo of the Grim Reaper. It was the source of his nickname. He turned back and stared at Cara. "Out with it."

"Where are you going?"

"That's what I want to know?" asked Axe.

Behind him stood Arenas. "Me too."

"I'm taking a couple of vacation days is all."

Cara removed her own vest, revealing her lithe form beneath it. She shook her head. "Nope, I know you better than that. You're up to something. And, if it is going to affect the team, then we deserve to know."

Kane sighed. "All right, I'm going to Washington."

"Why?" Cara asked as she removed her T-shirt.

"To see Jones."

"And why would you need to see him?"

Ferrero!

"Christ," Kane hissed.

"Everybody out. All except Reaper."

Cara replaced her T-shirt, gave Kane a worried glance, and followed the other two from the room. Ferrero stared hard at Kane and said, "This better be good, or by Christ, I'll have you out of here so fast you'll think you were shot."

"I'm going to see General Jones, Luis. We need to get out from under this three-headed umbrella and answer to only one man. Not the attorney-general, the secretary of state, or the president. Just one man. Someone who knows what it takes to get things done. None of those assholes have been on the ground before and know what it's like. They're going to get us all killed."

"And you think Jones can help?"

"If anyone can, it will be him."

"I agree with you, totally. But this is for me to do. Not you. If we can't trust each other, then we may as well shut the whole show down right now. So, I'll go to Washington and talk to Jones myself. In the meantime, if you ever try to pull shit like this again and go over my head, I'll shit can you. Understood?"

"Understood."

"Good. By the way, Swift got a hit on that dead merc."

"Yeah?"

"Looks like Chief Hunt was right. The man's name was Colter, ex-ranger. He's tied in with a bunch of ex-military assholes under the command of a Captain Ward Collins. He used to be a sniper before he was discharged under suspicious circumstances. The Mexicans call him The *Gringo*."

"Now they work for the cartels?"

"It would seem that way."

"Damn it. That's all we need."

———

CIUDAD JUÁREZ

The streetlights flicked by the armored Tahoe as it sped along the street. In the back, Sandoval remained silent for a long time before he spoke to Collins.

"I was unimpressed by your team today, *Gringo*."

"Sometimes things go that way."

"*Sí*."

More silence. Then, "I have heard from my contact. The *jefe* will be ready one week from today."

"That don't leave much time."

"No."

"Is everything in place?"

"*Sí*."

"I guess we better leave tonight then."

"It would be best."

CHAPTER 3

OUTSIDE EMBARGO, TENNESSEE—TWO NIGHTS LATER

THE EIGHTEEN WHEELER roared as the driver dropped it back another gear and turned off the interstate onto a single lane blacktop which would take them around Embargo instead of through it. Its headlights swept across the landscape until finding the road once more.

The driver accelerated and started to work his way back up through the gears until he had the vehicle up to fifty. Beside him, his passenger shook his head. "Damned if I know why we just can't drive on through the blasted town."

"Company policy," the driver said. "You already know that though."

"Yeah, but still. It ain't like anybody knows what the hell we're carrying."

"I don't make the rules, Billy. I just follow them."

"It's still crap, Harry. What happens if on one of these backroads someone wants to jack us just for the hell of it?"

Harry ignored the last comment. He'd been doing this for five years and had experienced no problem before.

A mile further along, the road climbed slightly to navigate the hills behind Embargo. The roadsides became festooned with trees and vegetation, and the blacktop narrowed. They crossed a bridge over a deep creek, and the road dropped down a hill then turned sharp left.

Harry grated through the gears to make the turn, and as soon as he'd traversed it, they were confronted with a roadblock. Flashing red and blue lights danced off the roadside trees. A sheriff's cruiser!

Harry cursed and started to bring the rig to a halt. In front of the cruiser stood a single deputy with a flashlight. When the eighteen wheeler finally stopped, he approached the truck from the driver's side.

"What the hell is this?" Billy growled.

"Must be a wreck or something," Harry stated as he opened the door, and the interior light blinked on.

He climbed down to the road and approached the deputy. They swapped a few words, the deputy pointed up the road, and they talked some more. Then Harry turned around and started back to the truck.

Billy watched on in horror as the deputy then pulled out his sidearm and shot Harry in the back of the head from close range.

The truck driver fell forward onto the road, the lights from the truck illuminating his body.

"No!" Billy screamed. "No! No!"

He grabbed at the door handle, and his hand slipped off it. He tried again, and this time the door flew open. He scrambled from the cab and slipped when he hit the blacktop. He felt his pants rip at the knees and skin peel away. Pain shot through his legs and into his brain.

Ignoring it as best he could, his jaw clenched, Billy came to his feet and started to run back along the truck's trailer. He was almost to the rear of it when another man appeared and stopped him in his tracks.

"Oh Christ," Billy gasped when the man before him brought up a handgun and pointed it at his head.

The weapon spat flame in the darkness and Billy's head snapped back. He fell to the ground, and the man looked at the other one in the deputy's uniform.

"Get the truck up here," Collins snapped. "We need to get this thing unloaded."

"Yes, sir."

The man disappeared, and Collins went around to the double-doors at the back of the trailer. He waited there until their truck was in position. One of his men used bolt cutters to cut through the padlock on the doors.

Collins swung them open, and the man who'd been dressed as the deputy shone his flashlight up into the back of the trailer.

"Nice," he said in a satisfactory tone.

"Get it changed over," Collins snapped. "I want to be moving within twenty minutes."

"Yes, sir."

―――

THE PENTAGON, WASHINGTON, D.C.

"I'm sorry it's so late, Luis, but it's been a bastard of a day."

"That's OK, General. I don't mind waiting. You kind

of get used to it if you spend enough time in Washington."

General Hank Jones nodded. "I forgot you'd been haunting the streets up here until recently."

Jones was a big man in his late sixties. Much bigger than he seemed when on the screen. He reminded Ferrero of the former general, Norman Schwarzkopf. His office was a traditional wood-paneled affair with a small American flag on a staff in the right rear corner next to a large window.

"Tell me what I can do for you, Luis," Jones said. "What brings you here?"

"I need your help, General."

"OK, before we start, call me Hank."

"All right, Hank. Like I said, I need your help."

Jones frowned. "I'll help in any way I can."

"You know about the other day. About what went down, and if it hadn't been for you, my team would be dead."

"I'm sure they would have handled the situation."

"That's just it, Hank. It should never have happened. The HVT should have been airlifted out of there. Not driven. And then, unknown to myself, the feed was being fed live back to Washington."

Jones nodded again. "It's not the first time that something like that has happened."

"Agreed. But when they start issuing orders that put my team at risk, it needs to stop. They aren't on the ground so they can't make the right call."

"What do you want me to do about it?"

"We need one commander. We don't need to be over-watched by the AG's office, the secretary of state, and the president," Ferrero paused, took a deep breath, and then continued. "Is there –"

Jones held up his hand to stop him.

"Leave it with me, Luis."

"Sir?"

"I agree. The other day was a complete clusterfuck. Through no fault of your own either. If your team was military, it would never have happened. Which is why I did what I did. When the decision was made to divert your team, no one gave any thought or two shits what would happen to them. I'll see what I can do."

"Thank you, sir."

"Don't thank me yet. It might come back to bite you on the ass."

———

WASHINGTON, D.C.— THE NEXT DAY

The cell phone rang, and Ferrero took it from his pocket. He placed it against his ear, and he said, "Hello."

"It's me."

Jones.

"I wasn't expecting to hear from you, General. Not yet anyway."

"Get your team together and have them come to DC. Tomorrow."

"Yes, sir."

Jones hung up.

———

They were all gathered in Jones' office as ordered, the next day; Reaper team as well as the Bravo elements. It was late in the afternoon when they'd been shown inside. However, the office was empty. The general had been detained, his secretary had said, but would be along directly.

"Hey, Reaper, get a look at this," Axe said, indicating a picture on the wall. In it were Jones and two other men. No more than kids really. They were in uniform, and Kane figured that it had been taken in Vietnam. They wore shoulder patches of the 75th Rangers.

"He was a Lurp," Axe said, admiration in his voice.

Kane was about to say something when the door to the office opened, and Jones entered. He left the door ajar and was followed in by of all people, another general. This one, however, was a woman. Maybe in her early forties, with her dark hair up in a severe-looking bun. She was athletically built, and her not-unattractive face bore no hard signs of aging. Her uniform though drew Kane's attention. Or rather her shoulder patch. It was a ranger patch. Since 2015, women had been allowed to go to ranger school. Arguably one of the toughest courses in the United States Armed Forces. Not many passed. But apparently, this one did. Which attested to her fortitude.

Jones took a seat and stared around the room. The general who'd entered with him took up a position behind and to his left.

"Good. You're all here," Jones acknowledged. "The young lady behind me is General Mary Thurston. She is your new commanding officer."

A murmur rippled through the room as the members of Team Reaper glanced at each other in confusion. Not Ferrero, however. Although he wasn't expecting this, he knew something was afoot.

"You all no longer work for the attorney general. You work for me. You'll still be classed as a DEA special operations team, and all your mission briefs will come from them. Whatever they want to be done, your team will do your best to accommodate it. However, what I saw happen the other day cannot be allowed to happen again. Which is why the change has been made."

"How is this meant to work, General?" Kane asked.

"Luis will be in charge of the team. Spencer, I'm sorry, but the CIA wants you back." Spencer said nothing.

Jones went on, "Out in the field, you, Gunny, are in charge. Whatever you say goes. If you want a damned nuke dropped on someone, you'll damned well get it. There'll be no desk jockeys running operations from afar."

"Yes, sir."

Jones continued. "General Thurston will be in overall command and will have final say on everything." Jones glanced at Ferrero. "I'm sorry, Luis, but to make it work, it has to be this way."

Ferrero nodded. "Fine by me, General. Whatever is best for the team."

"Good. Now, the general answers to me, and I answer to the president. From bottom to top, straight up the line. No interference from anyone. If you need something, take it to Mary. If need be, she'll kick it up to me. But, no matter what, she'll have your backs. Just as long as you've got hers. We've even given you a name. The World Wide Drug Initiative is the banner you'll operate under. And that is where you'll go, worldwide. Any questions?"

No one said a word.

An abrupt nod finished the meeting. "Good. You can leave. All except Luis, Kane, and Billings."

Once the door closed, Jones said, "Mary, they're your people now."

"Yes sir," Thurston said and then looked at the people before her. "Yesterday the DEA got a tip-off about a shipment of drugs and arms scheduled to leave Esmeraldas

Ecuador within the next week. They will be stowed in containers on board a Panamanian-flagged freighter called the Sea Fortune. I want you all to make yourself familiar with the specs of the ship."

"Can you tell us what we're meant to do, ma'am?" Kane asked.

"You'll insert yourselves upon the ship and stay out of sight until it reaches international waters. Once it does, you'll seize control of it. By that time, the Artoro should be on your radar, and she will rendezvous with you. You'll get more specific details before the mission."

"Sounds like fun," Cara said.

"I would say interesting," Thurston stated. "We'll all meet in El Paso in three days. We'll go over everything then. Any questions?"

There were none.

"Let me add this. I read all about what happened with the operation to do with the Montoya Cartel. I know you all work well together. I also know you lost a man down in Guatemala. All I can say is, I'm looking forward to working with you. Agent Ferrero, I'm not here to look over your shoulder twenty-four-seven. From what I can tell, you've made the right call all along the line. However, I will be with you on operations and expect to be kept in the loop at all times. I won't tolerate cowboys in my command. This is our chance to make a difference."

They were about to leave when Jones said, "I hope this works out for you all. Because if it doesn't, I've been ordered to shut it down."

Ferrero looked the general in the eye and said, "It'll work. We'll make sure of it."

CHAPTER 4

CHESAPEAKE SUPERMAX—THREE DAYS LATER

CHESAPEAKE SUPERMAX WAS like a giant hollowed-out cube surrounded by an electrified fence topped with razor wire. But that wasn't all. On the outside of that were more rolls of razor wire and another electrified fence. This one operated on a different circuit.

Then you could add in the nine guard towers, and the fact that the prisoners were locked in their cells twenty-three hours of the day. All of which gave you one of the most secure facilities in the country.

But the worst were kept in their own secure facility on the inside. Like a prison within a prison. This one was surrounded by an electrified fence too.

Then there was the main building.

Juan Montoya, head of the Montoya Cartel, rolled over on his bunk and checked his watch. It was almost time. He heard a door open along the hall, and then footsteps echoed on the concrete floor. They stopped outside his small cell, and the door rattled then swung open.

"It is time, *amigo*, yes?" Montoya said to the big man who filled the doorway.

The guard nodded. "Yeah."

"And my friend, *Señor* O'Brien?"

"He's in position with the others."

"You will be a very rich man after this, *amigo*." Montoya smiled.

"I'll be on America's most wanted is what I will be."

The smile disappeared. "It is better than the alternative."

The guard stepped aside. "Let's go."

They left the cell and walked along the hall to a steel door. The guard toggled his radio and said, "Open door six."

Juan Jesus Montoya wasn't a tall man at five-nine. His black hair and goatee were neatly trimmed, and his eyes dark and moody. Today, however, they had a spark.

There was a buzz, and the door lock sprang back. The guard pushed it open and allowed Montoya through. He checked his watch. "We've got five minutes until this thing kicks off."

They kept walking, passing through two more doors before coming to the indoor exercise area. Unlike the main population, the worst of the worst spent their free hour inside a large recreation hall.

There were three other men in the hall. Colin O'Brien stood with two other guards. They were the ones who would escort both prisoners outside into the yard when everything happened. The escape was timed to occur when the rest of the prisoners in Chesapeake were out in the yard. It would add to the confusion.

O'Brien, like Montoya, wasn't a big man by any stretch. His hair, once dyed black, was now streaked with gray. The appearance of his face put his age somewhere in the mid-fifties, although, since his incarceration, there were more lines on it.

O'Brien and Montoya shook hands. "Are you ready, my friend?"

Montoya nodded. "More than ready."

"Let's hope your men can pull this off."

Montoya turned to the guard who'd escorted him this far. "Thank you for your help. The money will be deposited to the account you have, within two days."

The guard nodded. He wasn't too worried about the money. He was more worried that the escape would fail and that the Montoya cartel drug boss would be stuck there.

"Good luck, gentlemen," the guard said and left them with the other two guards.

"How much longer?" O'Brien asked.

One of the guards looked at his watch. "One minute."

They waited in silence, Montoya silently counting off the seconds inside his head. When he had almost reached sixty, the first explosion boomed in the distance. He turned his head and stared at the Irishman. "It is time."

———

CHESAPEAKE BAY

Two helicopters came in low over the Chesapeake Bay. No more than thirty feet above the water.

The first one was a McDonnell Douglas MD500 Defender. Fully armed with rocket pods. The second was an Airbus H225M long-range tactical helicopter capable of carrying up to twenty-eight passengers.

Their destination, Chesapeake Supermax.

"Snake Eater Two, this is Snake Eater One, one minute to contact, over."

"Copy, Snake Eater One, one minute."

Collins heard the call over his headset and turned to his men. He held up a finger and called out, "One minute!"

The warning was relayed through nine earpieces, and they all nodded. Every man was dressed in full tactical gear and armed with Colt M4A1s. They also had FN Five-Seven handguns. Both weapons had five magazines each of spare ammunition.

"Thirty seconds," the call came over the comms.

At that point, the MD500 peeled off and sped up. Fifteen seconds later it made landfall. And fifteen seconds after that, it fired its first rocket.

———

CHESAPEAKE SUPERMAX

"Fuck!" Myles Carter exclaimed at the splotch of ketchup on his uniform shirt. Instinctively he wiped at it and smudged it further. "Ahh, Christ."

By rights, he wasn't supposed to have food in his tower, but he'd missed lunch. Now he'd dropped some of the contents of his sandwich down his front, and the stain would be there for the rest of his damned shift.

In disgust, he threw the sandwich in the bin and found a paper towel to wipe the offending spot away without much success.

For some reason, Carter felt the urge to look up. From where he was in tower four, he could see out across the Chesapeake Bay. But it wasn't the scenery which drew his attention. It was the two black dots above the horizon.

He frowned. "What the...?"

As they drew closer, they started to take shape. The one on the left broke away from the other and sped up. Suddenly Carter realized what they were. Helicopters.

He hurried across to the wall-mounted phone and took it off its cradle. He hesitated for a moment as the smaller of the helicopters grew large in his window.

Then: "Central, this is Carter in tower four. We have a situation. There are...oh shit!"

Suddenly there was a flash as the MD500 fired two rockets. Within a couple of heartbeats, Carter's world ceased to exist, as they slammed into tower four and exploded in an orange ball of flame.

The helicopter swooped in low over the prison and pulled up almost vertically. It spun one-hundred and eighty degrees in the air and swooped back in. The rocket pods launched two more of their contents, and another tower disappeared.

"Snake Eater Two, this is One. You are cleared to land. We'll keep their heads down. Over."

"Copy, One. Snake Eater Two, inbound."

The Airbus came in low over the prison and flared before setting down in the exercise yard, scattering prisoners. Collins and his team dispersed around the helo in a defensive perimeter. To their left, a third guard tower exploded.

"This is Cobra One. Cobras Two through Five on me, the rest of you protect the helo."

Collins started to move towards the main gate to the facility where the prison kept their best and brightest. Off to his left, a large man dressed in an orange jumpsuit started to approach. He pivoted and squeezed off a burst. The slugs stitched across the chest of the prisoner who collapsed like a sack of potatoes.

On the gate were two guards, in shock by what was happening around them. Collins and the man beside him raised their M4A1s and put them down with a burst of fire.

"Hold the gate," Collins barked.

Two men remained there while their leader and another pair walked through into a tunnel ringed with wire.

At the other end, a door opened, and two guards emerged along with two men in orange jumpsuits. Collins said, "I have eyes on the packages."

The MD500 swooped overhead once again, and another explosion rocked the prison compound. Collins said to Montoya, "We have to get out of here now before they regroup."

Montoya nodded. "Lead the way."

O'Brien said, "Do you have a gun I can use?"

Collins took out his Five-Seven and passed it to the Irish mob boss. He handled it like a seasoned veteran and swung it up and placed two bullets in each of the guard's heads.

"What did you do that for?" Montoya asked.

"Save money."

Montoya shrugged. "OK."

"Come on, move," Collins snapped.

"Just remember who you're talking to," O'Brien reminded him.

The former ranger ignored the mob boss and started towards the gate. A large figure blocked the way. He was dressed in orange and was almost six and a half feet tall. His head was shaven, and he had tattoos up his bare arms.

"Take me with you, Captain," he demanded.

Collins thought he recognized the big man. "Hall?"

"Yes, sir."

"Shit! All right, come with us."

"No," O'Brien snapped.

Once again, Collins ignored him.

"Thank you, sir," Hall said.

They broke out into the main exercise yard, and the former ranger noted the orange lumps scattered on the ground. His men had been busy. He said, "This is Cobra One. Prepare for exfil."

"Copy, Cobra One."

Bullets started to impact around them, and Collins stopped. He brought his M4 up and aimed at a guard on another tower who was spraying the yard with 5.56 rounds. He stroked the trigger, and the guard shuddered as the rounds slammed home.

"Move!" Collins shouted over the top of another explosion. Fires were starting to rage around the prison compound. Sirens blared above the sounds of battle.

Once more, Collins used his radio. "Snake Eater One, this is Cobra One. Copy?"

"Roger, Cobra One."

"If you've got a spare rocket put it in the main building, over."

"Copy, will do."

The MD500 swept in from the north and slammed two rockets into the main building which housed the warden's office.

A ball of fire exploded from the hole ripped in its side and seemed to shoot up the outside of the building.

A prisoner appeared in front of Collins. A Hispanic man with tattoos all over his face and neck. He snarled at the former ranger. "Take me with you, *puta*, or I will have your family killed."

Collins shot him in the head.

"That fucked him," Hall said.

"Who was he?" Collins asked as they closed on the helo.

"Guevara. MS-13. Dangerous motherfucker."

Dark smoke hung over the prison as the fires continued to grow. The mercenaries fell back to the helicopter and climbed on board along with Montoya, O'Brien, and Hall. No sooner had they done so when a handful of prisoners rushed at the Airbus.

Mounted on the side of the helo was an FN Mag. A general-purpose machine gun which fired a 7.62mm bullet at up to one thousand rounds per minute.

One of Collins' men opened up with it and the staccato sound hammered out across the yard. The bullets ripped into the prisoners and stopped them in their tracks. Their jumpsuits turned into bloody rags.

"Get us up, Snake Eater Two," Collins ordered.

"Copy. Snake Eater Two coming out."

The Airbus started its climb while Collins' men sprayed the yard with more bullets. Clouds of smoke rose into the air, sent off into the atmosphere to the accompaniment of blaring alarms.

Bullets smacked into the Airbus from all sides, and one passed through the open cabin door. Then, once it was high enough, it banked and headed back out over the Chesapeake Bay.

O'Brien stared at Hall, his hard gaze unwavering. The con noticed and said, "What the fuck you looking at?"

"Who the hell are you, boyo?" O'Brien asked.

"First Sergeant Ryan Hall, formerly of the Third Battalion, Seventy-Fifth Ranger Regiment," Collins said. "Best damned first sergeant I ever had."

"Where we headed, Captain?"

"After this, as far away as possible."

———

TEN MILES OUTSIDE ROANOKE, VIRGINIA

There were six black SUVs waiting when the Airbus H225M touched down in the field. All were pointing away from the aircraft to expedite the transfer and exit. The setting sun had the Virginian landscape doused in orange juice.

The first ones out were the mercenaries. Force of habit had them securing the already secure landing zone or LZ. They were followed by Montoya and O'Brien, both of whom were rushed across to one of the waiting SUVs.

Collins remained behind with the helo. Reaching back into the interior of the cabin, he retrieved a satchel and opened it to reveal a small improvised bomb made up of plastic explosive and a timer. Setting the timer for one minute, he left it in the aircraft and hurried away.

As the SUVs were pulling away, the bomb exploded, and the Airbus was ripped apart in a ball of flames and twisted metal.

———

TEAM REAPER HQ, EL PASO, TEXAS

Every news channel in El Paso was broadcasting the prison break on a constant loop. Pictures of fires and bodies lying in the yard flashed up on the screen with ticker headlines rolling across the bottom.

So far, reports revealed that at least twenty-five people had died in the escape, with an additional thirty wounded.

But that number was expected to rise. As yet there were no reports identifying the three escapees.

The whole of Team Reaper sat back watching the large screen. They had set up in a large warehouse in an industrial district on the outskirts of town. Now they were waiting for Ferrero and General Thurston to brief them before their flight to Ecuador.

"We still have no information on the identities of the escapees, however, it seems to have been a well-organized and -executed escape plan."

"Do we have any idea of the origin of the helicopters?"

"Not yet, Lance. All we can say for sure is that they were military."

Kane hit mute on the television again.

"Fuckers were well-organized all right," Axe grated. "It would take military precision to pull something like that off. Look at those pictures."

Grainy security camera footage flashed up on the screen. It showed men setting up a perimeter around the helicopter, and another team of shooters heading towards the secure internal facility.

"They set up a perimeter and shot anybody who came within their security zone. They're decked out in full tactical gear, and they're not shooting wildly like some half-assed cowboys. They're making sure of their shots. Damned shame we can't see their faces. Pictures are shit."

Cara stared at the pictures. Another feed showed two guards getting shot. She said, "That one just shot those guards."

"They were escorting them," Kane said. "They were in on it."

"How do you know that?" Reynolds asked.

"Why else would they be taking them outside in the middle of a shit storm like that?"

"Did you see that?" Teller asked.

"What?" said Cara.

"That big feller they're taking with them. He's an add-on. He blocked their way, and instead of shooting him, they took him with them."

"What does that mean?" Swift asked.

Cara said, "It means he knew them."

"Then why not just shoot him?"

"Maybe he was a good friend," Axe proposed.

"Must've been," Traynor said. "That feller out front just shot a prisoner who did the same thing."

The door to the warehouse opened with a loud bang, and almost every one of those present dropped their hands to their sidearms instinctively. Ferrero and Thurston walked into the cavernous space, closely followed by Spencer.

"What the fuck is he doing here?" Axe asked none too softly.

"I guess we'll find out," Kane said.

"I see you're all watching the news about the breakout from Chesapeake Bay Supermax," Thurston said.

Kane stared at her. Gone was the perfectly-pressed uniform. Her casual attire included a green T-shirt and jeans, which did not detract from the air of authority about her.

"Like what you see, Sergeant?" she asked Kane.

Suddenly uncomfortable, he saw the flicker in her eyes. "Just looking, ma'am."

"Just because I'm military doesn't mean I have to look it, Reaper," she told him.

"Do they know what went on with the escape, ma'am?" Cara asked.

Thurston glanced at Ferrero. He cleared his throat and

said, "We can do better than that. We now know who it was that escaped."

"Who?" asked Traynor.

"Montoya and O'Brien."

"Well, fuck me," Axe said, the awe obvious in his voice.

"My thoughts exactly, Burton," Thurston agreed. "The third man was an ex-ranger named Hall."

"Kane!" Cara's alarm was evident.

"Easy, Cara, we don't know."

"Don't know what?" Thurston asked.

Kane said, "We have family up in Maine. We figure that O'Brien won't stop until he finds them."

Thurston nodded. "I read that in your file. Luis and I talked, and we agreed that we should send a couple of you up there until this mess can be cleaned up."

Kane and Cara stood up. Ferrero stepped forward. "But, not you two. You are going on this mission. That's where you're needed."

"The hell I am," Kane snapped.

"Me neither," agreed Cara. "That's my son up there."

"I will go," a voice said.

They all turned to look at Arenas. He shrugged. "They will both be safe with me. I will guard them with my life, *amigo*."

"I'll go too," Pete Traynor put in. "Ferrero is right, Reaper. The team needs you running point on missions."

"Which is why Spencer is back," Thurston told them. "He'll take the place of Arenas in the field."

"Who gives the orders?" asked Kane.

"You do."

Kane turned his gaze upon Spencer. "You good with that."

He nodded. "I'm fine."

"Cara?"

Kane could see the internal conflict in her eyes. She looked at Arenas. "Can you protect my son, Carlos?"

He gave her a reassuring smile. "Like he was one of my own, *querido*."

She glanced at Kane and nodded.

"All right," said Kane, "we'll do it your way."

Ferrero said, "Pete, you and Carlos leave now. There'll be a plane waiting for you at the airport."

Cara stopped them as they started to turn away. "Take all you need from the armory."

"Don't worry, Cara," said Traynor. "They'll both be fine."

Once they were gone, Thurston said to the team, "Right, let's get about this mission."

Kane held up his hand. "Before we do, General, have you read the report about what went down on our last prisoner transfer?"

Thurston nodded. "I did."

"So you also know that we had some trouble with American mercenaries?"

"Yes. And before you ask, the one you killed, I knew of him. He was a ranger, as you already know."

"What about Collins? You know him too?"

Thurston nodded. "I did. Quite a capable officer."

"Capable enough to pull something like that prison break off?"

"Are you trying to connect the two, Kane?" Thurston asked. "It's a bit of a stretch."

"OK. But don't it seem funny to you that after what happened down there, that a bunch of military guys then break Montoya out of prison?"

"How do you know they're military?"

"Have you seen the damned footage?" Axe snapped.

Thurston glared at him.

"Ma'am," he added.

"I have."

"Then you tell us why they wouldn't be," Kane said. "We've all seen it. They formed a perimeter around the helo. Used controlled fire to hold the prisoners back, and didn't waste one shot."

"I agree. But it doesn't mean that Collins was involved in it."

"If it does," Cara pointed out, "shit just got real because he won't stop until he gets us all."

"I think he'll scurry off back to Mexico for a while and lay low. If he does, then that'll give us time to prepare."

"Prepare for what?" Teller asked.

"To find out where he is and go after him. Until then, we have a mission to complete."

Ferrero stepped forward, and another big screen came to life with a picture of a cargo ship tied up at a dock. It was black and white, but the words on its stern were clearly visible. *Sea Fortune.*

"This is your target," he said. "The *Sea Fortune.* At this point in time, it is tied up in Esmeraldas Ecuador. It looks like any other Panamanian-flagged freighter on the exterior. But below her main deck is a secret cargo hold which is used to store containers full of weapons and drugs. We have intel that there are three in there as we speak."

"Is the intel good?" Cara asked.

"Both Mary and I have been assured that the intel is good, yes."

"Who the fuck is Mary?" Axe growled. Then he realized. "Oh, shit. Sorry, General. I forgot."

She frowned at him, then said, "Continue, Luis."

"As you know, we want you to slip on board, confirm

that everything is there, and find a place to lay up until she sails."

"When might that be?" asked Kane.

"In three nights. Once it is in international waters, you are to seize it and bring it within range of Artoro."

"What if there's nothing there?" asked Kane.

"Then we abort."

"Where will you be?" Cara asked him.

"We'll be holed up in a CIA safehouse. We will direct everything from there. Once you're at sea, we'll be flown out to the Artoro to wait."

"What about support?" Axe asked.

Thurston shook her head. "You're it until you get into international waters. After you leave the safehouse, you're on your own. They don't really like us down there, so it has to be as covert as possible."

"Rules of engagement?" Kane asked.

Thurston's face set like granite. "If you have to fight, Sergeant, fight like hell."

APPALACHIA MOUNTAINS, WEST VIRGINIA

Double gates were opened by armed guards, admitting the six black SUVs which drove through in a screen of dust. The sun had set three hours prior to their arrival.

Pulling onto a large turn-around, the vehicles crunched gravel beneath their tires, and their headlights washed over the white façade of a large building before coming to a halt. The doors swung open, and the first ones out were Collins' mercenaries. Setting up a perimeter around the SUVs, they waited for all of those within to alight.

From the front of the building, there was movement when four men emerged from a doorway. They stopped directly beneath an exterior light that was swarming with insects. Three men were armed with a variety of semi-automatic weapons, from a Colt M4, an HK 416, and the third had an AK-47. All three had bushy beards and were clothed in camo gear. The fourth man was obviously their leader.

He was a middle-aged man with graying hair and a thickening waistline. He was clean shaven and carried an air of authority about him. He too wore camo pants, but a T-shirt was his upper body attire, over which he wore a shoulder holster that carried an H&K USP.

Collins approached him, and they shook hands. "Good to see you, Colonel."

"You too, Ward. Come on in. My men will get you squared away."

"Yes, sir."

Collins issued orders to his men who started to move. All except Hall. "What you want me to do, Captain?"

"Go with the others."

"Yes, sir."

Collins, Montoya, and O'Brien followed the man inside. They were led into a room filled with the aroma of cigar smoke. It was lavishly furnished with wood-paneling, leather furniture, and a large timber desk with a polished top. On the wall was a large map of the Appalachia Mountains. Dotted on it were small flag pins.

The man sat behind his desk and asked, "Would you care for a drink, gentlemen?"

Montoya stared at him and said, "Who are you?"

"My thoughts exactly," agreed O'Brien.

The man took the SIG from its holster and laid it on the desktop. His gaze settled upon each man in turn and said, "Gentlemen, my name is Colonel Luke Webster. When Captain Collins came to me and asked for my help, I didn't hesitate to say yes. Don't make me regret that decision."

Montoya shrugged. "It was just a simple question."

Webster nodded. "Here's another simple question. When are you people going to be leaving?"

Collins said, "I'll be leaving with Mr. Montoya tomorrow."

"I wish you luck with that. The stunt you pulled today stirred up a damned hornet's nest. They'll have the border shut down tighter than a fish's ass."

"We've got it covered."

Webster stared at the Irishman. "What about you?"

"Maybe we could come to some beneficial arrangement," O'Brien suggested.

"How so?"

"If I'm not mistaken, this is some kind of militia outpost or some shite like that?"

The colonel's face remained passive. "We are the United Patriot Front of America. That is who we are."

"Well then, how about I donate to your cause? Say, ten million dollars."

Webster's gaze grew as hard. "You have my attention, Mr. O'Brien. But you'd better not be shitting me, or I'll pick up my gun and shoot you in the fucking head. Now, what is it that you want from me?"

"Men."

"Men?"

"I have a job that I want done before I end up back in prison or dead."

"And it is worth ten million to you?"

"It is."

"Then I guess we can come to some arrangement."

"That's what I like to hear."

"When do you want it done?"

"Yesterday."

"Impatient?"

"Fucking oath I am."

Collins cleared his throat. "If it is all the same with you, Colonel, I've got some things to sort out before we leave in the morning."

"Fine. When you're ready, sing out, and I'll have someone show you to your rooms."

"Thank you, sir."

"Meanwhile, it seems that Mr. O'Brien and I have some business to discuss."

———

Once they were outside and on their own, Montoya said to Collins, "Is everything ready?"

"Yes. We have the UAV hidden away, ready to use when needed."

"What about the pilot?"

"He is under surveillance."

"And you will have him when required?"

"Yes."

"I will need to send Gallo a big thank you for all of his help."

"Gallo is dead. Sandoval is in charge now."

Concern settled on Montoya's face. "Tell me what happened."

When Collins was finished, the cartel boss said, "That is too bad."

Collins shrugged. "It is what it is."

"What about the other parts of the plan?"

"There is another team still in Mexico. But the one we

have here will split up and take care of other matters until we return."

"Your new man, can we trust him?"

"Hall? Yes."

"Good. Once the plan is executed, the American government will finally realize that Juan Jesus Montoya is not a forgiving man."

CHAPTER 5

BIGGS AIRFIELD, OUTSIDE OF EL PASO

THE BLACK SUV came to a halt inside the HC-130 aircraft, and Brooke Reynolds climbed down from the driver's seat. She slammed the door and tossed the keys to Ferrero.

"Fully-armored and drives like a dream," she commented.

Towards the front of the aircraft, Kane and Cara ran through a checklist of equipment. They had suppressed HK 416s, two M110 semi-automatic sniper systems, HK MP7s, flashbangs, a box of M67 fragmentation grenades, tactical vests, boxes of ammunition, plus night vision and comms gear. Not to mention the gear for the electronics geeks. Every one of them wore their own personal sidearms in holsters strapped to their thighs. After all, it was the wild west they'd be flying into.

Ferrero asked, "What's the score, Reaper?"

"Seems like everything is there," he said.

"Good."

"Any news from Carlos and Pete?" Cara asked.

Ferrero shook his head. "They won't arrive until later today."

Thurston appeared and started to climb the ramp. Instead of jeans, this time she was dressed in camo pants and a green T-shirt, with a holster strapped to her right thigh; in it, an M17.

"Wheels up in twenty minutes, people," Thurston said in a loud voice.

Kane turned to Thurston and said, "Ma'am?"

Thurston halted. "What is it, Mr. Kane?"

"Are we sure that the CIA will have a truck with enough room, at the other end?"

"That's what they told me," Thurston confirmed. "If they don't I'll kick someone's ass."

The plane was flying into an airstrip twenty miles outside of Esmeraldas. The CIA used it when required. It would be their people meeting the team and ferrying them and their equipment to the safehouse.

"I was thinking, ma'am, that once we land, Cara and I might take a drive to the port. Do some up-close recon."

Thurston nodded. "That's fine. Take a satellite phone with you just in case you need it."

"Yes, ma'am."

She checked out their attire. "You might want to change before we land. I'll see if they can spare a man to go with you, act as a guide."

"Ahh shit!" Axe cursed from behind the stack of gear.

The three of them glanced at him. He looked up, an anguished expression on his face. He saw them staring at him. "What?"

They remained silent.

"I forgot my fucking I-Pod, OK? Got a bitching eight-hour flight and nothing to listen to," he growled.

Thurston said, "I'm sure you can find something to play with."

Kane tried to suppress a smirk as Axe looked confused until it dawned on him what she was getting at. He gave her a broad smile. "You're good. I like you."

"I don't like you," Thurston said and turned away with a smile on her own face.

Cara and Kane both chuckled at the expression on Axe's face. He glanced at them. "She didn't mean that, did she?"

Kane shrugged.

"No, she didn't mean that. Cara, did she?"

Cara gave the ex-marine sniper a sorrowful look. "Don't worry, Axe, I still love you."

"Fuck off the pair of you," he growled. He started to follow Thurston. "Ma'am, did you mean that?"

Ferrero shook his head.

Kane said, "That was funny. It would seem the general has a sense of humor."

Ferrero nodded. "She seems nice from what I can tell since we've been working closely together."

"Are you OK with how it's all changed?"

"Yeah. I think it's for the better. Anyway, too late now, let's get this all finished. We've got a plane to catch."

———

MOOSEHEAD LAKE, MAINE

The white Tahoe crunched to a stop on the gravel turn-around, and the two Reaper Team men climbed out. Arenas looked around. The building before him was built like an old fifties style hunting lodge and was surrounded by tall pines. It was sited in a secluded cove where the lake was fringed with a rocky shore.

In reality, it was a retreat for the terminally ill. And it was where Kane had hidden his sister when Irish mob boss Colin O'Brien became an all too real threat.

An older man in his fifties exited the building and approached them. He stopped in front of Pete Traynor. The bulges where their personal weapons were tucked inside shoulder holsters under their coats hadn't been missed. He eyed them warily and said, "I'm David Harper. I'm in charge here. You are?"

Traynor said, "I'm Pete Traynor, and my friend is Carlos Arenas. John Kane sent us."

Recognition showed in the man's eyes. He held out his right hand for Traynor to shake. "Pleased to meet you both. It would have been better under different circumstances, but that's the way it goes sometimes. My friends call me Doc."

He shook with Arenas and said, "Come with me, and I'll show you where you'll be sleeping."

"One minute, Doc. We just need to get our gear."

Harper nodded. "Sure."

Both men went to the back of the Tahoe and retrieved their large duffels. Then they dragged their tactical vests free. Harper had seen such equipment before, but the concern on his face was still evident.

They started to follow him towards the main door when Arenas said, "Maybe, Doc, you have another way for us to go?" He held up the vest. "We would not want to worry the patients."

There was a hint of relief on Harper's face. "Yes, quite. Follow me this way."

He deviated to the left, and they circled the large building until coming to the back entrance. They were about to enter when Traynor pointed to a small cabin probably fifty yards from the main building. "What's that there?"

Harper shrugged. "It is nothing. Just an old shack that doesn't get used."

"Good. It'll do us just fine."

"But..."

"Don't worry, Doc. We're better off out of the way."

Harper shrugged. "If that's the way you want it. I'll just get a key for the lock."

They watched him walk inside and then, Arenas said, "It is a hard place to defend with just the two of us. We have been here five minutes, and I have already counted four different ways of infiltration. I think we can discount the lake, though. We could see them coming from a long way if they chose such a route."

"So, which one is the most likely then?" Traynor asked.

"If I was them, I would use two points. The road in and the trees to the north," Arenas explained. "They will need to get out fast, so I would park back along the road and wait for an all clear. The snatch team would circle around and come in through the trees to the north. Once the packages were secure, they'd just have to radio the extraction vehicle."

"That's what you would do?"

Arenas nodded. "Yes. But unfortunately, they are not me."

"Once we get unpacked, we can set up some cameras. Maybe do some roving patrols through the night. The main objective is not to get surprised by the bastards."

"Here's the key," Harper said when he emerged from the doorway.

Traynor took it and said, "We'll take it from here, Doc. You go see to your patients."

"Are you the guys my mom sent?"

They turned to face the doorway and saw Jimmy Billings standing there.

Harper started to protest the boy's presence, but Traynor cut him off. "He's fine, Doc. Maybe he can give us a hand. Take his mind off things."

Harper shrugged. "Sure. Dinner is at six."

"We'll be there."

After Harper had disappeared, Traynor looked at Jimmy and said, "Well, you want to help or not?"

Jimmy stared at the big, unshaven ex-DEA agent with all the tattoos, and hesitated. Then he said, "Why not?"

Jimmy was no older than fourteen with a boyish face and dark hair like his mother's. Traynor tossed him his tactical vest and said, "Good, carry that."

Arenas could see the boy's chest swell at being asked to carry the loaded vest. It was heavy, but he caught it with ease. They began walking toward the shack. Traynor asked, "What's the food like here?"

"It's OK, I guess."

"Do they take care of you?" Arenas inquired.

"Sure. The doc is great."

They reached their destination and Traynor unlocked the door. It swung open, and the scent of dust and damp reached their nostrils. Once inside, Arenas screwed up his nose. "I think maybe inside would have been better, *amigo*."

There was clutter everywhere, and the windows had so much grime they were almost opaque.

Traynor picked up an old broom which looked as though it had been savaged by a bear. He examined it and said, "It just needs a clean."

Passing it to Jimmy, he said, "There you go, kid. Make a start."

———

OUTSIDE ESMERALDAS, ECUADOR

The HC-130 touched down shortly after 1400 hours on a long, but pot-holed dirt airstrip which would undoubtedly be very dangerous to use in heavy weather. The plane came to a stop, and the ramp at the rear lowered with a whir.

Beside the strip, waiting in the intense humidity, were three CIA agents with a truck and a battered Ford pickup. Their names were White, Brown, and Black. Obviously not their real names, but they weren't forthcoming with those.

The plane was unloaded, and all of the equipment put into the back of the tarp-covered truck. Ferrero approached Kane and said to him, "Thurston just asked our friend Black about giving you and Cara a guide to go to the port. Brown's going to take you in the pickup."

Kane looked at the battered vehicle. "OK. When are we leaving?"

"Now," said Brown.

Brown was big and athletic with a trimmed beard. If he'd had to guess, Kane would have pegged him as a SEAL in a previous life. Or maybe Delta.

Kane and Cara had changed their clothes on the plane. They both now wore jeans. Kane had on a green t-shirt, and Cara wore a form-hugging white singlet top which accentuated her curves. Sunglasses shaded their eyes, and both had their personal sidearms tucked into the backs of their pants.

"We're ready when you are," Kane said.

"All right then, load up. Let's go and have a look at this ship of yours."

———

ESMERALDAS

It took them an hour to get to the port. An hour of bumping and bouncing in a truck with shot suspension, over pot-holed streets which were in desperate need of repair. Kane sat on the outside while Cara was in the middle. Brown grated and ground the gears with monotonous frequency as they drove along.

"Sorry about the roads," he apologized. "They might see a repair crew once a year. With all of the trucks going back and forth to the port they don't last long."

When they reached the port, Brown pulled the truck over next to a large stack of shipping containers. "That's your target, down there. The other side of the wire."

Roughly a hundred yards ahead of them was a large fence split by twin gates. On the other side was a large container ship.

"Here," Brown said and passed Kane a pair of field glasses.

Kane put them to his eyes and looked at the stern of the ship. Painted in big white letters were the words: **Sea Fortune**.

He let his gaze wander over the ship. The bridge was roughly three stories above the main deck at the stern. It had two cranes on deck as well, to handle its own cargo. The ship looked to be half-loaded on deck, and the dock workers were still busy loading it.

Then he noticed the armed guards. They were

acting as security just inside the gates. There was another at the gangplank, and two more on the wings of the bridge.

Kane passed the glasses to Cara and said, "That's a lot of security. I will assume that there are more there somewhere."

Cara said, "Five times three. That's what I figure anyway."

"Very good," Brown acknowledged. "Five guards on duty at any one time. Three shifts."

"I don't like it," Kane said. "They want us to get on board that thing and hide out until we reach international waters. Then take the damned thing over. I say we plant explosives in the hold and blow it. Take out all their guards and do it that way."

"Glad it's you and not me," Brown said.

"What do you think, Cara?" Kane asked her.

"I can set up on top of these containers with the SASS and provide overwatch. From here, Spencer and I can provide backup. You and Axe go in over the bow. Do your business and get the hell out of Dodge."

"I suppose the CIA hasn't got a UAV up their sleeve by any chance, Mr. Brown?" Kane asked their tour guide.

He chuckled. "Not a chance. Best we could do is maybe a satellite."

Kane nodded. "A satellite I'll take."

Brown was about to suggest they leave when a four by four appeared, the words: **Policia** stenciled on the side.

"This looks interesting," Kane said in a low voice.

"The *Policía Nacional del Ecuador*," Brown told them. "The most crooked sons of bitches around at the moment. If you get caught by them, you'll be in a whole world of hurt."

They watched on in silence and saw the guards open

the gates without hesitation. The vehicle passed through and then stopped near the gangplank.

Two men climbed out dressed in gray uniforms with gray caps. They met a man from the ship at the gangplank's base, and the three talked briefly before the man from the ship handed over an envelope.

"Looks like they're picking up a payment," Cara said.

"Let's get out of here," Kane said. "Before we draw any attention to ourselves."

CIA SAFEHOUSE, ESMERALDAS

Thurston stared at Kane and Cara thoughtfully before she spoke. "Are you sure it's the only way, Reaper?"

Kane nodded. "Yes, ma'am."

"Tell me about it again."

Kane looked at the whiteboard on the wall. He pointed at it, "May I?"

"By all means."

He walked over to it and marked out different areas of the docks. Putting a cross on it, he said, "The ship is here. Gates are here, containers here. Now, they've got lookouts at the gates, the gangplank, on the bridge wings. The only way aboard is over the bow. Then we have to find a place to hide. The easy way is to take them all down. Have Cara and Spencer here with Cara on overwatch. If we get into trouble, they'll be backup. They have fifteen armed men on the *Sea Fortune*. I say we get on, plant the explosives and blow the son of a bitch up."

"What about the local police?" Ferrero asked. "You go making a lot of noise, and they'll come down on you like a ton of bricks."

"We'll have to deal with that if it happens."

Thurston's face grew serious. "I won't have you lot shooting local police. Even if they are crooked. Understand?"

"Yes, ma'am," Kane acknowledged. "Brown also said he can get us access to a satellite to watch over us."

"That would be handy," Ferrero said. "That way if the police dispatch officers we could keep track of them and any other responders."

Thurston shifted her gaze to Ferrero. "What do you think, Luis?"

"I trust Reaper's judgment, Mary. But ultimately it's your call."

Thurston nodded. "OK, we'll do it your way. When will you go?"

"Tomorrow night."

"Fine. But do me one favor, Mr. Kane. Bring me back a canary. Preferably one that will sing. We have no idea who's behind this thing down here."

CHAPTER 6

PORT OF ESMERALDAS

"REAPER TWO, Bravo Three is online, and the picture is clear, over," Teller's voice came through the comms loud and clear.

"Copy, Bravo Three. Reaper Two and Five are in position," Cara responded in a soft voice. "How's it look? Over."

"So far so good, Reaper Two. The sentries all look to be where they're supposed to be. Bravo Four is monitoring all radio frequencies, so we don't get any nasty little surprises."

"Copy, Bravo Three. Reaper Two out."

Beside Cara lay Spencer. He was armed with an HK 416, dressed in full tactical gear, complete with night vision, though it wasn't down because of the bright lights used to flood the ship. "We should be seeing Kane and Axe soon," he whispered.

Cara shifted the SASS and focused her scope on the

bow. Even though the ship was stern on, she could still see some of the hawsers. "Nothing yet."

She swept back to her left along the ship. The sentries were still in place.

Suddenly Cara's comms crackled to life. "Reaper One and Reaper Four are on station. Preparing to board."

"Copy, Reaper One. Reaper Two and Five in an over-watch position. Out."

Cara focused her scope back on the front hawsers and saw Kane start to make his way along it towards the bow. Behind him was Axe. The latter carried the explosives in a waterproof bag. Both were armed with suppressed MP-7s.

The M110 moved back in a long sweep as Cara checked on the sentries once again. All seemed good. None of them had moved.

With her focus now back at the bow, she watched Kane and Axe climb aboard and disappear from her line of sight.

"Reaper Two? Reaper One. We're both aboard and making for the hold. Over."

"Copy, Reaper One. All clear to move. Tangos still stationary. Good luck. Out."

———

THE SEA FORTUNE

Kane brought the suppressed MP7 up to his shoulder and raised his right hand to signal Axe to move. They walked in a crouch along the row of deck containers, their black wetsuits glistening with sea water. When they came across a gap, they slipped into it, using the double stack of twenty-foot boxes for cover.

They kept moving until they ran out of cover and then paused. There was an open area of around thirty-feet. All flat deck. At the far end was a door which would lead them below decks and down into the hold. The only problem was that they would be in full view of the sentries on the bridge wings.

Reaper depressed his talk button. "Reaper Two, keep an eye on the bridge sentries. If they move funny, take them down. Over."

"Copy, Reaper One."

Kane waited for what seemed like an age before both of the sentries weren't looking their way. Kane and Axe ran forward until they reached the door, paused, and then Kane opened it.

All clear.

The next five minutes were spent traversing passage-ways, ladders, and hatches until they reached the hold.

"What color box do we want, Reaper?" Axe whispered.

"Red. Glad to see you listened at the briefing, Axe."

Axe smiled. "Didn't need to. You were coming."

Kane shook his head.

Within one minute of searching, they'd found the container. "Over here, Reaper."

Kane abandoned his search to join Axe who stood before their target.

Axe said, "You get the feeling that this was too easy, Reaper?"

"You too?"

"We saw no one on the way down here. Kinda like the way was cleared for us."

"Let's get this open, and we'll have a look."

Axe and Kane worked the handles, and one of the doors swung open with a dry groan.

"What the fuck," Axe said with disbelief.

"Reaper One? Zero. What do you have? Over."

"We have nothing, Zero. I repeat, nothing. The container is empty."

———

CIA SAFEHOUSE

Ferrero snapped a look at Thurston. "What the hell is going on?"

She was as concerned about it as him. "I don't know. The intel said it was there."

"Fuck!" Ferrero cursed. "Bravo One this is Zero. Confirm your last transmission, over."

"The container is fucking empty, Luis. I can't say it any plainer than that."

Suddenly Teller's voice cut across the conversation. "Bravo Three to all Reaper callsigns. You have trouble inbound. I say again, you have trouble inbound. I count two trucks headed your way. Repeat two trucks. Get ready for company."

Ferrero stared at Thurston in realization. "It is a fucking trap."

"Yes, get them out. Now!"

"Bravo Three? Reaper Two. What is the ETA on the trucks? Over."

"Two minutes, Reaper Two."

"Copy."

Ferrero came over the comms. "Reaper One abort. I repeat, abort. Get the hell out of there."

"Copy."

Behind him, Ferrero heard Thurston curse, "What a damned fuckup."

THE SEA FORTUNE

"Time to go, Axe," Kane snapped.

"Shame to waste these explosives, Reaper."

"You've got one minute."

"Roger," Axe said and reached inside the bag he carried.

He withdrew the device and set the timer for five minutes. Then he set his watch. After which he tossed the device behind the container.

Axe looked at his watch to make sure the timer was running properly.

4:58...4:57...4:56...

"How long, Axe?" Kane asked him.

"Just under five minutes."

"Hell, you didn't give us much time."

"I guess we'd better move."

Then all hell broke loose as gunfire erupted and bullets started to ricochet throughout the hold.

———

PORT OF ESMERALDAS

"Cara, the sentries are moving towards the gates," Spencer warned her when the call for an abort came through.

She focused on the sentries. "They're opening them for the trucks."

"We need to stop them from letting them in. That way it might slow the trucks down."

Cara nodded. "One step ahead of you."

She sighted the M110 on the first of the sentries and

stroked the trigger. He fell as though he'd been hit by the hand of God when the 7.62mm NATO round slammed into him. She then shifted aim to the second target, and another bullet dropped the man midstride.

The sound of automatic gunfire sounded from deep within the ship. "They're taking fire."

She pressed her talk button. "Zero? Reaper Two. Reaper One and Four are taking fire."

"Copy, Cara. Do what you can."

"There's movement on the deck, Cara. Starboard side, amidships."

Cara brought the weapon around. She could see the movement Spencer was talking about and said into her comms, "Reaper One? Reaper Two. You've got more Tangos moving your way. Maybe up to ten, over."

A mess of noise filled her ear, and an incoherent babble followed it.

"Say again. Over."

This time the voice was clearer. "Copy, Reaper Two. We're a little busy right now. Out."

No sooner had the comms gone quiet when another louder noise arose. The whine of truck engines. They came in with a roar and a blaze of headlights. Instead of slowing, the first truck crashed through the gates, the forceful impact throwing them wide.

The second truck followed the first through, and they both skidded to a halt not far from the gangplank. Armed men spewed from the back of both vehicles.

"Shit!" Cara cursed. "Targets of opportunity, Spencer. Shoot whatever moves."

———

THE SEA FORTUNE

A stream of bullets whined off the bulkhead not far from Axe. "These fuckers mean business, Reaper."

Kane fired a burst from his MP7 and saw a man drop. "We need to get out of here, Axe. How much time do we have?"

Axe looked at his watch.

3:31...3:30...3:29...

"Fuck all."

"Lay down some fire!" Kane shouted.

"What do you think I've been doing?" he shouted back and leaned around the side of the container where they were sheltering. He laid down a long burst of fire until the thirty-round magazine ran dry. "Changing," he shouted.

As soon as Axe's gun went silent, Kane pressed forward towards the door in the bulkhead. A man appeared, and Kane squeezed the trigger on the MP7. The would-be killer jerked violently and tumbled back out of sight.

Another man appeared, and the same fate befell him.

Kane reached the door and looked along the passageway. It was clear. But instead of heading back the way they'd come, Kane broke to the right, Axe hot on his ass.

"Keep an eye on that countdown, Axe. I don't want to be down here when that thing blows."

...2:30...2:29...2:28...

"Reaper One, Zero. You need to get out of there now. There are at least twenty more Tangos about to board the ship. Over."

Axe shot a man on their six and growled, "Does he think we're playing with our dicks down here?"

They reached a ladder and climbed it to find a clear

passageway. Moving on until they reached the main deck level, they paused just inside the exit.

"Reaper Two? Copy?"

"Copy, Reaper. Where the hell are you?"

"We're just about to break out onto the main deck."

"Negative, Reaper. Main deck is full of tangos."

"Shit!" Kane cursed. He glanced at Axe. "Talk to me."

Axe glanced at his watch.

...59...58...57...

"We go now or die."

Kane gave him a wry smile. "On the way through, don't forget to grab the boss a canary."

"Ha. Fuck you."

Kane opened the door and raised his MP7. He was about to step through when flying lead filled the void. He drew back. "Shit."

More rounds hammered the interior bulkhead with a metallic staccato sound. Axe tapped him on the shoulder. "After you."

"Yeah, right."

...45...44...43...

"Reaper Two, copy?"

"Copy."

"I need you to clear us a path. You've got thirty seconds."

"Copy that. What happens after thirty seconds?"

"We die."

———

PORT OF ESMERALDAS

"*We die.*"

The words filled Cara's mind and spurred her

instantly into action. She came to her feet and began to run along the tops of the containers closer to the ship.

"Where are you going?" Spencer shouted after her.

Without looking back, she shouted, "Come on, move! They need our help!"

"Christ," the CIA man cursed and followed.

Bullets ricocheted from the containers in small explosions of orange sparks as shooters from the docks followed their route of travel. Cara reached the fence where there was a gap in the containers, and she leaped across. She landed hard, gathered herself, and lined up on the deck with the M110. She stood there like a female Adonis. Illuminated and a clear target.

Her first shot tore through the air and smashed into the chest of a man armed with an AK-47. By the time she lined up on a second target, Spencer was alongside her. He opened fire with the HK416 on full auto and sprayed the deck with a hail of lead.

Over the top of the din, he heard Cara shout, "Reaper, go!"

From where he stood, Spencer saw the two figures erupt onto the deck. They moved fast, firing as they went. Muzzle flashes sparkling across the ship.

Then it blew up in a giant ball of orange flame.

Her face lit by the orange glow, Cara was stunned. She just stared at the ship which was now burning. In her comms, she could hear Ferrero's voice.

"Reaper One, this is Zero, come in."

Nothing.

"Reaper One, this is Zero, come in."

Cara said, "Zero, this is Reaper Two. Reaper One and Four are down. I repeat, Reaper One and Four are down. No one could survive that."

"Reaper Two? Bravo Three. You have more vehicles

headed your way. I think they're Ecuadorian Police. You need to get out of there now."

Cara stood staring at the burning ship in stunned silence.

"Reaper Two?"

Dead air.

"Reaper Two?"

"Cara," Spencer snapped and grabbed her shoulder.

"Huh?"

"We have to go. Police incoming."

She nodded. "Sure."

"Zero, this is Reaper Five. We're moving now."

"Copy, Reaper Five."

Cara and Spencer hurried back along the tops of the containers. They leaped across the gap now illuminated by the flames from the cargo ship. Another explosion rocked the port, and a large fireball erupted skywards. Sirens sounded as the police grew closer.

Cara paused atop the containers and looked back at the burning ship.

"Come on," Spencer urged her. "We don't have time for this."

She shook off his hand and kept her vigil, hoping that Kane might suddenly appear like a Phoenix from the ashes.

It was the police that brought her back from the edge. The arrival of four police vehicles, each with four officers inside, that skidded to a halt not far from their position.

Immediately, one of them looked to the stack where she and Spencer were. He pointed to them and said something which made his compatriots turn.

Instead of shouting at them to stop or surrender, they brought up their guns, and a stream of semi-automatic fire raked the containers where they stood.

This time Cara reacted and ran. She got to the edge of the stack and jumped down, with Spencer close behind. They took shelter behind the containers as more shots clanged from the metallic sides.

"They have us pinned," Spencer said desperately.

Cara leaned around the corner of their shelter and was forced back by more bullet strikes. She pressed her talk button and said, "Zero? Reaper Two, copy?"

"Copy, Reaper Two."

"We are pinned down by heavy fire, over."

"Copy, wait one."

"Christ!" Cara hissed. "Am I cleared to shoot back?"

Thurston came on the comms. "No. We don't want any police casualties."

"They're closing in," Spencer growled.

"Zero, we really need a way out of here," Cara snapped with urgency.

"Wait one, Reaper Two. Bravo Three is working on it."

"Well, work faster."

"Reaper Two requesting permission to open fire."

"No. Permission denied."

"You're tying my fucking hands here."

"They haven't tied mine, Reaper Two," a voice said over the comms. "Get ready to move."

The Reaper was still alive.

————

PORT OF ESMERALDAS

"Reaper, go!"

The voice filled Kane's head, and he didn't hesitate. Both he and Axe came through the door with fresh magazines in their weapons, fire in their belly, the will to live, and fuck all time left on the counter.

They opened fire as soon as they came clear of the doorway. The deck was awash with blood and corpses. Still, there were enough gunmen to go around.

"We're not going to make it, Reaper!" Axe shouted as he shot another killer.

A man stepped in front of Kane to block his path. Before he could fire, Kane shot him point-blank in the face.

They'd almost made it to the side when the charges detonated. At first, Reaper felt the heat of the blast. Then came the brutal force which hit him in the back, followed by a sense of weightlessness.

Things went black for a moment before his senses rushed back when he hit the water with a hard slap.

When Kane's head broke the surface of the water, he saw the flaming ship almost directly above him. Another explosion rocked the vessel, and amongst the orange flames, he thought he saw a couple of human torches, well alight, and writhing with the pain of their melting flesh.

Axe! Where was he?

Kane did a full circle in the water as he looked for his friend. "Axe? Where are you?"

Axe broke the surface a few feet away. "Shit, Reaper. That was big."

Relief washed over Kane at the sound of Axe's voice. "Are you OK?"

"Sure," Axe confirmed. "What do you want me to do with this fucker?"

Kane gave him a confused look. "What?"

From below the surface, Axe raised a muscular arm and dragged up a man, coughing and spluttering to get his breath and rid his lungs of sea water.

Kane gave him a wry smile and shook his head. "Shit. Bring him along."

They swam to the edge of the dock about fifty meters from the burning *Sea Fortune*. The gunfire was still raging. As they pulled themselves over the edge of the dock, Axe encouraged his prisoner to do the same. Both team members had their MP7s, held in place by the shoulder strap attached to them.

Kane observed the carnage before them. The police had arrived and were now concentrating their fire on Cara and Spencer's position, where they were pinned down behind a container. The problem was, the pair weren't returning fire.

"Reaper Two, copy?"

Static.

"Reaper Two, copy?"

More static.

"The damn comms are screwed."

"Zero, copy?"

Axe brought up his MP7 to cover the police who were still firing at Cara and Spencer's position.

"Reaper, we've gotta move. They're closing in on the others. Why don't they shoot back?"

"'Cause they're under orders not to."

"Fuck orders."

Kane smacked at his comms, and they crackled to life. "Got them."

"We are pinned down by heavy fire, over."

"Copy, wait one."

"Christ! Am I cleared to shoot back?"

"No. We don't want any police casualties."

"They're closing in."

"Zero, we really need a way out of here."

"Wait one, Reaper Two. Bravo Three is working on it."

"Well, work faster."

"Reaper Two requesting permission to open fire."

"No. Permission denied."

"You're tying my fucking hands here."

Kane pressed his talk button. "They haven't tied mine, Reaper Two. Get ready to move."

"Reaper, is that you?" Cara called back.

"In the flesh. As soon as we open fire, get the hell out of there."

"Don't shoot the police, Reaper One," Thurston said.

"I'll do my best, ma'am. Cara? Now."

Axe and Kane opened fire with their MP7s, and the police scattered. Beyond them, Kane could see Cara and Spencer break cover. As soon as they disappeared Kane said to Axe, "Shoot out them damned floodlights."

"Copy."

Axe fired burst after burst at the lights which exploded with each spurt. Soon it was all dark, and once more Kane pressed his radio button. "Bravo Three, we need a way out."

"Copy, Reaper One. Ten meters to your right there is a ladder. It will take you over the edge of the dock to a walkway. The maintenance crews use it to keep an eye on things under the dock itself."

"Roger, Bravo Three," Kane replied and turned to Axe. "Time for us to go. Bring your friend."

They moved along to the ladder before the Ecuadorian police could regather themselves, and climbed down over the side of the dock to the platform below.

Kane said, "Give us some directions, Bravo Three."

"OK, track straight ahead for fifty meters until you reach a T-junction."

"Copy. Axe this way."

"On your six, Reaper," Axe said. He shoved his prisoner and growled, "Move asshole."

They worked their way along the walkway until they reached the junction. "Which way, Bravo Three?"

"Turn left and keep going until you find another ladder. Climb that, and you should be clear. One click along the road is an old petrol station. I'll have Reaper Two meet you there. See you when you get back."

"Copy. Come on, Axe, let's go home."

CHAPTER 7

CIA SAFEHOUSE

REYNOLDS PUT a sticking plaster on Kane's left shoulder and patted it, making him wince. "Easy."

She smiled at him showing her even teeth. "Toughen up, stud. I've had more skin off my knees."

Kane stared over at Axe who was getting a bandage wrapped around his forearm by Cara. "I can't believe you only put five minutes on that thing. You dick."

"It would've been plenty of time if those other pricks hadn't turned up."

Spencer came into the room and took off his tactical vest. He was followed by Thurston. Axe looked at her and asked, "How's my little buddy?"

"All ready," she replied. "One question though."

"What's that?"

"How the hell did you manage to capture him?"

"Right place, wrong time. He happened to be in my way, and I sure wasn't going around him."

Kane said, "What I want to know, General, is where that intel came from. That was a set up if ever I saw one."

She nodded. "I'll get someone onto it. You're right. This was meant for us. Someone doesn't like you at all."

"And I figure I know who," Cara said in a dry tone.

"Are you thinking Montoya?" Reynolds asked.

"Yes. Who else would it be?"

"But when we got the intel he was still behind bars," Thurston pointed out.

"If he can organize a breakout as he did," Cara said. "he can sure organize something like this."

Thurston stared at Cara. "Let's go and find out, shall we?"

————

The man was tied to a chair in a spare room. He had been stripped down to his waist and was being watched over by Brown. Directly in front of him, a few feet away, there was a camcorder on a tripod.

Three of them walked into the room. Thurston, Ferrero, and Kane. They stood before the sweating man and waited in silence.

Ferrero spoke first. "Who are you?"

The man stared past them at the wall.

Ferrero tried again, this time in Spanish. *"Quién eres?"*

The man glanced at him and then spit on the floor at his feet.

Kane stepped in closer and hit him across the face. *"Necesitas tener respeto.* You need to have respect."

This time the man spit blood.

Kane hit him again. "I can do this all day."

"Fuck you," the man snarled.

"English," Thurston said. "That's a start."

"Fucking *puta*."

"Who set up the ambush?" Thurston asked.

The man just stared at her.

"I'll ask you again. Who set up the ambush?"

The man swore at her again.

"What happened to the drugs that were on the ship?"

Nothing.

"Ma'am, give us a go, and we'll get him to talk," Brown said.

Thurston's eyes grew hard. "I'll not have him tortured."

"No, ma'am. Wouldn't dream of it."

She looked at him skeptically and then nodded. "OK. Give it a go."

They left the room, and White joined Brown. They were in there for thirty minutes before Brown emerged.

"His name is Alejandro. He doesn't know who ordered the setup," Brown explained. "However, he does know where the drugs and weapons went to."

"Which is?" Ferrero asked.

"Puerto de Topolobampo in Mexico."

Kane cursed. "Sinaloa. Should have fucking guessed."

"Well, that's their destination anyway. It seems that they are to be delivered to a warehouse in Juarez from there."

"Did he say exactly where?" Thurston asked.

Brown shook his head.

"Rattle his cage some more and see if he knows."

"Yes, ma'am," Brown said. Before going back in, he looked at Kane. "That was some serious shit you all went through out there."

Shrugging, Reaper said, "What is it they say? All in a day's work."

Brown smiled. "Yes, sir. Serious shit. I'll go and see what else our friend knows."

"Once we're done with him," Thurston said, "he needs to disappear. Can't have him back on the street telling what he knows."

They stared at her.

Thurston shrugged. "What? I said I don't abide torture. Didn't say anything about killing. As soon as we know everything there is to know, we're back on that plane."

———

MOOSEHEAD LAKE, MAINE

There were ten in total. Black-clad figures fitted out in tactical vests and armed with Diemaco C8s, made in Canada then shipped across the border and into the laps of the United Patriot Front of America.

For some reason, none of them wore night vision goggles. Maybe they considered them superfluous to their needs. After all, it was just a hospital.

As they slipped through the trees, they split into two groups of five. The first stopped in place one hundred yards from the building while the second circled around to the back so they could affect a double-pronged attack.

Ten minutes after they split, a radio message came over the comms from the second team. "Team Two in position."

The leader of team one depressed his talk button, "Copy. On my mark. Three, two, one, Execute."

Then all hell broke loose.

———

"We have movement on one of the cameras, *amigo*," Arenas said as he shook Traynor awake.

It was a touch after 2 a.m., and the only sounds to be heard were the loons on the lake. Traynor came out of his bedroll and to his feet. As he did so, he scooped up the suppressed HK416.

Arenas was already in his tac vest and had his helmet with night vision in place. He checked his weapon and made sure he had a round in the chamber with the safety on.

While Traynor prepared, Arenas kept an eye on the camera. "They've gone out of view."

"If they get inside, we're going to have trouble," Traynor pointed out as he rammed his SIG M17 home in its thigh holster.

"I hope that will not happen. Let's go and make it so, *amigo*."

They walked out the door and into the night, to the darkness being torn apart by gunfire.

"Shit!" Traynor cursed as he hit the dirt, the thud of bullets all around him as they dug deep into the ground. He flicked his NVGs down. Ahead of him in the green haze formed by the goggles, he could see five forms. All were armed, and all were shooting at both him and Arenas.

A burst spewed forth as he squeezed the trigger. One of the attackers jerked violently as the bullets struck home. The problem was that all impacted the vest and even though it put the shooter down, he was by no means out of the fight.

Beside Traynor, Arenas used a different method. He had the selector switch on his 416 set to single shot. With his NVGs down, the laser sight on the weapon stood out like a beacon. He dropped it onto his first target's head and fired. The shooter's skull snapped back, and his body dropped like a stone.

He shifted aim within a couple of heartbeats and fired again for the same result.

The effect was instant, and the two remaining shooters emptied their magazines in a wild spray. Traynor felt a bullet tug at his sleeve. He cursed under his breath and fired off another burst. This time the bullets struck the shooter just above the vest and opened a horrific wound in the man's throat.

Although they couldn't see it, the man clutched at his throat, striving to stem the gouts of arterial blood.

The remaining shooter died with a bullet in his brain.

As the gunfire died away across the lake, Arenas and Traynor came to their feet. They advanced on the fallen attackers; their weapons raised and ready to fire. When they reached them, the man who'd taken the burst in the vest was starting to squirm. Arenas reversed his 416 and hit him between the eyes with the stock.

"We'll come back for him," he said.

"They fucking split up," Traynor cursed. "The second team will be inside already."

"On me," Arenas snapped, and he ran towards the rear entrance to the hospital.

The doorway took them in through the kitchen and out into a large dining hall. From there they exited into a foyer with three passageways running off in different directions.

It was in the foyer that they found the first casualty of the unwanted intrusion. On the floor was a night nurse. A man. His white clothes stained red with blood. They flipped up their NVGs.

Arenas lowered his HK416 and let it hang by its strap.

Traynor followed suit and both then drew their M17s from their leg holsters.

There was movement along each of the halls as the gunfire had disturbed the patients. Each passage had dim night lights which ran horizontally at the base of the walls.

Further movement behind them made Traynor swing around, his gun up and ready to fire.

Harper's arms were raised, and he said hurriedly, "Easy, it's me. What's going on? What happened to Michael?"

Michael was obviously the male nurse on the floor.

"Take care of your patients," Traynor urged him. "They're inside."

Without waiting for a reply, Arenas and Traynor made their way along the passage. Inquisitive patients were ushered back inside their rooms when the men reached them. At the end of the passage, there was a turn to the left.

A person wearing full tactical gear appeared suddenly and was surprised to see the two men.

He tried to bring up his gun, but it was already too late. Arenas and Traynor opened fire together. The man jerked with the bullet strikes and dropped to the floor. While one bullet hit his vest, the second punched into his face, deflected upward, and ripped through his brain.

Another man leaned around the edge of the hallway and opened fire with his Diemaco C8. The bullets burned along the passage, forcing the two Reaper team men to dive for the nearest doorway.

The firing stopped, and Arenas put his head around the corner of the doorway. The end of the passage was empty. With hand signals to Traynor, he indicated his intent to move further along.

The M17 came up to eye level, and Arenas started

forward. Behind him, Traynor emerged and covered his back.

When Arenas reached the corner, he peered around it and saw that the passage that way was empty. He took a knee beside the downed man and felt for a pulse. There was none.

With his gaze focused back on the passage, Arenas said, "Moving, *amigo*."

Halfway along, he reached the room where Melanie Kane lay. He looked inside and saw that she was as OK as she could be, given her state. Relief flooded through Arenas, and he moved along to the next doorway. Jimmy's room.

It was empty. "Shit."

The bed was mussed, and there were signs of a struggle.

Traynor was at his shoulder. "What?"

"The boy is gone."

The curtain flickered in the breeze of the open window. "They got out that way."

Hurrying across to the window, they looked out and were immediately assaulted by spraying glass and bullets as the rattle of an automatic weapon rang out, peppering the pane and punching holes in the wall.

They dove to the floor, and Traynor shot out the ceiling light which had illuminated them. Then they flipped down their NVGs and worked their way back to the window.

The firing had stopped, and they peered cautiously through the opening. The hazy green view revealed retreating figures. And the boy.

"They're making for the lake," Arenas said hurriedly. "We need to stop them."

The two Reaper men climbed through the ruined

window frame and started after the kidnappers. The head start was too great, however, and by the time they reached the shore of the lake, the group had already boarded the waiting boat, and it was roaring off across the water.

———

Arenas placed the muzzle of the M17 against the man's thigh and growled, "You tell me what I want to know, *amigo*, and I won't shoot you in the leg."

The man gave him a wry smile which more or less said, I dare you to. So he did. Arenas shot him right through the solid mass of thigh muscle.

The report reverberated around the small shack, followed by a high-pitched scream. Arenas slapped his face and said, "I don't have time for this, *imbécil*. Tell me what I want to know."

"You fucking shot me, asshole!" the man shrieked.

"And I'll shoot you again if you don't tell me what I want to know," Arenas snarled.

"All right, all right. I'll tell you."

"What's your name?"

"Mickey."

"Where have your friends taken the boy?"

"Appalachia Mountains. We have a compound there."

"Who's we?" Traynor snapped.

"United Patriot Front of America," Mickey said.

"Shit," Traynor hissed.

Arenas stared at him. "Who are these people?"

"Bunch of fucking gun nuts," Traynor explained. "Want to take the country back from the politicians. You know, usual bullshit."

"But why have they taken him?" Arenas asked, his focus back on their prisoner. "Why have you taken him?"

"Ten million dollars."

"What?"

"The colonel was offered ten million by some Irish-man, to get the woman and the boy."

Arenas said, "O'Brien?"

The man shrugged. "I don't know."

"Tell me about him," Traynor said.

"He arrived the other day with a bunch of mercs. And some other Mexican guy."

"Christ," Traynor hissed. "Was it Montoya?"

The man nodded. "Maybe. But he left."

"Where'd he go?"

"Don't know."

The barrel of Arenas' weapon pressed down on the wounded leg. The man shrieked, "I don't know! Honest. He and the mercs left the next day."

The former DEA agent took out his cell. "We've gotta call this in."

CIA SAFEHOUSE, ECUADOR

Thurston was dozing on a cot when Ferrero woke her. He switched on the light and said, "Sorry, Mary, but we've got a problem."

She gathered herself for a moment and sat up, swinging her legs over the cot's side. She asked, "What is it, Luis?"

"There's an issue with the team in Maine."

Her face grew serious. "Talk to me."

He placed the cell down and said, "Tell her, Pete."

Traynor's voice came over the speaker. "Ma'am, we

were hit by two teams of militia. We stopped one but the second got away with Jimmy. Reaper's sister is safe."

"Shit!" Thurston growled. "How many shooters?"

"There were ten in all."

"And they were militia?"

"The feller we questioned said they were a group holed up in the Appalachian Mountains. United Patriot Front of America."

Thurston glanced at Ferrero who winced. She nodded. "You said you have a prisoner?"

"Yes, ma'am."

"Did you get anything else out of him?"

"He more or less told us where they were holed up," Traynor answered. "And there was one more thing."

"What?"

"A team of mercs arrived at their compound a few days ago. They brought with them a couple of passengers. Montoya was one, the other we can be sure, was O'Brien."

"Are they still there?"

"Montoya left the next day. The second man is still there. He paid ten million to get to Reaper's sister and the boy."

"Is that it?"

"Pretty much."

"OK. Hang up and wait for a phone call."

"Yes, ma'am."

The line went dead.

Ferrero said, "How do you want to play this?"

"Keep it under your hat for now. I need everyone on this team with their eyes forward. I'll make a call and get them some help. They're going to need it. The man who heads up those damned nuts was a ranger. His name is Luke Webster. He was a colonel and has mostly military personnel under him."

"Who are you going to call?" Ferrero asked.

"Jones. If anyone can help, it'll be him."

———

MOOSEHEAD LAKE, MAINE

The cell rang, and Traynor picked up immediately. "Hello?"

The deep voice on the other end said, "You know what I hate about getting a phone call at three in the morning? It's generally always bad news. Tell me yours and don't leave anything out."

Traynor related the events of the evening to General Jones. When he'd finished, the general said, "I'll send some transport for you. Most likely a helo. You'll be taken to a secure place where you'll find Scimitar waiting for you. Both he and Pop-Eye will help you out with this one. Do whatever it takes to get the kid back. Even if you have to kill all those fucking gun nuts to do it."

The line went dead.

Traynor looked at Arenas and grinned. "I guess we're going to kick some militia ass."

———

SINALOA, MEXICO

Team Reaper was swapped over from CIA to DEA the following night. A three-vehicle convoy sped along the gravel road, leaving a rooster tail of dust behind it. The HC-130 had landed on a strip ten miles from Puerto de Topolobampo. Their gear was loaded into the backs of the three Chevy Suburbans before starting out for the DEA safehouse which overlooked the port.

Headlights cut through the dark as they rounded a bend in the road and the gravel changed to blacktop. Reaper sat in the front with the driver of the first vehicle, a man named Wells. In the back were Thurston and Cara. The suburban behind them carried Ferrero, Axe, and Reynolds. The third vehicle carried Swift, Teller, and Spencer.

Countryside gave way to the streets of Topolobampo, and that was when it happened. The small convoy swung around a blind corner and was faced with four armed men standing in the middle of the street. Behind them, blocking any further advance was a battered old Ford truck.

Wells cursed and brought the Chevy to a halt. Kane took out his M17 and placed it on his lap. Behind him, he sensed Cara and Thurston do the same.

"Out back of us," Wells said.

Kane looked in the side mirror and saw another truck fall in behind the third Chevy. Reaper pressed his talk button. "Axe, Spencer, be prepared but hold your fire. We don't want a damned firefight just yet."

Axe's voice came over the coms, "You ruin all my fun, Reaper. Can't I shoot just one?"

"If this goes south, shoot as many as you want."

Two of the armed men approached the Chevy. They split and stood at each side window. Kane wound his down and stared out at the tattooed man standing before him.

The Mexican had a mirthless smile on his face. He said, "What have we got here? A car full of *gringos*, yes? What are you doing out here after dark? Do you not know that it is very dangerous to do this?"

Kane smiled. "What can we do for you, *amigo*?"

"You can get out of the car for a start, eh?"

Shaking his head, Kane said, "Can't do that."

"But what if I insist?"

"That would be a mistake," Kane told him.

The man stared at him as he weighed up what to do next. Stops like this relied on fear to be successful. But this American showed anything but fear. He shrugged. "I will ask you again nicely, *gringo*. You and your friends get out of the car."

Instead of getting out, Kane said, "What's your name?"

The man frowned. "Pablo."

"Well, Pablo, have you ever seen what one of these can do up close?"

The Mexican was confused, and before he could blink, Kane raised the M17 and pointed it straight at Pablo's face. He was armed with an AK-47 and reflexively made to bring it up.

"I wouldn't," Kane snapped. "Not unless you want to see the sun come up."

Pablo's face screwed up in anger. "If you kill me, *gringo*, Ernesto will kill you and everyone in the car."

"I don't think so. You see, he'll already be dead."

"Are you going to shoot him too?"

Kane shook his head. "Nope. I won't. She will."

Pablo looked into the back and Cara waved her own sidearm at him. She asked him, "Does your friend have a mother? I'll send her a letter about how he died."

"Fucking *puta*," Pablo hissed. He stepped back from the window and shouted out, "*Déjalos ir!*"

"Cara, neutralize the threat," Kane said in a low voice and squeezed the trigger on his M17. He fired two shots which punched into the Mexican's face. In the back, he heard Cara's sidearm crash twice and felt the draft rush through the Suburban as the window blew out.

"Go! Go! Go!" Kane snapped, and the doors on the Chevys were flung open.

The professional shooters of team Reaper were out in an instant. Kane and Cara took the Mexicans to their front, while Axe and Spencer took the rear-most vehicle. Taken completely by surprise, the two in front of the small convoy jerked violently with each bullet strike.

They collapsed to the ground, and Kane shifted his aim. Just as he did, the truck roared to life. Then Reaper blew through the rest of his magazine, dropped it out and reloaded another. Cara did the same, and loud clangs sounded as their bullets peppered the vehicle.

It lurched forward then came to a sudden stop.

Behind Kane and Cara, Axe and Spencer did the same with the rear-most truck. By the time they emptied two magazines each into it, it looked more like a sieve than an automobile. Except what ran through it were fluids and blood.

Kane strode purposefully forward; the M17 still raised and ready to fire. On his way, he checked the corpses. Cara skirted the front of the Ford, her M17 never wavering from the shattered windshield.

She opened the driver's door, and the man behind the wheel slumped sideways, half in and half out. She checked him. "He's dead, Reaper."

"Reaper One and Two are clear," he said over the net.

"We're clear back here, Reaper," Axe said. "We've got two down."

"Let's get them off the street before we get an audience."

Wells came out of the driver's seat in a rage. He walked

up to Kane and growled, "What the fuck was that? He was letting us past. Christ!"

"He would have followed us to look for another chance," Kane said. "We don't need that."

Wells whirled about and stalked across to Thurston who had climbed from the back seat of the suburban. "Are you going to do something about him?"

"He's right," she said to Wells. "They would have followed us and tried again. Losing face is something that he wouldn't have let go."

Knowing when he was beaten, the DEA man walked away to cool down. Thurston, on the other hand, walked over to Kane and said in a low voice. "The next time you do something like that, let me fucking know. I hate surprises."

"Sorry, ma'am, but there was no time."

"Damn it, Reaper," Ferrero said. "What was that shit?"

"That was me doing my job. Now, if you don't mind, I'll help clean this mess up."

Thurston nodded. "Fine, do it. See if you can find out who they are, while you're at it."

"That's easy enough," Kane said. "They'll be West Coast Cartel."

"Just see if you can confirm it."

"Yes, ma'am."

CHAPTER 8

PUERTO DE TOPOLOBAMPO, SINALOA, MEXICO

"HEY, REAPER," Axe said, waving a plate of food at Kane. "You've gotta taste this shit, man. It's better than freaking MREs."

Kane glanced at it and winced. It was a crude breakfast of pancakes, syrup, beans, bacon, and eggs. "Christ, Axe. Are you really eating that shit?"

Axe looked hurt. "This is good food you're insulting, man. I'm offended you would even say such a thing."

Brooke Reynolds said, "It looks like something bikini-clad women would wrestle in."

Cara hid a smile behind the book she was reading.

Winking at Reynolds, Axe said, "Are you offering?"

"Not in this lifetime, baby."

"I can take the bacon off if you don't like it."

Reynolds walked up to him and ran a finger through his food and slipped it seductively into her mouth. She withdrew it slowly, and his eyes lit up. Smiling at him, she walked away. He said, "Is that a maybe?"

His eyes fixed on her ass as she walked away, her hair halfway down her back in a ponytail. He glanced at Kane. "That's a definite maybe."

Kane nodded. "Yeah, buddy. You keep at it."

All the while, Cara was smiling broadly behind her book.

The team was outside in the pool area of a hacienda-style house used by the DEA as a base. At any one time, there were four agents housed there. It was quite a magnificent area with a clear pool and lots of leafy foliage in the garden. The pavers all around were sandstone, and the path to the house led to a large set of bifold doors.

Teller was seated on a banana lounge with his shirt off, catching some rays in the Mexican sun. Spencer was off on his own doing the same. Swift had his feet dangling in the pool, whilst doing something on his smartphone.

Cara lowered her book and said, "Reaper, have you heard anything?"

He stared at her. "No."

She looked about for Reynolds. "Brooke?"

"Yes?"

"Has Luis heard anything from Maine?"

Reynolds gave her a sorrowful look. "Not that I know of. He hasn't said. Sorry."

"Gather around, team," Ferrero said as he and Thurston emerged from inside. A DEA agent named Tobin joined them. In his hand was a folder. He tossed it onto an outdoor table and pointed at it. "These are aerial photos of the warehouse that we believe the drugs have been taken to. Whether they're still there or not, we can't be certain."

Axe fought to speak around a mouthful of food, but it came out jumbled. Thurston looked at him and the mush on his plate. She reached out and took both the plate and fork from him. He looked at her as though she'd stolen his last piece of candy. Ignoring him, she started to eat it. He smiled and puffed out his chest. "Now that's what I call a connoisseur of good food."

She said, "It tastes like shit, but I haven't eaten since yesterday, and at the moment I could eat the crotch out of a low-flying duck."

"OK, listen up," Ferrero said. "Make yourselves familiar with the warehouse and its surrounds. You're going in to have a look tonight."

"Who is?" Kane asked.

"You and Cara. The rest of the team will be backup. I want this to be done quietly. We establish that the drugs are there first, then get out. If we can confirm that they are, then the DEA will take over."

"Why the fuck are we even here?" Axe asked. "Why can't the DEA send one of their CIs in there to have a look?"

"It's how it's going to be," Ferrero told him firmly.

"I'll go on my own," Kane said.

"No," Cara told him.

"I agree," said Ferrero.

"The last thing we want is the team getting caught in another shit storm like Ecuador. I slip in, take a look and then exfil. Less chance of being seen that way."

"And if you are, what then? You'll be out on a limb," Cara pointed out.

Ferrero turned to Thurston. "What do you think, Mary?"

"I agree with you, but if Reaper wants to go on his own, well..." she let the rest of the sentence hang whilst pointing the fork.

Ferrero studied Kane and then said, "All right. We'll do it this way. We'll put Cara on overwatch. She can find a place to lay up and then if you do get into trouble, she'll be on hand. Good enough?"

Kane was about to disagree when Ferrero cut him off. "I didn't say it was negotiable, Reaper."

"Fine."

"Good, now let's sort out the particulars."

"Hang on a moment," Axe interrupted. "How is it that Cara gets to go and not me?"

"Because she's reliable, sweetie," Reynolds told him.

"I'm reliable."

Ferrero's gaze fixed on him. "We need this done quietly, Axe. When we need a one-man free-fire zone, I'll send you. Now, let's get back to it."

———

DOVER AIRFORCE BASE, DELAWARE

Arenas finished stuffing the last of the 5.56 NATO rounds into the magazine and placed it in the remaining empty pouch on his tactical vest. Across from him, Traynor was doing the same.

"Are you sure you want to do this, *amigo*?" Arenas asked him.

"What? Jump out of a perfectly good plane from God knows how many feet in the air, attached to some crazy SEAL who isn't going to open his chute until the trees are about to jam up my ass?"

Arenas smiled at him. "That's it."

Chief Borden Hunt smiled at him. "Pete, if I didn't know any better, I'd think that you were nervous."

Traynor looked up at him. "Tell me again just how the fuck we're meant to stop when we're packing all of this equipment."

"The ground is usually good for that," Popeye said.

"Fuck you very much," Traynor growled. "It's all right for you pricks that have done this shit before."

"Hey, Pete," another SEAL named Rucker called across to him. "If you get to ten feet and the parachute hasn't opened, don't worry about it. You should be right to jump from there."

"Bite me, asshole," Traynor cursed.

"All right," Hunt said. "Game faces on. We've got thirty minutes until wheels up. Doublecheck your equipment."

There would be five of them going into the Appalachian Mountains that night. Hunt as team leader and Popeye would act as team sniper and provide over-watch. Rucker was a trained combat medic, just in case.

Hunt had gone over the plan with them earlier in the day. Their landing zone, LZ, was about two kilometers from the compound. Once on the ground they would hump in and should be in position soon after midnight.

From there they would insert and extract the boy. And if possible, neutralize O'Brien. If they couldn't, then they were to just get out. Drone surveillance had the Irish mob boss in a small building on the east side of the compound.

Their exfil was approximately fifteen hundred meters to the north where there was a clearing large enough to put a Blackhawk down in.

Admiral Joseph had also seen fit to supply them with a UAV should it be required.

Ten minutes later, Hunt called them around a table to go over the blown-up photo of the compound one more time.

"OK," he said. "This is the high ground to the east. Popeye will set up there. Once we're in position at the fence, Popeye will neutralize the guards. From there, Pete and I will go after O'Brien. Carlos and Rucker will get the kid. If all goes well, we rendezvous back here at the fence. If not, we get out as best we can and rendezvous on the high ground with Popeye who will provide cover for us. If it does go south, Pop, any target of opportunity. Those are the admiral's orders."

"Copy that."

"All right, let's go."

———

PUERTO DE TOPOLOBAMPO, SINALOA, MEXICO

Kane hid behind a stack of steel drums and waited for the guard to walk by. There were three guards in all, doing roving patrols. The trouble being that between Kane and the warehouse was a hundred feet of open, floodlit ground that trucks used as a turnaround.

"Hold, Reaper," Cara said softly. She had set up position on the rooftop of a building four-hundred meters away from the target. It was less than ideal but gave her a full field of fire with the M110. "Hold."

"Come on, Cara, get me in there."

"Patience, Reaper," Ferrero said over the comms. Even though the rest of the team had no eyes on, they could still listen in. Behind him stood Axe and Spencer. He turned to see them both dressed in combat gear and fully armed. He frowned. "What are you doing?"

"It's called being prepared," Axe told him. "We're the QRF."

Meanwhile, another guard walked past.

"There's something going on here, that's for sure,"

Cara said. There are lights on inside, and I saw a shadow move."

"If you want to call this off, Reaper, just say the word," Ferrero said.

"Negative."

"Your call."

"Ready, Reaper?" asked Cara.

"Just say the word."

Cara was about to give the all clear when the roar of a large diesel motor sounded, and headlights flashed into view. A flatbed truck with a battered shipping container on back swung into the warehouse yard and stopped in close proximity to the building's door.

"What's going on?" Ferrero asked.

"A truck just pulled up," Cara told him.

Two men climbed out of it and walked towards the back. They stopped at the double doors and swung them open. There were some shouts and Cara watched on as the human cargo was unloaded forcefully from the back of it.

"Shit," she cursed. "Can you see this, Reaper?"

"I've got it."

Ferrero came back over the comms. "What can you see?"

Cara said, "There are six women who have just been manhandled from the container on the back of the truck. And they're not Latino."

"Say again, Reaper Two?" This time it was Thurston.

"They're Caucasian females, ma'am. If they're not American, I'd say European. That would be my guess."

"Trafficking for their brothels?"

"Yes, ma'am."

"OK. Stand down for the moment. We'll see how this unfolds."

Kane said, "I'm not going anywhere."

———

APPALACHIAN MOUNTAINS

Traynor was still shaking after the drop, and they'd been on the ground for the best part of an hour. At least he was still alive.

Popeye was on point as they moved silently through the trees, aided by the green haze of their NVGs. Somewhere a night-bird made a sound that was accentuated by the stillness of the darkness.

Traynor readjusted his grip on the suppressed HK416 and took another step forward. And froze as Popeye's voice came over the net. "*Scimitar hold! Danger close! Danger close!*"

"Copy," said Hunt and then there was silence.

The comms were quiet for around a minute before Popeye came back on. "Tango down."

"Copy, tango down."

They moved forward, and Popeye was waiting beside the dead militiaman. The SEAL had used his Strider SMF marine corps knife, won in a card game a few years before, to neutralize the immediate threat.

"Roving patrol of one," he said to Hunt.

"I guess we'll need to step this up a bit then. We can't be far away. Lead out, Pop."

"Roger."

Hunt pressed his talk button. "White Shark, this is Scimitar, over."

Hunt's comms crackled to life. "Copy, Scimitar."

"Is that UAV up? Over."

"Roger. The UAV should be overhead in the next five mikes."

"Copy. We've just neutralized a tango. We're moving on to target at best possible speed before this blows up in our faces."

"Roger, Scimitar. White Shark out."

Hunt walked over to Arenas. "As soon as that dead guy doesn't check in on time, they're going to get suspicious."

Just then the dead militiaman's radio came to life. "Lima Four, do you read?"

"Fuck," Hunt breathed.

Arenas leaned down to pick up the radio.

Hunt reached out to stop him. "What the hell are you doing?"

"If we don't do something they will get suspicious."

"And you're going to fucking talk to them?"

"No. Just wait."

Arenas picked up the radio just as the voice came across it again. "Lima Four, do you read?"

Arenas pressed the squelch button twice and waited.

"Lima four, come in?"

He did it again.

"What's going on, Morris?" the voice asked. "I can hear the squelch, but I can't hear you."

Arenas repeated his last.

"Christ, Morris. All right. Listen, when you finish your watch get the damned thing fixed. I'll check back in an hour."

Hunt looked at Arenas and said, "That'll work. Now let's get the hell out of here."

———

PUERTO DE TOPOLOBAMPO, SINALOA, MEXICO

The darkness swallowed the red of the truck's tail lights, and once the sound of its powerful motor died away in the distance, all grew quiet once more. From arrival to departure, twenty minutes had elapsed.

The women had been unloaded and taken inside the warehouse. The count on tangos had risen to seven without the two from the truck.

"What is your intention, Reaper?" Cara asked him over the comms.

"Call it when we're clear, Reaper Two," he told her. "I'm still going in to have a look."

"Copy. You should be clear in three, two, one, go."

Hunched over in a low crouch, Kane emerged from his hide and moved towards the door. A black-clad figure with a suppressed M17 raised and ready to use.

He was still ten feet from the door when it swung open, and an armed man appeared. Kane dropped to a knee, and before he could fire, the SASS Cara was armed with fired and the Mexican dropped like a stone.

"I suggest you get him stowed away, Reaper."

"Thanks."

He hurried to the door and paused for a moment, listening for any sign of alarm. There was none, and he leaned down, picked up the AK-47 the cartel man had dropped, slung it over his shoulder, and then grabbed him by the collar.

Kane dragged him behind a pile of crates just inside the door. He leaned the AK there as well. Then he hurriedly closed the door just as another guard came around the corner.

The first thing Reaper did was scan for security cameras but saw nothing. He relaxed slightly.

Kane switched his comms to VOX and said, "I'm in. All clear."

"Good luck."

The interior of the warehouse was lit by large bell-shaped lights suspended by chains from the metal-framed roof. They threw a warm white rather than cool white light. To his right, there was another big stack of crates. Starting to work his way over to them, the sound of a sneeze caused him to freeze.

Kane looked up and saw an armed guard on a long catwalk which ran the width of the warehouse. He ducked behind a pallet of barrels, out of sight. *How the fuck did I miss him?*

He waited for a moment to make sure that the man wasn't looking in his direction and then went across to the crates. Checking to see whether he could get a look inside any of them, he noted that they were battened down tight.

Above him on the catwalk, the guard was on the move to the far side. It gave Kane a chance to slip along the wall behind him and over towards another stack of pallets. He checked them over. Tied down on them were forty-four-gallon drums. Their lids were sealed by a spring-release fastener.

Using his knife to cut through some of the plastic wrap around them, Kane tried to access one of them. With the wrap cut away he quietly unclipped the lid fastener and pulled it free. Next, he lifted the lid away just far enough to get a look inside. It was loaded with pills. Little pink ones with love hearts pressed into them.

Ecstasy. And judging by the number of barrels, there was one hell of a lot of money tied up in them. He whispered, "I just found a shitload of ecstasy, Zero."

"Copy."

Behind them were more drums, different to the one

he'd checked out. He crept over to them and read the labels. They were a mix of chemicals that your everyday garden variety drug lord would use in the manufacture of product.

He peered around the corner of the stack and saw a guard outside a door. His guess was that the girls were being kept in there. There was, however, no way of getting inside without being seen.

Kane momentarily pondered his next move. Decision made he said into his mic, "Reaper Two, kill the guards."

"Say again, Reaper."

"Kill the guards, Cara."

"Copy."

"Damn it, Reaper," Ferrero hissed in his ear. "What are you doing?"

"I'm going hot."

CHAPTER 9

"POPEYE IN POSITION."

"Copy," Hunt said. "Tell me what we've got, Pop."

The night vision scope on the MK11 Sniper Weapons System (SWS) picked up two guards. "There's a guard to your ten o'clock and another to your two, Chief. If you want to get in there unseen they'll need to go."

Hunt eased through the foliage and swept the perimeter with his CQBR, also known as the Close Quarters Battle Receiver, a variant of the M4A1 assault rifle which the SOCOM operators used. He picked out the two militia guards and said in a low voice. "Eyes on."

Popeye was right. There was no way of getting past them and through the fence without being seen. "Popeye? Scimitar. You take the one at my ten. On my mark, copy?"

"Copy, Chief."

Hunt raised his CQBR and laid his laser sights on the second of the two guards. Behind him, the other three team members waited in silence.

"Three, two, one, mark."

The count was slow and deliberate, and when he finished, his finger squeezed the CQBR's trigger at the same time Popeye did.

When fired, silencers don't make weapons silent. Unlike their portrayal in the movies. They suppress. There is still some noise. And to those standing behind Hunt when he fired, it sounded almost deafening.

The two guards dropped as one, no shouts or screams. They just fell where they'd stood. Popeye's voice came over the comms, "Tango down."

Hunt said, "Copy. Two tangos down. Moving in."

Emerging from the brush like wraiths out of a mist they approached the wire, and three of them, including Arenas and Traynor, took up a defensive pose while Hunt clipped the wire so they could gain access to the compound. When he was finished, he depressed his comms button and said, "White Shark, this is Scimitar, over."

"Copy, Scimitar."

"We're breaching now, over."

"Copy. Your bird is overhead and ready when required. White Shark out."

Hunt turned to Arenas and Rucker and nodded. "Bring that kid out in one piece. Go."

With Rucker in the lead, they slipped through the hole.

———

PUERTO DE TOPOLOBAMPO, SINALOA, MEXICO

Cara squeezed the trigger on the M110, and the first guard dropped to the ground. He spasmed and went still.

Shifting aim to the second guard, Cara repeated her actions, and he died like the first, the recoil of each shot punching into her shoulder. Now she waited for the third and final guard to appear from around the back. It was only seconds later, and he too died when a 7.62mm round blew through his head.

"Three tangos down, Reaper. All clear."

"Copy. I'm going hot."

———

Kane took a deep breath and came clear of the cover of the drums. His suppressed M17 lined up on the guard near the doorway. Before realizing that deadly peril was on approach, the man was slammed in the chest by two 9mm slugs. He jerked under their impact and slumped to the warehouse floor.

Without hesitation, Kane turned and searched the catwalk for his next target. He'd disappeared. Reaper cursed under his breath. Where the fuck was he?

And then Kane caught sight of him. Stepping into the light, the man had an AK-47 raised to his shoulder.

The suppressed M17 in Kane's hand fired, and the shooter lurched. Reaper shot again, and the man toppled silently over the rail of the catwalk. He hit the hard floor with a sickening thud and the clatter of his AK.

By Kane's calculations, that left one more man, but with no idea where he was, he was the most dangerous one of all.

Reaper moved, sweeping the warehouse as he went. He began working his way across to a room in the left far corner, which could be the only place left for the last man to be.

He was right.

There was a window in the room's front wall, and glass exploded outward when the shooter within opened fire with his own AK-47. The air all around Kane was full of lead, and in an evasive move, he dived to his right. He brought the M17 up and snapped off three fast shots at the opening. More 7.62mm bullets peppered the floor at Kane's feet. Others slapped close to his head.

Kane fired the rest of his magazine at the invisible target and scrambled to his feet. He ran for the shelter of a pallet stack on his left. Reaching it, he dropped out the empty magazine and replaced it with another one loaded with 17 rounds.

"Reaper One? Reaper Two, come in, over."

"I'm still here, Cara," Kane answered as another burst of automatic fire chewed splinters from the wooden pallets.

"What's going on?"

"Meeting a little resistance. This tango doesn't want to give up without a fight."

"I'm coming to you, Reaper. Hang in there."

"Copy. I'm hanging."

"Reaper? Zero. Do you want backup?"

"We'll need transport to get these women out of here," Kane got out before an additional burst from the shooter's AK smashed into the boards, sounding like a manic person with hammer and nails.

"On its way."

"Roger," Kane acknowledged and leaned out to fire a couple of shots.

The shooter fired more of his own and Kane cursed. He was pinned down. "Stupid fucking idea," he hissed.

"Cara, can you hear me?"

"Copy, Reaper." Her voice sounded funny as she ran towards the warehouse.

"I'm pinned down behind a stack of pallets inside. The shooter is in a room at your ten o'clock as you come through the door."

"Copy. Be there in two mikes."

In a dry tone Kane said, "No rush, I'm not going anywhere."

———

PUERTO DE TOPOLOBAMPO, SINALOA, MEXICO—
DEA SAFEHOUSE

When the request for transport for the women came through from Kane, and after Ferrero told him it was on its way, the team Reaper second in command turned to Axe and Spencer and snapped, "Go!" then "Wait!"

"Make up your fucking mind, boss," Axe said. "This ain't the time to dick around."

"I know," he said and turned to his other people. "Reynolds, Teller, gear up. You're going with them."

The two Bravo members nodded and hurried away to get their tactical vests. Axe pointed out that they only had their M17s.

"That'll have to do. Now get going," Ferrero ordered. He turned away to Swift and barked, "Find me a fucking satellite. I want to know what's happening."

"Is there a reason you sent them?" Thurston asked from behind Ferrero.

He turned to look at her. "Yes. I don't like it."

She nodded. "Fair enough."

On their way out, Axe stopped and grabbed his M110 and ammunition. At the vehicles, he took Reynolds to one side and thrust his 416 in her hands. "Here, take this. I'll use the SASS."

"You are better off with this than me," she argued.

Axe ignored her and started to load the tactical vest with suitable mags for the weapon.

Behind him, Wells appeared. "Come on, I'll drive, and you guys follow in the second Suburban."

Axe smiled at Reynolds and said, "Load up, sweet cheeks. Let's go to war."

"You did not just call me that, did you?" Reynolds asked and turned away to climb into the Suburban.

Axe slapped her on her rump, and she jolted. "You wait until we get back, asshole. I'll belt you one."

With a chuckle, Axe said, "How about we try out that wrestling thing with the food?"

"You're unbelievable."

"I know," Axe replied and slammed the door.

———

PUERTO DE TOPOLOBAMPO, SINALOA, MEXICO—
THE WAREHOUSE

When Cara opened the door to the warehouse, a spray of bullets from the shooter's AK slammed into the frame around it. She quickly retreated and hugged the wall. "Reaper, give me some cover so I can get in there."

"Give me a moment," he said.

A few heartbeats later a flurry of gunfire erupted from within. This time, Cara made it inside and took up position behind the same stack of crates where Kane had left his first body. "I'm in, Reaper."

His voice came over her comms. "Good, now maybe one of us can shoot this fucker."

Cara peered around the edge of her stacked refuge. She saw movement through the busted window as the shooter fired at Kane again. She thought for a moment and said into her mic, "Reaper, you feel like playing Bugs Bunny?"

"What do you want me to do?"

"Nothing," Ferrero said. "Backup is on its way."

"Talk to me, Cara," Kane said.

"Reaper, you hear me?" Ferrero tried again.

"I need you to break cover to your right, Reaper," Cara told him. "So our shooter will have to lean around to get a shot at you."

"OK. Let's do it."

"On my mark," Cara told him and eased up her M110. "Three, two, one, mark."

Kane broke cover and ran as fast as he could towards the door which he assumed concealed the girls they'd seen brought in. The Mexican with the AK leaned around to follow his progress and was about to squeeze the trigger on the weapon when Cara fired.

The man disappeared from view, and Cara said, "Tango down."

"Check him," Kane said over the comms. I'll check this room."

"Roger."

With his M17 raised up just in case, Kane opened the door to the room. It was dark and the outside light flooded in as the door swung wider. Half-squeals of fear emanated from the girls. Lowering his gun, Kane said, "It's OK. I'm a friend."

He ran his gaze over the occupants, and a quick head count came to ten. Which meant that some had already been there when the others arrived. Kane spoke into his mic, "Zero? Reaper One. Building secure. I have ten hostages, repeat, ten hostages."

"Copy, Reaper One."

There was movement beside him, and Cara appeared. She took one look at the girls and said in a soft voice, "Holy shit."

PUERTO DE TOPOLOBAMPO, SINALOA, MEXICO—
DEA SAFEHOUSE

Ferrero watched the feed from the satellite as the SUVs halted and disgorged their passengers. He counted them in his head. Sixteen. Sixteen figures climbed out, and fourteen moved with fluid ease.

"Shit," Swift swore. "Did you see that?"

"They're military," Thurston said.

"Collins' mercs, ma'am?" Swift inquired, knowing the answer.

"Yes, damn it. Put them on loudspeaker. I want to listen in."

"That means it was another trap, or they knew we were coming," Ferrero said. "Which could also mean they know where we are too."

Just at that moment one of the DEA agents burst in. There was a look of grim determination on his face. "We're compromised. We've got at least eight shooters outside closing on the house."

Thurston drew her M17. "Luis, tell Reaper he's on his own. We'll take what we can. It's time to get out."

"Yes, ma'am. Reaper One, copy?"

"Copy, Zero."

"We're compromised at the safehouse. You're on your own. Will contact you if possible."

"Copy, Zero. Good luck."

"You too, John."

CHAPTER 10

APPALACHIAN MOUNTAINS

THE KNIFE IN ARENAS' hand slid up under the militiaman's ribs, piercing the heart while his opposite hand clamped over the dying man's mouth to stifle any noise which might escape.

He took the weight of the corpse and eased it to the ground. Then he withdrew the knife and wiped it on the dead man's shirt before replacing it in its sheath.

Rucker moved up beside him and took a knee. "Drag him into the shadows next to the building. I'll keep an eye out."

While Arenas hid the body, Rucker spoke into his mic, "White Shark, this is Scimitar Three, copy? Over."

"Copy, Scimitar Three."

"About to move on the target building, over."

"Copy, Three. Looks all clear from here."

"Roger, Three out."

Arenas re-joined him, and they began to move stealthily on the building, wherein all probability, the boy was being held. The guard they'd just taken care of was the second since breaching the compound. They didn't know how Hunt and Traynor were doing, but all was still quiet which was a good sign.

They reached the target building which appeared to be no more than a small one-room hut. With hand signals, Rucker indicated the door, and they took up position on either side. Rucker reached out and tried the door handle. It turned. He nodded at Arenas who came away from the wall and raised the suppressed 416. Rucker's head dipped, and he swung the door wide.

Arenas entered and swept the room, his laser sight looking like a thin straight rod through his NVGs.

The boy was asleep on the floor. Crossing the room, he knelt beside Jimmy and placed a hand over his mouth and felt the kid stiffen. "It is OK, Jimmy. It is me, Carlos. We're taking you out."

Jimmy relaxed, and the hand came away. "Carlos? Is my ma with you?"

"No. We've got something just as good. SEALs. You must do everything we say, OK, *amigo*?"

He nodded. "OK."

"Arenas, we've gotta go."

"Copy. Come on, Jimmy, follow me."

Rucker said, "This is Three. We're coming out with the package."

White Shark came over the comms. "Copy, Three."

No sooner had they emerged from the hut when a burst of gunfire erupted from the other side of the compound. Then Hunt's voice came over the net. In the background, more gunfire could be heard. "Scimitar has been compromised. I say again we've been compromised. You might want to bring that UAV online about now."

"Copy, Scimitar. The Pred overhead is armed with

two Hellfire missiles. Just let us know where you want them."

The Hellfire missile was a laser-guided weapon which was used widely by the U.S. military. It got its name from the earlier *Heliborne, Laser, Fire and Forget Missile.* The two on the Predator UAV were AGM-114N Hellfire IIs. They had a range of eight thousand meters with a top speed of approximately fifteen hundred, ninety-one kilometers per hour.

"Can you see my laser, White Shark?"

"Copy."

"That's where I want it."

"But that's your position, Scimitar."

"That's where the fucking tangos are. Light them up."

"Copy, Scimitar. Keep your head down."

Rucker said into his mic, "We'll come to you, Chief."

"No. Get the kid out."

"Popeye, can you see what's going on?" Rucker asked.

"I got them, Ruck."

"Can you help?"

"Already on it."

Arenas and Jimmy knelt next to Rucker. A figure appeared from around the corner of one of the buildings and the SEAL let go a short burst with his CQBR and whoever it was collapsed onto their face.

Another militiaman appeared to take his place, and Rucker repeated the dose. He turned to Arenas who was shielding Jimmy with his body. "Let's go, Carlos."

They stood up to move, and there was a loud whump! The earth trembled and then a huge fireball erupted as the first Hellfire hit.

———

Traynor rose from behind the truck and fired a burst from his HK416 at a militiaman who was trying to flank their position. The man stumbled and fell as his left leg kicked out from beneath him. He then started to drag himself out of the firing zone, but another burst stopped him cold.

"Pete, we've got a Hellfire inbound. You need to stay down," Hunt shouted across to him as he opened up with his CQBR at another running figure.

Ever since breaching the compound, all had gone well. That was until they'd been forced to shoot a guard who'd appeared unexpectedly. His death was quiet enough, but the result of his finger squeezing the trigger on his M4 which rattled off a burst, brought it all undone.

Hunt and Traynor were still probably thirty meters from their target at the time. Now there was no chance that they would make it, due to the swarming militia.

Hammer blows on the truck they sheltered behind sounded like a fierce hailstorm, only instead of ice, it was bullets. Muzzle flashes appeared all around, and there was soon no refuge from incoming fire.

Then the Hellfire hit and the whole world seemed to explode.

The force of the explosion forced both men flat against the ground. Their ears rang, and their heads spun. The heat from the fireball washed over them, and the air was forced from their lungs.

For a moment Traynor thought that he was about to die and the heat was the earth opening to let him into Hell. Then the noise rolled away across the darkened landscape.

"Pete?"

The voice sounded far away.

"Pete, you OK?"

"Yeah," he moaned.

"Stay down. I'm ordering another strike."

"Copy."

Traynor gathered himself and poked his head around the corner of the truck. Buildings burned and he saw a flaming figure stagger about and then fall. His stomach lurched as the sickly-sweet smell of burnt flesh filled his nostrils.

"White Shark, this is Scimitar, over," Hunt said into his mic.

"Read you, Scimitar."

"I'm going to light up another target for you, over."

"Copy."

A militiaman appeared around the front of the truck, and Traynor's 416 ripped a burst into his guts. The man doubled over and collapsed. Another man, much bigger than the last, stepped into his place with a Colt M4 in his hands. He depressed the trigger and dirt and debris flew into the air about the former DEA agent. The whack-whack-whack of bullets burying into the earth sounded loud in his ears.

"Shit!" Traynor cursed and fired his weapon. The burst missed and to his horror, the militiaman sighted along his weapon.

The CQBR in Hunt's hands sent a single shot into the man's face, dropping him cold.

"Thanks, Bord," he said loud enough to be heard over the intense firing.

As he dropped the magazine out of his 416 and replaced it with a fresh one, he heard a voice shout, "They're still behind the truck! Kill them, now!"

Traynor took a look and saw a man standing there barking orders. In his right hand, he waved a gun around and pointed it at the truck where they were sheltered. "Who the fuck is that, Hunt?" he shouted.

Hunt fired at a militiaman and caught a glimpse of the man. He dropped back down and said, "Fuck knows. Obviously, he thinks he's in charge."

Hunt said into his mic, "Scimitar to Eagle One, read me, Pop?"

"Copy, Chief."

"Can you see the son of a bitch directing traffic on this side of the compound? Over."

"Roger, I got him."

"Frag his ass."

The man was in mid-shout when his voice was cut off. Pop-Eye came over the net. "Tango down."

Then a shout. "They got the colonel!"

A few moments later a voice came over the net. "Scimitar, this is White Shark. Second Hellfire is inbound."

Hunt called across to Traynor. "Get your head down, Pete. The second package is on its way."

Seconds later, the night lit up once more.

———

Arenas covered Jimmy with his body as the second Hellfire exploded. Beside him, Rucker let loose a burst which cut down a militiaman in a flail of arms and legs. The bullet strikes were quite audible and came across as a quick thunk-thunk-thunk.

"Get the kid up, Carlos!" he shouted. "We've gotta move."

"Come on, Jimmy."

"I can't!" he almost screamed.

"You have to."

Without waiting, Arenas hauled the boy to his feet

and started to drag/carry him towards the compound's fence, with Rucker on their six. Every now and then he could hear the CQBR cough.

Suddenly a figure appeared ahead of them. He wore a torn suit and the orange firelight illuminated the side of his face enough to show something wet. He held a handgun in his right fist, and when he spoke, his voice was laced with rage. "Hold it right fucking there, boyo."

"What the hell?" Rucker snapped.

O'Brien shifted his aim and shot him in the chest. Rucker grunted and fell to the ground. Jimmy screamed as the weapon snapped back into line with Arenas. The Irishman said, "Give me the boy."

Arenas shuffled Jimmy around behind him. "I can't do that."

"Last chance, Mex. Give me the boy."

In a soft voice, Arenas said into his mic. "Eagle-One, copy?"

"Copy."

"Need your help."

O'Brien snarled, "What did you fucking say?"

Arenas stared at him. "I said, goodbye."

The shot whistled out of the night and smashed into the Irishman's head. The side opposite to the entry wound exploded outwards, and he fell to the ground.

"Tango down."

The words filled Arenas' head. "Thanks, Eagle-One."

Rucker moaned and rolled onto his knees. "That hurt."

"Are you OK?" Arenas asked.

"Yeah, just got my vest."

"Come on, let's get out of here."

Rucker said into his mic, "Pop-Eye, we're coming to you."

"Roger, come away."

———

"Scimitar, this is Eagle-One. Copy?"

The transmission was met with silence, and Pop-Eye tried again. "Scimitar, Copy?"

There was movement in the brush to his right, and the SEAL rolled onto his side and brought up his M17. A voice sounded, "Friendly."

Pop-Eye put the weapon away as Rucker, Arenas, and Jimmy emerged from the leafy-green screen. "You fellers seen the chief?" he asked as they settled down beside him.

"Not a lick," Rucker said.

"I can't raise him on the comms."

Rucker nodded. "Scimitar, copy?"

Silence.

"Scimitar, copy?"

Silence.

"Scimitar, copy?"

The brush moved, and Hunt and Traynor appeared. "Will you guys shut the fuck up?" the chief growled.

"It would help if you answered the radio," Rucker told him.

"That last Hellfire was a little too close. Screwed something up and our comms are jacked up. You get the boy?"

"We have him," Arenas said.

Traynor looked at Jimmy. "How are you doing, kid?"

"OK, I guess."

He seemed shaken but unhurt. Traynor said, "When we get back, don't tell your mother about this."

Jimmy smiled.

"What's funny?" Hunt asked.

"My mom would kick his ass if she knew about this."

"How about we get you on that chopper then before she does."

———

PUERTO DE TOPOLOBAMPO, SINALOA, MEXICO—
DEA SAFEHOUSE

The front door of the safehouse was blown in amid a shower of razor-sharp splinters and orange flames. The sound of it made all within the house wince as the blast jarred their senses.

The DEA men tried to meet the incursion head-on, but the trained mercenaries were too good. The three agents died in the passageway in a hail of blazing gunfire. The mercenaries started to file through the shattered opening, dressed in tactical gear, and armed with Colt M4A1s. These weapons were a modified version of the M4. Where the M4 had a safe/semi-auto/3-round burst selector, the A1 had a safe/semi-automatic/fully automatic one.

Thurston leaned around the corner of the living room and blew through half a clip on the M17 before she took cover again. Her bullets brought down two men. One took two shots in his tactical vest, and though still alive, he was out of the fight for the near future. The second man took a round to his vest, and as he fell, another blasted through his face.

Across the hall in another room, Ferrero leaned out to fire his sidearm. He was forced back by a sustained burst of gunfire ripping into walls and raining debris down onto the floor tiles.

Ferrero tried again and snapped off a couple of shots.

Behind Thurston, Swift was busy downloading files onto a thumb drive. It was easier to do it that way than to drag the computer with them. "Are you finished yet?" she shouted over her shoulder.

"Almost."

A mercenary stepped over the body of a fallen DEA man and fired another long burst at the hidden team members.

Thurston fired three more shots at the man before she was forced to drop out her empty magazine. "Changing!" she shouted. Ferrero leaned out and fired shots of his own.

The general slapped home a fresh magazine and was about to lean back out when something thudded onto the floor near her feet. She looked down and froze. Coming to a slow stop was an M67 fragmentation grenade.

"Shit! Grenade!" Thurston shouted at the top of her voice and dived for cover. The explosive device went off with a roar, sending steel slivers scything through the air.

Part of the ceiling and some of the wall came down with the blast. The concussion from the explosion knocked the air from Thurston's lungs, and it took a while for her to recover. Quicker back on his feet was Ferrero, shielded from most of the blast by the wall. He leaned around and through the dust and crap he saw the outline of an advancing killer. He aimed high up with the M17. Three shots rocked the passage, and the man shouted out in pain. While the intruders recovered, Ferrero moved across the passage to where Thurston was slowly coming to her feet.

"Are you OK?"

"I'll live," she moaned. "That was fucking close."

"Swift, are you done?"

The computer tech dragged himself erect, drew his

M17 and blew the shit out of the equipment he'd been using. "I am now."

"Right, get out," Thurston snapped.

"Where are we going?" Swift asked.

"Anywhere but here. Move."

Ferrero led the way out the rear entrance. He crashed through the door, and as expected, there were two shooters there. Raising his sidearm, he pumped two shots into the first man. One into the vest and the second into the stunned man's head.

He pivoted and lined up on the second killer and squeezed the trigger.

Nothing happened.

"Shit!"

Behind him, Swift emerged and took in the situation before him. He brought his gun up and with a crazed howl, fired six wild shots. Four missed. Two managed to find a home in the killer's arm and throat.

"Over the fence," Thurston urged them, and they ran towards the brick wall. They scrambled over it just as a fusillade of gunfire peppered it, sending chips flying through the air.

"Go! Go!" Thurston shouted.

The three of them ran along the alley and disappeared into the darkness. Behind them, their pursuers vaulted the wall and halted. Their leader, a big man with a shaved head, took out a cell phone and punched in a number. When it was answered, he could hear the gunfire on the other end.

"It's me," Hall said. "They got away. We'll keep looking for them."

Then he hung up.

He stared at the team members that remained. "Split up. Find them."

CHAPTER 11

PUERTO DE TOPOLOBAMPO, SINALOA, MEXICO

"REAPER, WE'RE TAKING HEAVY FIRE!" Axe shouted in his ear.

"Copy, Axe. Fall back."

"Roger."

Axe, Teller, and Spencer drew back into the warehouse. Axe was the last in, a thin trickle of blood running from his brow. Kane pointed at it and asked, "You OK?"

He gave him one of his weird grins as he slapped home a fresh magazine and said, "You should see the other dude."

Cara's voice came over the comms. "Reaper, we've found a way out the back. It seems to be clear."

"Copy. We're on our way."

He turned to Teller and said, "Give me your 416 and some spare mags. Then get to the back. They've found a way out."

Teller passed them over and hurried away. Behind Kane and Axe, Spencer was still firing through the doorway. Bullets peppered the warehouse, making it sound like a severe storm had descended overhead.

"Axe, get going. If we get separated, try to make contact with Bravo. The safehouse was attacked, and they had to vacate."

"Copy. Don't hang around too long."

"I'll be right behind you."

That left Spencer and Kane to watch their six. He reached the CIA man's side and said, "What have you got?"

"We've been able to thin them out some, but not a whole lot," he said. "There's still probably at least ten of the bastards out there."

Kane took a look around the edge of the doorway and caught a glimpse of muzzle flashes from behind one of the SUVs. There were others spread out in a broad perimeter. He rattled off two bursts and saw the rounds impact the second of the vehicles. It brought forth a rise in the attacker's rate of fire and made him duck back.

Then Spencer shouted, "Get back! RPG!"

The whole world seemed to explode in a bright orange glow. The air rushed from Kane's lungs as he was flung violently backward. When he landed, his head smacked against the hard floor. Bright lights flashed before his eyes and darkness seemed to consume him. In the distance, he could hear more gunfire which slowly diminished and then ceased.

Kane moaned. He opened his eyes, and the roof above him swam in circles. He closed them again and waited to see if it would clear. But before he could open them again, everything went quiet as he passed out.

————

The explosion rocked the night. Cara and Axe whirled around to see the flaming cloud rise into the sky.

"Christ!" Cara swore and pressed her transmit button. "Reaper One, come in."

There was silence over the comms.

"Reaper One, come in."

She waited for what seemed an extraordinary amount of time before she said, "Spencer, come in."

He too was silent.

"Spencer, this is Reaper Two. Come in."

"This is fucked, Cara," Axe growled. "Let's go back."

He started to move when she grabbed his arm. "No."

"What?"

"I said no. That's an order."

"It's bullshit, Cara," he hissed. "That's what it is. I ain't leaving Reaper or Spencer back there."

"Axe, damn it. If he was still there then it's a good possibility he's dead," it pained her to say. "If he isn't, then they'll have him, and we'll find him. They were ready for this. It was a trap. Bravo got hit too. We all need to regroup."

He knew she was right. "Shit. Where to?"

"I don't know. We'll work it out. Lead out. We need to get the girls to safety."

———

When Kane came to, he was laying on the pavement outside the burning warehouse. The first noise he heard was familiar and disconcerting. It said, "We meet again, *gringo.*"

Kane moaned as the figure swam before his eyes. He blinked to clear his vision, and the face came into view. "Son of a bitch."

Another figure appeared next to the cartel boss. An American. From the pictures he'd seen, it was easy to make him out as Collins.

Before Kane knew it, Spencer was hovering over him and helping him to his feet. The CIA man had a cut above his right eye with still-tacky blood halfway down that side of his face.

"I'm not sure if you being alive is such a good thing, Reaper," he said.

"I guess we'll find out. The others?"

Spencer shrugged.

Kane faced Montoya and saw the smug look on his face. He said, "It is a shame that my plan failed to net all of your people. But I have you, and the others I'm certain will not be a problem to my future plans."

"What plans are they?" Kane asked casually.

A wicked smile touched the Mexican's lips. "You do not need to know."

"I see you got yourself some new help. Last feller kind of went to pieces on you. Are these guys any better?"

"What the fuck are you doing?" Spencer hissed.

Kane knew exactly what he was doing. Get Montoya mad enough, and he might flip out and shoot him. Better than the alternative prospect.

"If you're going to kill me, Mex, just get it over and done with. I ain't got the time or the inclination to swap sentences with a murdering son of a bitch like you."

Montoya smiled again. "*Amigo*. Be assured that I am not going to kill you. What I have intended for you is much worse. I am sending you both to *Las Puertas del Infierno*."

"Christ almighty," Spencer breathed.

Kane raised his eyebrows and said, "No shit? You're

sending us to The Gates of Hell? What the fuck is that? A volcano by the sea or some bullshit?"

"Looking at your friend, *amigo*, I see that he knows exactly what I mean."

Kane glanced at Spencer whose expression had worsened.

"You see, my *Americano* friend, The Gates of Hell refers to a prison on the *Isla del volcán*. It is off the coast of Peru. This is where they send all of the *presos malos*. Bad prisoners. If you live out the week when you arrive, it will be something, yes? Especially since you are *gringos*."

Surprisingly, Kane felt relieved. While there was life, there was a chance, albeit a slim one.

Montoya barked, "Get them into the trucks."

Collins stepped forward. "So, you're the one they call Reaper?"

"I've been called that."

"Were you the one in Juarez?"

"Yeah. You were there?"

"Uh huh. That was some ballsy move jumping off the building like that. Too bad you aren't working for me."

"Yeah, too bad."

Collins indicated to one of the SUVs. "After you."

PUERTO DE TOPOLOBAMPO, SINALOA, MEXICO

A dog barked and brought Cara to a halt. She held up her left hand and signaled the others behind her to stop as well. She lowered herself to one knee and brought up the M110. With her right eye to the night scope, she swept the area ahead of her.

The alley looked deserted. A rundown wooden fence

ran along the left of it with a dumpster pushed up against it. On the right side was a long brick wall, the rear of some kind of building. Movement caught her eye ahead, and a cat slunk across in front of them.

The sound of boots on gravel sounded beside her and Axe said in a low voice, "What's up?"

"I'm not sure," Cara whispered back. "I have a feeling."

"I'm not surprised. I mean, look where we fucking are. Sinaloa. Christ, the only ones who last down here would be drug lords and my mother-in-law."

Cara lowered the M110 and stared at him incredulously. "You have a mother-in-law?"

"Nope. I meant if I had one."

She shook her head and brought the scope back up to her eye. She focused it on the alley mouth and waited a few more heartbeats. That was when she caught the movement. "There," she said.

Axe lowered his night vision goggles and peered through the green haze. Three men had appeared when they turned into the alley. They were armed with what he thought were AKs. "You figure they're part of the ones who attacked us?"

Cara didn't answer straight away. Instead, she studied them for a while longer. One of them had his weapon canted back onto his right shoulder while another held his pointed to the ground. The third man passed his to the first and then proceeded to take a piss on the fence.

"I don't think they are," Cara finally said.

The dog barked again. The noise was followed by a string of invective in Spanish as its owner cursed its noise. From the end of the alley came muffled laughter as the three armed men shared a joke.

"What's happening? Are we in trouble? Is it those men?"

Cara and Axe turned to face one of the girls they had rescued. She had crept up on them while they were concentrating on the three men ahead of them. Cara said, "You need to go back and wait for us to tell you it's all right to move."

"I was just curious," she said, hoping that it would make everything OK.

"Go, now." This time her voice was firmer.

The girl turned to walk away and kicked a discarded tin can. The noise it made was accentuated by the narrowness of the alley, and the echo rolled all the way along it.

"Shit!" Axe hissed and grabbed her by the shoulder and forced her down.

Anger surged through Cara because she knew that the three armed men to their front couldn't miss the damned racket. She looked through the scope again and saw that the men were all looking their way. Not that they could see them in the darkness. And maybe they wouldn't investigate the source.

Not to be. They had already started along the alley.

"Axe," Cara whispered in a harsh tone. "We have incoming."

Axe turned back around and stared straight ahead. "Damn it, that's all we need."

Cara spoke into her mic, "Teller, Reynolds, get the girls under cover. We've got three tangos inbound."

"Copy," Reynolds said.

"Don't do anything until I say, Axe," Cara said. "Wait until they get up close."

They waited in silence and watched on as the three men grew bigger in the green haze of their NVGs. When they were close enough, Cara said, "Now."

The M110 punched back into her shoulder, and the armed man on the left of the trio dropped like a stone. On her right, Axe fired a burst from his suppressed 416 and the second Mexican went down without a sound. The third man turned to flee, and bullets from both weapons caught him in the back. He was flung forward, and he skidded to a stop with his head jammed up against the dumpster.

"Moving," Cara snapped and strode forward. She shouldered her M110 using the strap and drew her M17. Axe did the same.

One at a time, Cara checked for life on the fallen Mexicans. Once she'd established that they were of no further threat, she reached into her pocket and drew out a small flashlight. She then rechecked each of them.

All three were covered head to toe with tattoos. A sure sign they were cartel. She riffled through their clothes and found a cell in the second man's pocket. She put it in her jacket and turned him over.

He was young, maybe in his early twenties, and yet his face was covered in tattoos, and he had a string of skulls around his neck. "Hey, Axe, get a look at this."

He crouched beside her and stared at the tattoos. "Trophy chain," he said.

"I thought so."

A trophy chain was testament to each kill that a cartel man had. This one had at least nine, possibly more. Cara felt a vibration in her pocket. She reached in and took out the cell. It trembled in her hand and the backlit screen said unknown.

"Shit," she whispered in a low, harsh tone.

"What's up?"

She showed Axe the cell. "You going to get that?"

"Yeah right."

Axe reached out and took the cell. He hit the connect button and answered as only Axe could, "Speak, motherfucker."

Cara rolled her eyes, but a smirk touched her lips at the same time.

"Dónde está Emiliano?"

"Emiliano can't come to the phone right now; he's a little fucked up."

"Quién eres?"

"Who am I? I'm the son of a bitch who killed him. Who are you?"

"I am Marco Antonio Ramos," the voice hissed.

"Nice to meet you," Axe said and hung up. He tossed the cell to Cara. "Asshole."

"Who was it?"

"Some feller called Marco Antonio Ramos."

"Christ, Axe, do you know who he was?"

"Damn it, I just said, didn't I?"

"Ramos is one of three lieutenants in the damned cartel."

"OK. I guess we'd better get moving then," he suggested.

"You think," Cara said. She pressed the transmit button and said, "Brook, you and Teller bring the girls up. It's time we got the hell out of here."

"Copy."

"Axe, find us some transport. I'm sick of walking."

———

Thurston and Ferrero had the same idea. And they had their eyes on the perfect ride. A 2015 Ford Mustang F-35 Lightning II. The only problem was that there were five armed men standing around it.

"That is one sweet ride," Thurston said with more than a hint of appreciation in her voice as she peered around the corner of the large building.

"Are you a car nut, ma'am?" Swift asked her.

"I can appreciate the finer things in life, Slick," she said to him. "All we have to do is get it."

The sound of boots on gravel sounded behind them, and Ferrero appeared. He said, "There's company coming up behind us. Four shooters that I could see as they passed under the street lamp."

"I guess we'd better get this car then," Thurston said and tucked her M17 in the back of her pants. Then she let her hair down and shook it out. It fell down to her shoulder blades, and the transformation was almost complete. Finally, she grasped the top of her T-shirt with her hands and gave it a sharp pull. What followed was the sound of tearing material as it ripped down to just below what Swift adjudged to be her well-rounded breasts, revealing a lacy black bra. She adjusted them in their cups, pushed them up a touch and stared at Swift. "How does that look?"

The corner street lamp showed the dumb expression on his face and Thurston nodded. "I'll take that as OK."

"Ahh, yep. Yes...I mean yes, ma'am."

"What are you doing, Mary?" Ferrero asked her.

"Going to steal us some wheels. Just be ready in case it goes south, and I need help."

Ferrero took his own M17 out of his pants and said, "If it gets too hot, get out."

Thurston smiled, "I've got this."

She walked around the corner and out of sight. Swift turned to Ferrero and said, "She's hot."

The ex-DEA man said, "Shut up."

Meanwhile, Thurston strode purposefully towards

the five men crowded around the Mustang. They saw her coming and stretched out into a line in front of her. Which suited her just fine.

One of them gave a low whistle when she emerged into the orange light of the street lamp. He ran his gaze over her, letting it linger long enough to take in her semi-exposed breasts.

"*Hola, Cielo. Hablas Español?*"

Thurston gave a giggle and shook her head, making sure it was hard enough to give her breasts another jiggle. She said, "Sorry, sweetie, I don't, and I'm a little lost."

Every last one of them had some sort of tattoo on display. The man who'd spoken had the most, and she guessed that he was their leader and the owner of the car. She also noted that they all had handguns tucked into their pants.

"We can help you, *Chica*," the Mexican said.

"Really. That would be great. At least I'll be safe with some big strong boys like yourselves."

They all gave each other knowing looks. The leader said, "Sure. You come with us, and we'll keep you safe."

Thurston casually moved both her hands around behind her back which in turn thrust her chest further forward. It had the desired effect, and every last one of them diverted their gazes right where she wanted them.

The familiar feel of the M17 came into Thurston's hand, and she brought it forward. She figured that the way the five were bunched together it should be over in a matter of seconds and take six or seven shots at the most. Her first one would be a double, however. Cut the head off the snake.

The SIG M17 crashed twice, and two 9mm rounds blew into the group's smiling leader. The first punched into his chest, the second his head. Without waiting for him to fall, Thurston shifted her aim and fired again.

BLAM!

Shift.

BLAM!

Shift.

BLAM!

Shift.

BLAM! BLAM!

The last man fell with two bullets in his chest.

Thurston knelt beside the man whom she believed to be their leader. She went through his pockets and found what she wanted. The keys jingled as they came free and she stood erect. Behind her, Ferrero and Swift hurried along the street.

The general turned and threw them to Swift. He caught them, and she said, "I presume you can drive?"

"Sure, but I thought you would want to drive."

Thurston shrugged. "I've got one at home."

Swift raced around to the driver's side door of the Mustang. Before he climbed in, he asked, "Where are we going?"

"To the airfield. We need to get the fuck out of this country."

After she climbed in, Thurston pulled her cell from her pocket. She punched in a number and waited. There was an answer from the other end, and she said, "We've been compromised and need extraction."

Silence.

"Yes, as soon as possible."

More silence and then she hung up. She turned to face Ferrero. "The C-130 will be on the ground in two hours. Let's hope we can last until then."

Ferrero nodded. "I just hope the others think of rendezvousing there. And since they don't have cell phones, for operational security, we won't know."

"I guess we'll see."

CHAPTER 12

APPALACHIAN MOUNTAINS

"HAMMERHEAD ONE-ONE, this is Scimitar, do you read? Over."

The Black Hawk pilot's voice sounded over the comms. "Scimitar? Hammerhead One-One, copy? Over."

"Hammerhead One-One, we're two mikes out from the LZ," Hunt said. "We have the package with us."

"Roger, Scimitar. You're two mikes out with the package. Hammerhead is inbound. Out."

"Copy. Scimitar out."

Hunt turned to the others and said, "Let's keep going."

They moved out once more with Pop-Eye in the lead and Rucker bringing up the rear. Jimmy walked in the center of the small column, between Traynor and Arenas. Suddenly their comms crackled to life.

"Scimitar? White Shark, over."

"Copy, White Shark."

"Chief, you've got an estimated eight tangos about to crawl up your rear, over."

Shit. "How far out are they, White Shark?"

"They'll be upon you before you can board the helo, Chief."

"Copy, White Shark. We'll take care of it."

"Roger. White Shark, out."

"Pop, on me," Hunt said into his mic.

From the thick foliage ahead, the SEAL appeared. "What's up, Chief?"

"We've got tangos coming up on us from behind. I need you to watch our six until the helo touches down."

"How many?"

"White Shark says eight."

"Won't be that many by the time I'm finished, Chief."

"Just don't miss the chopper."

They kept on until they reached the clearing where the Black Hawk would put down. In the distance, they could hear the WHOP!-WHOP!-WHOP! of the rotor blades. Once again, Hunt spoke into his mic, "Hammerhead One-One, Scimitar is in position, over."

"Copy, Scimitar. We'll be on the ground shortly. Hammerhead One-Two will provide air cover."

It wasn't long before Hammerhead One-One was on the ground. Just before it touched down, Hunt ordered Pop-Eye back for extraction. He appeared from the brush and ran across to the helicopter. Overhead, Hammerhead One-Two flew a steady circle. Suddenly a loud Brrrrp! sounded and a stream of tracers streaked across the sky like red-hot lances.

"Looks like he found something," Hunt said to Pop-Eye.

"Yeah."

Hunt looked back into the chopper to do a quick

head count to ensure that everyone was there. They were. He gave the crew chief a windup signal, and before he knew it, the Black Hawk lifted into the sky.

———

SINALOA, MEXICO—JUST OUTSIDE OF PUERTO DE TOPOLOBAMPO

The old battered Ford truck hit a hole in the road, and the crunch of the undercarriage was felt throughout the vehicle. It slowed slightly as Reynolds' foot slipped off the gas pedal and she cursed before jamming it back on, and with a roar, the truck shot forward.

"I thought you said you could drive this thing," Axe growled.

"I got it hot-wired, didn't I?" Reynolds shot back.

They had come across the truck soon after taking down the cartel *soldados*. Reynolds had weaved her magic when no keys could be found, and the old beast had roared to life.

The back was packed with the girls, Teller, and Cara. Everything was going to plan so far, as they made their way to the airfield where the HC-130 had dropped them.

The truck hit another hole, and the headlights bounced wildly across the landscape. In the back, a couple of the girls gave out a yelp of panic.

Cara said into her mic, "How much further you think, Brooke?"

Reynolds said, "About two minutes."

Nodding, Cara let her mind wander back to Reaper and Spencer. Maybe they had got away. Escaped. Maybe.

Axe's voice filled her comms. "Heads up, we're coming in. Just over the next rise."

"Stop and kill the lights," Cara snapped.

The brakes were applied, and the truck slid to a halt on the gravel. The lights went out, and Reynolds made the engine stall. Cara climbed over the side of the truck and brought the M110 up to sweep the area ahead of her. She could see nothing for the slope and the brush which adorned it.

"Pete, get the girls off. We're going the rest of the way on foot."

"Yes, ma'am."

"Axe, on me."

The ex-recon marine climbed from the truck. "Yes, ma'am?"

"Take the SASS and give me your 416. Then get on your bike and get to the top of that low ridge and have a look. We'll join you shortly."

"Ma'am," Axe said as he took the M110 and melted into the darkness.

"Where's he off to?" Reynolds asked.

"Trailblazer," Cara said. "Get the girls moving and have Teller bring up our six."

"Copy that."

Ten minutes later, Cara stopped them just below the crest of the rise. They'd taken a weaving route which took them through the brush. She found Axe lying on the crest with his eye to the scope of the SASS. She hunkered down beside him and asked, "What do you see?"

"Someone's down there," he told her. "They're in a flash-looking car. Mustang I think."

"Can you tell who they are?"

"Not from this angle. They're still in the car, and I can't make out what they look like."

Cara said, "We'll wait for a moment and see what happens."

"Copy."

After ten minutes of watching and waiting Axe said, "We've got movement, ma'am. Someone's getting out."

He observed a while longer and then chuckled. "I'd know that oddball anywhere. That's Slick, ma'am."

A sigh of relief escaped Cara's lips. "Get down there and let them know we're coming in."

"Roger," Axe acknowledged and climbed to his feet.

———

Swift had been busting for a piss for some time when he squeezed out of the Mustang. He hurried around the back of it and started to relieve himself. A wave of satisfaction washed over him as the floodgates opened.

For a time it felt as though he wouldn't stop, but eventually, the stream slowed and then ceased. He put himself away and turned around to walk back to the passenger door when he was confronted by the large smiling face of Axe. "Boo!"

Swift's heart lurched in his chest. "Fucking hell, Axe. Don't do shit like that, man. I almost died."

The doors opened on the Mustang and Thurston, and Ferrero climbed out. Axe gave the general a big cheesy grin and said, "You sure are a sight for sore eyes, ma'am."

"You too, Axel," she said. "Where are the rest?"

Axe winced. "Most of them are right behind me, ma'am."

"Most?" Ferrero said.

"We lost Spencer and Reaper."

"Elaborate," Thurston said, her voice filled with concern.

Before he could say any more, Cara appeared out of the darkness with the girls, Reynolds and Teller.

"Ma'am," she greeted her commander. "Good to see you. You too, Luis."

"And you, Cara," Thurston told her. "Axel was just about to explain why you are two men short."

Cara hesitated and then said, "We got separated from them. They were laying down a rearguard when there was an explosion. They never joined us."

"You didn't go and look?" Ferrero asked.

"I made the call not to, sir," Cara explained. "We were outgunned and had the girls to worry about. It was my decision, and I'll wear it."

"Do you think they are dead?" Thurston asked.

The question was blunt, straight to the point.

Cara opened her mouth to speak, but her voice caught in her throat. It was the first time she believed there to be a real possibility that Kane wasn't coming home. She said, "Yes, ma'am, it's possible. But I'm not sure."

"When we get back to El Paso, I'll make a few calls and see if it can be confirmed."

"We're headed back, ma'am?" Axe asked.

"Yes, I'm sorry. We have no choice. This thing was a clusterfuck from the beginning. It's time to regroup and re-arm."

"Ma'am, have you heard anything about Jimmy?"

Thurston sighed. "That is a whole other story."

CHAPTER 13

MEXICO CITY—TWO DAYS LATER

UNITED STATES AMBASSADOR Karen Day walked out of the large concrete and glass embassy towards the three black SUVs which awaited her. Her high-heeled shoes clacked against the hard surface of the footpath with each step.

Normally she would have been protected by DSS agents who watched over ambassadors across the globe. But this was Mexico and the cartel activity of late had been intense. So, she had put in a special request for private military contractors in the hope that they would discourage the Mexican drug lords from any notion of making her a target.

They issued Karen with six men. Combat veterans who'd served on the ground in all corners of the known world. Two of them rode in the front SUV, two with her, and two in the follow-up vehicle. Also, for the day's trip to a government-funded orphanage on the outskirts of the city, they would have units of the *Policía Federal* along as well.

The orphanage was having an opening day on a newly-built dormitory funded by the U.S., to accommodate the influx of children who'd lost parents due to the escalation in the Narco wars. The project had cost ten million dollars.

Karen was a very athletic forty-four, worked out every day at the embassy gym, ate healthily, and swam five kilometers twice a week in the pool.

That morning she wore a navy pantsuit, her dark hair was blown down below her collar, and she had on her favored aviator sunglasses.

A smile touched her lips as she arrived at the middle SUV. The big man with the shaved head and tattoos on his forearms waited for her with the rear door open. "Morning, Brick. Sleep well?"

The big security man decked out in full tactical gear returned her smile. "Like a baby, ma'am."

She stopped and stared at him. "I think we should do it again this evening."

Brick Peters stared out from behind his own sunglasses and shook his head. "No, ma'am. You've got me licked in that pool."

"I thought you SEALs were meant to be tough?"

"Even the best of us can get waterlogged, ma'am."

"Pussy."

"Yes, ma'am."

"Shall we go?" Karen said and climbed in the back.

Brick pressed his talk button and said into his mic, "We're moving, mount up."

The security team got into the vehicles. One man would drive, while the other rode shotgun. Brick sat his

M4A1 down beside him after he settled into the passenger seat. He looked over at his driver, a Texan named Brett, who came from somewhere near Houston. "You ready?"

"Let's do it."

Brick said into his mic, "Zed, let's roll."

The vehicle in front started to move away from the curb. The other two SUVs pulled out behind it. Two armored humvees eased away from the sidewalk and fell in front of the first SUV. The same happened behind the last. They were all mounted with machine guns which made the convoy look as though it was driving along a street in Afghanistan, not Mexico City.

Inside each was two other Mexicans, fully armed and ready for battle.

"How long will it take us to get there, Brick?" Karen asked.

"It'll take about forty mikes, ma'am."

"Mikes?"

"Minutes."

"Yes, right."

Driving along the street for a couple of blocks before turning east, they then stayed on that route for another three miles and crossed over onto the freeway which took them to the outskirts of the city.

Brick's comms came to life with sudden traffic. One of the rear humvees reported a black Ford van following them. He picked up his scanner and turned it on. It was filled with chatter. He glanced at Brett. "They're dialed in on us. Keep an eye out."

Brett nodded and kept driving.

Pressing his transmit button on his radio, Brick said, "Listen up. We've got cartel assholes watching our every move. Keep an eye out and call in anything suspicious."

The other two SUVs called in while Brick picked up his M4 and checked its load.

"What is it, Brick?" Karen asked.

"It's nothing, ma'am. Just a few unfriendlies."

Brick trained his eyes forward so he could scan the side streets before they reached them. The chatter continued on the scanner as cartel soldiers called out the progress of the ambassador's column.

"I don't like this, Brick," came the call from Zed in the front car. "We've got traffic backed up in front and some roadworks at the on-ramp."

No sooner had Zed finished speaking when the brake lights to their SUV came on.

"Brick, copy?" Miller from the third SUV said over the comms.

"Copy."

"Eyes up left, Brick. I'm pretty sure I just caught sight of a Mexican with a weapon on a rooftop."

"Copy, Miller. Keep an eye out."

The column came to a halt, and Brick cursed under his breath. Before him lay the line of traffic stopped at the workmen. A prickle of nervous concern heightened his senses. He hadn't experienced the feeling since his last Afghanistan tour when his team was about to be hit. His gut never lied.

The rooftops to Brick's left held a lot of signage, and some even had crenellations. His eyes were skimming over a sandstone building with an insurance sign on it when he saw movement. It was only a flicker, but the sight of a man with binoculars to his eyes, who looked as though he was talking into a cell or a radio, jolted him into action.

"We've got to get off this street," Brick murmured to Brett. Then into his mic, said, "Zed, get off the damned street. The crossover alley to our left. We'll circle back to the embassy."

"Copy, turning now."

The black SUV reversed slightly before turning left and rocketing forward. Brick snapped, "Brett, follow them."

The second SUV lurched forward, and Karen called from the back, "What's going on, Brick?"

"We're headed back to the embassy, ma'am. The cartels are up to something."

"No. Keep going to the opening."

"Sorry, ma'am. Your safety is my call. I say we head back."

In a low voice, Karen hissed, "This is fucking bullshit."

"Miller? Copy?"

"Go, Brick."

"Do we have an eye in the sky?"

"I think so. Call the embassy."

"Roger," Brick acknowledged. The SUV entered the alley with a large bump and motored along. "Eagle Base, this is Eagle One, over."

"Got you, Eagle One," a voice came back.

"I need to know if we have a bird in the air, over."

"Wait one, Eagle One."

Christ.

"I'm bringing up a satellite feed now, Eagle One. What seems to be the problem?"

"I'm pretty sure we've got multiple Tangos on rooftops. We're turning back and bringing the ambassador home."

The SUV in front smashed through a pile of wooden crates, scattering them. Bags of rubbish were ripped to shreds as the motorcade careened over the top. Brick glanced into the rearview mirror and saw the third SUV on their tail, followed by the Humvees.

"Oh shit!" A voice came over the open comms from the comms room at the embassy. Obviously on VOX.

"Say again, Eagle Base."

When the voice came back, there was a nervous edge to it. "Eagle One, you need to get out of there now! The rooftops are covered with Tangos. I'm dispatching DSS agents to your location."

Brick felt a surge of adrenaline flow through him. "Waste of time, Eagle Base. We'll be lon—"

The rest of the sentence remained in Brick's throat when an incoming RPG blew the lead SUV up with devastating consequence.

Brett jammed the brake pedal all the way to the floor, and the vehicle stopped suddenly. Brick shouted into his mic, "Back up! Back up!"

He turned in his seat just in time to see one of the rear humvees take another rocket-propelled grenade and explode, tossing the machine gunner out of his hatch.

"Christ" Brick snapped. "Eagle Base, we're taking heavy fire. I say again, we're taking heavy fire. We've lost one SUV and a Humvee. We're trapped in this fucking alley."

"Copy, Eagle One. Backup is *enroute*."

The security team leader twisted in his seat and stared at Karen. Fear was etched on her face. "Get on the floor, ma'am. Do it now."

"Brick, I…"

"Do it!"

Karen slid onto the floor and curled herself up into a ball. Bullets started to rain down on the SUVs, the staccato rhythm sounding like a drummer's convention. Brick took one last look at the burning vehicle in front of them. He needed to compartmentalize right now and would mourn the loss of his friends later.

"Brett, let's go. We can't fight back from in here."

Brett nodded. "Let's kill us some of these mother-fuckers."

The last thing Brick said to Karen was, "Keep your head down, ma'am. We'll be right back."

They flung the doors open and slid from their seats. Behind them, the other team did the same. They set up to cover opposite sides, taking aim at the shooters on the rooftops. Back along the line, a Humvee opened fire with a .50 caliber Browning.

The bullets chewed great chunks from the edge of the rooftops as it sprayed them wildly. Brick saw a cartel soldier take a hit from a round and disappear backward in a spray of red.

Another rocket-propelled grenade streaked through the air overhead leaving a white contrail. An ear-shattering explosion rolled along the alley when it struck home. The second Humvee flew apart with razor-sharp shards of metal scything through the air.

"Eagle Base, where's that fucking support? Over." Brick shouted over his comms.

"They're still five minutes out, Eagle One."

"We'll be dead in five minutes, over," Brick told him as rounds ricocheted all around him.

"Sorry, Eagle One. Five minutes is the best I can do."

Brick cursed under his breath and raised his M4A1. He shot the first cartel soldier he saw through the face, shifted target, and did the same again. Miller's voice filled his earpiece. "Brick, we need to get out of this shit, buddy. It's a fucking deathtrap in here."

"We still have about four minutes before help arrives."

Yet another RPG ripped overhead. This one hit the side of the building and sprayed the alley with debris. They'd got lucky with that shot.

"Fuck it," Brick hissed and hurried towards the back of the SUV. He opened it up and reached inside. When he withdrew his hand, it was filled with a kevlar vest. "Miller, move up. We're getting out of here."

"Copy, we're coming to you."

Brick opened the back door of the SUV and leaned in. "Here," he said to Karen, passing her the vest. "Put this on. If we stay here, we're all dead."

As though proving his point, bullets rained down on the roof, one of which opened up Brick's right forearm. He hissed with the burning sensation but shook it off. Karen took the vest and put it on without so much as an argument. The security team leader noticed her hands trembling while she worked. He looked into her eyes and said, "You can do this. Just follow our instructions, and you'll be fine."

Karen gave a hesitant nod and slid out from the back seat.

Brick said into his mic, "Eagle Base, we're moving. Follow us with the bird. Direct QRF to us, over."

"I suggest you stay put, Eagle One."

"You ain't the ones neck deep in shit. Direct them to us. Brick out."

The security leader felt the impact of an AK round strike a glancing blow to the back of his kevlar. It made him stagger forward into the crouched form of the ambassador. He gritted his teeth and said, "Sorry ma'am."

"It's...it's OK."

Brick turned and shouted, "Miller, get us the hell out of here!"

Miller started to move towards the burning wreckage

of the first SUV. Black smoke billowed skyward from it in a heavy pall. The burning upholstery and melted acrylonitrile, butadiene and styrene of the dash, gave off a strong chemical stench. Behind him came his driver from the third SUV, a young, experienced Kansan named Jenkins. The team called him Billy after Billy the Kid because of his age.

"Ma'am," Brick said to Karen, "keep your hand on my shoulder at all times, just like we practiced, OK?"

Karen gave him a tentative nod.

"Right, let's go."

The security team leader raised the M4A1 to his shoulder and walked away from the cover of the SUV. Bullets chewed chips of pavement out around their feet and spanged off in different directions with high-pitched whines. Every time Brick saw a target above him, he fired two quick shots at it. A 5.56 NATO round smashed into a tattooed face, slamming its owner back out of sight.

Behind him, he could hear Brett firing bursts from his own weapon. Then he called out over the gunfire, "Brick, changing!"

While he slapped a fresh magazine into the M4, Brick kept a closer watch to cover him. Then Brett was back at it, returning fire.

The team leader saw his two men ahead of him skirt the burning SUV and disappear from view behind the orange flames and charcoal smoke from the burning tires. He called back over his shoulder to Karen, "Keep your head down, ma'am. This will be a little warm, but you'll be fine."

"Brick? Miller. We've got a doorway the other side of the bonfire. Going to check it out."

"Copy."

As they navigated the narrow passage between wall

and flames, the heat grew in intensity. Brick heard Karen cry out when a flame flashed out and singed her hair. "Easy, ma'am, we're almost there."

"Man down! Man down!" the shout over the comms echoed through Brick's head.

"Who, damn it?" Although he knew the answer because the voice belonged to Billy.

"It's Miller. He's dead."

A cold wave settled over the team commander. That made the body count three of his men. Shit!

He broke free of the smoke and flames to find Billy crouched near Miller. His M4A1 ripping round after round at the rooftops. Around him, Brick could see the impact of frequent bullet strikes.

"Billy, get the damned door open, now," Brick snarled as he squatted beside his fallen man to doublecheck his vitals. Apart from being team leader, he'd also been a combat medic for his SEAL team back in the day. There was no pulse. The bullet had entered at the top near the junction of shoulder and neck. Its trajectory would have carried it down through Miller's heart.

The sound of a shotgun's roar made Brick's head snap around in time to see Billy flung back. He'd kicked the door open, only to be greeted by an armed cartel soldier who let go with a charge from a 12 gauge pump.

"Brett, the ambassador," Brick shouted, and came up from his crouched position. The M4A1 in his grasp hammered into life. His thumb flicked the fire selector onto auto, and he let his anger burn freely.

The doorway became the epicenter of hell, with round after round passing into it as the Colt chewed its way through the magazine. It ran dry, and Brick changed out the mag. He brought the weapon back up in time to see a Mexican stagger forward; his top half shot to ribbons. The man toppled forward, dropping the shotgun as he went.

"Brett, inside! Get her inside!"

With Brick giving them cover, Brett and Karen Day hurried towards the doorway. They almost made it.

The first bullet punched into the kevlar vest Brett was wearing. It knocked the air from his lungs and forced him forward onto hands and knees. Behind him, Karen stumbled and straightened, took a step and went down when a slug tore into her throat.

"Oh no! No! No! No!" Brick cried out and scrambled over to the fallen ambassador. The wound in her throat ran a river of blood, but he could do nothing about it at that point. Not when the cartel men were peppering his position with bullets.

Brick grabbed Karen's hand and dragged her inside, a stream of slugs kicking up at her heels. He discarded the M4A1 and concentrated on the wound.

Karen's eyes rolled in her head as she tried to comprehend what had happened. Blood started to fill her mouth and spill from the corner of it. Her teeth turned pink.

"Hang in there, ma'am," Brick told her as he started to work on her. "I need to see how bad this is."

He reached up with a bloody hand and switched his comms to VOX. "Eagle One to Eagle Base, do you copy? Over."

"Copy, Eagle One. Report."

"The ambassador is wounded. I say again, the ambassador is wounded and in a bad way. I need medivac ASAP, over."

"We'll see what we can do, Brick. How bad is she?"

Close to him, he heard Brett groan. "Are you still in this fight, buddy?"

"Yeah, I think so."

"Make it happen."

"Brick, are you there?"

"The ambassador has a throat wound and is bleeding out. I have my fingers in it at the moment trying to keep her alive. Is that bad enough?"

"Hang in there, Brick. Help is a minute out."

The security team leader realized they had taken cover in a stairwell. The thunder of footsteps on the stairs gave that much away. He looked up to his right and saw a dancing shadow on the wall as a figure descended.

"What the fuck now?" he growled, changing hands on the wound in Karen's throat. He reached down with his right hand and freed the SIG M18 from the thigh holster. His hand was slick with blood, and he almost lost his grip on the weapon as he brought it up.

A cartel soldier holding an AK-47 appeared on the stairs. He started to bring it to the firing position when the M18 in Brick's fist spat three bullets at him. The Mexican jerked and dropped onto the steps. He slid down them until he reached the bottom and remained still.

Brick glanced down at Karen and saw that her eyes were closed. Her face was a pasty gray. His heart beat a little faster. "Ma'am, can you hear me?"

Nothing.

"Karen?" Louder this time.

Her eyes flickered open. He smiled reassuringly at her. "You'll be fine, ma'am. Help is almost here."

By way of recognition, she blinked her eyes and then closed them again. Brick's eyes drifted to her chest. It still rose, and fell but her breathing was shallow. "Brett, how are we looking?"

"Firing dropping off, Brick. I reckon they've caught sight of the DSS reinforcements."

Then the gunfire stopped. Just like that.

Brick heard SUVs pull up at the mouth of the alley. Then he heard shouts between men as they disembarked and organized themselves. He looked back down at Karen. He said in a soft voice, "You'll be OK, ma'am. The cavalry has finally arrived."

CHAPTER 14

EL PASO, TEXAS

THE TEAM WAS in a somber mood. It had been two days since they'd returned from Mexico and there was still no news about what had happened to Kane and Spencer. Most were now congregated in their large rec-room, watching developments unfold on the television as reports of the United States Ambassador to Mexico's ambush broke over all the news channels.

Scenes cut from a burnt out SUV to a helicopter evacuating the critically-wounded Karen Day across the border to a medical facility where it was hoped that she could get the life-saving surgery she required.

Reports said that four of her security team had been killed in the firefight, along with an unknown number of Mexican law enforcement officials. A picture of a man with a shaved head flashed up on the screen. The name beneath the picture said Richard "Brick" Peters. It said that he was an ex-Navy SEAL and leader of the ambassador's security team.

"This is fucked up," Axe commented. "You know what's going to happen next? They'll blame the security team for everything that happened out there."

Reynolds turned in her chair to stare at him. "Why do you say that?"

"Because that's what happens. Instead of blaming the cartels, the fallout will come down on the one thing they can get to, the team. Don't get me wrong, they'll make a song and dance about the cartels, but it happened on the team's watch."

"Surely not," Reynolds said. "If it wasn't for them she'd be dead."

"He's right," Thurston said from where she stood in the doorway to the room. "People on the hill will be out for blood, and if they can't get it from the cartels, then the team will do. It's like a bloodsport up there at times."

Reynolds shook her head. "That's fucked."

"Amen," said Axe.

Thurston caught Ferrero's eye and signaled for him to follow her. She disappeared as he rose from his seat. Cara watched them go. Beside her sat Jimmy who'd arrived back that afternoon along with Traynor and Arenas. The excitable kid had filled her in on everything, including being in the middle of a firefight with real Navy SEALs.

At least they would never have to worry about O'Brien again. Just having her son there helped with the pain of uncertainty about Kane.

Arenas had apologized for what had happened. But Cara had insisted that it wasn't his fault. Besides, Jimmy was safe, and that was all that mattered.

Upon learning about the occurrences during their absence, the pair had been stunned at the prospect of losing their field commander and friend.

"Do they know who did this yet, or what?" Axe asked.

Cara stopped stroking her son's hair and stared at Axe. "I've not heard."

"What about Slick?"

Traynor said, "He's working around the clock to find something on Reaper and Spencer."

"I had to fucking ask," Axe mumbled.

Teller joined the conversation. "I reached out to a friend in the NSA to see if there was any chatter about what had happened, but they've heard nothing."

"And the DEA are trying to clean up the mess with their safehouse," Traynor said.

"And the warehouse was burned down, so the Mexican authorities have only DNA to go by to identify the bodies which were found inside," Arenas told them. "Knowing them, it will take weeks."

"So, in the meantime, we sit here with our thumbs up our asses and do nothing," Axe growled. "I hate this shit. But what I hate more is that we have no idea who is fucking responsible."

———

Ferrero found Thurston in her office. She sat behind her desk, and the flatscreen t.v on her wall was frozen on a picture of Brick Peters. The former DEA man studied it and asked, "What's going on?"

"We need to make a decision about the team," she told him.

He nodded. "I know. You're in charge. What do you want?"

"It needs to be a joint decision, Luis," she told him. "I may be in charge, but you put the team together. It needs to work."

"I agree, but we don't even know whether Reaper is dead yet."

"Let's assume he is."

Ferrero sighed and sat down in a chair opposite her. "Then we make Cara team leader. They all respect her, plus she has leadership experience."

"And her deputy?"

"Carlos. Special forces training and again, leadership experience."

"We'll do that then."

There was a brief silence before Ferrero said, "That leaves a hole in the team. I gather our friend on the screen is there for a reason?"

Thurston stood up and walked around the desk. She stopped in front of the television and stared straight ahead. "Brick Peters would be a good fit."

"How do you propose to get him here?"

"I made a couple of calls, and he's flying to Washington to be debriefed. I'm heading there tomorrow to meet with Hank Jones. I want to see if I can nail down some air assets for us. Black Hawks, an HC-130, plus our own drones and such. Something we have on hand full-time. Not relying on other branches to play taxi."

Ferrero was impressed. "That would be great, Mary. Lord knows we could use them."

"While I'm there, I'll set up a meeting with Peters, test the waters. The man is an ex-Navy SEAL Plus he was a combat medic. Something the team could use on missions."

"Granted. What do I tell the team?"

"Nothing until I get it all worked out."

A knock sounded at the door, and Swift appeared. He closed the door behind him, and both Thurston and Ferrero couldn't help but see a hint of excitement on his face. "Sorry for the intrusion, ma'am, but I think I might have something."

Swift had their attention and continued. With a couple of swipes on the tablet in his hands, the flatscreen changed to show a dark satellite image with what appeared to be figures on it.

"What are we looking at?" Thurston asked.

"This is from the other night at the warehouse."

"Where did you get it?"

"I'd rather not say."

Thurston stared at him and then said, "OK. Talk to us."

Swift walked closer to the screen and used the index finger on his right hand as a pointer. "These here are the bad guys. You can make out the flashes from their guns."

He touched the screen on the tablet, and the satellite image started to play. "Just about *now*...there it is."

A big flash lit the screen up and then died away. "That was the explosion which we thought might have killed Reaper and Spencer. But, if you keep watching, you'll see *this*."

Again the video paused, and Swift pointed at a group of figures who looked to be walking towards a vehicle. "You see this group of people here? Look closely at them and see if you see what I do. Make sure that I'm not making it up."

Both Thurston and Ferrero moved in to take a closer look. There was silence for a good two minutes before Ferrero said, "These two here. They're being escorted by these two."

Swift smiled with relief. "That was my thinking too."

Thurston asked, "Do you think they could be our guys?"

"It's quite probable, ma'am," Swift said.

After a brief silence, Thurston said. "Good work, Slick. However, keep this to yourself. I want to be sure before we say anything. See if you can track them and whoever is in those vehicles. And before you say it, I know it's going to be virtually impossible, but try."

"Yes, ma'am."

"Is there any news on the other front?"

"You mean Montoya, ma'am?"

"Yes."

Swift shook his head. "No, he's disappeared."

"Well, it was mercs who broke him out of prison, so we can assume that it was the same ones who attacked us at the safehouse. I'm guessing that they were the ones at the warehouse too. If they are, then it is a fair bet that Montoya is involved in it up to his eyeballs. Find the mercs, and maybe we find the Mexican motherfucker too."

"I'm on it, General."

"On your way out, tell Cara and Carlos we want to see them."

"Yes, ma'am."

A few minutes later, Cara and Arenas entered the office. "You wanted us, ma'am?" Cara asked.

"Yes. You're the new commander of Reaper Team. Carlos is your second."

"But that's Reaper's job, ma'am."

Thurston's voice hardened. "Until we know one way or the other what has happened to him, you're it. Understand?"

"Yes, ma'am."

"Are you good with that, Carlos?"

"*Sí.*"

"OK. The team will stand down for a few days to rest and recuperate. I don't care what you do as long as you leave your cells on. I want you to be contactable at all times."

"Yes, General."

"That is all."

They left, and Thurston turned to Ferrero. "You too, Luis."

———

TEXAS ROSE MOTEL, EL PASO

Reynolds' fingernails raked deep furrows in Axe's back as she sat astride him, grinding hard. Axe's face was buried between her milky-white breasts, muffling his moans. Both were coated in a sweaty sheen. The night was hot, and the ceiling fan did nothing to cool it down. Finally, Reynolds arched her back with the release that shook her lithe form. An incoherent, "Christ!" escaped Axe's lips as he achieved his own.

They rolled apart and lay there staring at the stained ceiling, listening to the sound of their breathing. It was Reynolds who broke the silence. "Do you think they're still alive?"

Axe took a while to answer, not wanting to admit what he was thinking. "No. If he was, we'd know by now."

"How long have you known him?"

"Reaper? Eight, nine years. I first met him when I filled a hole on his team in Africa. Hammer had been wounded on a previous op."

"Who's Hammer?"

"He was Reaper's best friend in the whole world," Axe explained. "He's gone now. Hell, they're all gone."

"I've heard the name," Reynolds said.

"Uh huh. He was killed when all of this shit started with O'Brien."

"Oh."

"Anyway, we were in the DRC chasing some really bad people. At first, it was meant to be all about recon. We were inserted to take a look over a new revolutionary group who were killing their own people to scare them into joining up. They were called The Men of the Congo Revolution. Original, huh? We were four days in the field when we came across this village. All of the young men had been forcibly taken from it to boost the MCR's ranks. They killed everyone else. Old ones, women, children."

Reynolds said, "How awful."

Axe nodded. "Yeah. Anyway, Reaper just gathered us together and told us he was going after them. He said we could either stay or come with. We weren't about to leave him out there with his ass in the wind, so we all went."

At the thought of it, Axe's mouth formed a smile. "He drove us damned hard to catch up to them. We reached the border into Burundi and just kept going. I guess once we caught up to them, they knew what it was like."

"What was like?"

Axe's voice grew hollow, distant. "What it was like to have the Reaper hunting you. Death stalking your every move."

Reynolds shivered at the thought.

"When we found their camp, it was early morning, and the fog on the ground was thick. There was no way I could set up an overwatch, so we just assaulted their position. Somewhere along the way, I got separated from the rest of the team. I was confronted by these three MRC types who got the drop on me. I was dead, no two ways about it. Then there was this burst of gunfire, and the guys just dropped. That's when I saw him. The sun was just starting to cut through the mist, and he stood there all shrouded in fucking fog. That's when I first knew that the Reaper was real."

———

SMOKIN' HOT BAR AND GRILL, EL PASO

Arenas was sure that the bump was deliberate. What else could it be? There was enough room to park a truck at the bar. But the smart-ass young Texan just couldn't help himself. Arenas turned, and there he was, a shade over six feet, strong as a bull, and a shit-eating grin spread across his face. Behind him stood his friends, nudging each other, the same expression on their faces.

"Sorry, Pancho. I didn't see you there."

Arenas nodded and then turned away. He was about to pick up the tray when the big asshole did it again.

From where they sat, Cara, Teller, and Traynor watched it all unfold. Traynor reached into his pocket and pulled out a crumpled fifty-dollar note. He placed it on the scarred tabletop and said, "Fifty says the guy doesn't walk away from the bar."

Teller dug deep and found what he wanted. He placed it beside the first fifty and said, "I'm in."

Traynor stared at Cara. "What about you?"

"I can't believe you lost my fucking son," she said to him.

"We can only apologize so many times," Traynor said. "Now, are you in or out?"

"He's a family man. He'll let it ride," she offered and threw her own note on the table.

They had been in the bar for an hour. Just a few quiet drinks to blow off some steam.

The bar was full of cowboys and smartasses. Bowls of beer nuts sat atop the bar, and in the corner, a t.v. screen still had rolling coverage of the attempt on Karen Day's life. Tomorrow, Cara would fly with Jimmy and take him back to Maine. Then she would fly back. After that, they were going operational again. And who knew what would happen. Then there was Kane.

Back at the bar, Arenas loosened his grip on the tray and left it where it was on the drip mat. He turned once more, and the punk said, "Sorry, I did it again."

He turned and smiled at his friends. Arenas said, "Would you like to try again so I can see you coming this time, *amigo*?"

The punk's face hardened. "Are you saying I'm doing it deliberately, *amigo*?"

His voice was raised, and his friends moved to the edge of their seats in anticipation of what was about to happen. But they were wrong.

Arenas shook his head. "No, no. I would not even suggest that. I think that maybe you are a little crosseyed and can't see for shit."

It took a moment to register, but when it did, the punk lunged forward with a snarl. Arenas was ready for him, and as his attacker moved, he reached up and grabbed a handful of hair. He used the punk's momentum to pull his head down hard, smashing his face into the bartop. The impact sounded loud, and those at the table, Cara, Traynor, and Teller, winced.

The punk reared back, the bridge of his nose mashed in a spray of blood. Arenas pulled the head back savagely, and the stunned man dropped onto his back. Arenas' right foot rose and stomped down with brutal force. The punk doubled up as the boot smashed into his guts.

"Guess I win," Traynor spruiked his good fortune.

Cara and Teller both let out muffled curses before the former said, "Double or nothing we're about to end up in a fight?"

"What?" Traynor said, snapping his head around. The punk's friends had already started to move. "Shit!"

———

THE PENTAGON, WASHINGTON, D.C.

Hank Jones was sitting behind his desk when General Mary Thurston was shown in. He stood up and said, "Mary, good to see you."

She returned his smile and said, "Thank you, sir. Good to see you too."

They both sat down, and Jones said, "Any news about your MIAs?"

Thurston shook her head. "No, sir. We believe that they were taken away from the warehouse alive, but so far that's it. There is a good chance that they are dead."

Jones' expression was grim. "I'm sorry, Mary. Kane was a good man. What are you going to do?"

"I'm promoting Billings to team leader and Arenas to her second."

"Good choice."

"Also, I'm meeting a hopeful replacement here, if that's OK, sir?"

Curious, Jones asked, "Who might that be?"

"Brick Peters. I thought, with your permission, that I could bring him onto the team."

The general nodded but remained silent.

"I do have another request, sir?"

"Go ahead."

Thurston said, "It's for more assets for the team."

"You'd best just tell me, Mary, so I know what I'm in for."

"Sir. I would like a couple of Black Hawks, an HC-130, two UAVs, and other drones that we might need."

"Don't you have access to that already?"

Thurston nodded. "Yes, sir. But not when we require them. I'd like the Black Hawks at my fingertips. The HC-130 will be a good asset to have when we have to fly out of the continental US. We can load all of our gear on it and be gone within hours."

"Roger that," Jones said. "I almost hesitate to ask, but, is that it?"

"Armored Humvees and Tahoes?"

"You're killing me, Mary."

"I want us to be as independent as possible, General."

"I'll see what I can do."

"One more thing."

Jones sighed. "There would be."

"Luis and I are of the same opinion that all of what has happened to us of late is the work of Juan Montoya."

"What brings you to that conclusion?"

"Ever since we left for Ecuador, we've been walking into one shit storm after another. Then there's the thing with O'Brien and the militia. All of this happened after they broke out of prison using Collins and his mercenaries. I know he's involved somewhere, sir. Have you heard anything?"

"Not a word."

"What about the ambassador?"

"She's going to live, thanks to Peters. Plugged her

wound with his fingers and stopped her from bleeding out."

"Are there any clues who was responsible?"

"Without a doubt, it was cartel related. We just don't know which one."

A knock at the door stopped their conversation, and when it opened, Peters was shown in. He looked at the two generals and asked, "Am I in some kind of trouble, sir, ma'am?"

They both shook their heads. "No, son," Jones said. "Quite the opposite. We have a job for you."

———

CHIHUAHUA, MEXICO

A thin-faced Mexican set up and tested the camera to make sure that it was working. Behind him stood Juan Montoya and Ward Collins, both men watching him work. They were in one of the cartel boss' many safe-houses. For one kilometer in every direction, he had men positioned to warn of any incursion into the secure zone.

"Is it ready yet?" Montoya asked.

"Soon, *Jefe*. I just need to make sure that the Americans cannot trace it back to us."

The cartel boss seemed satisfied with the explanation and nodded abruptly. He then turned to Collins and asked, "Are the *equipos* ready?"

"The teams are in place. In a few days, when the time is right, my men will pick up the package and take it to where it needs to be."

"What about the other jobs. They must be completed over the next couple of days, so the *gringos* are looking towards Mexico, not in their own *patio trasero*."

"It will be done."

"Good."

The Mexican who'd been fiddling with the camera cleared his throat and said, "It is ready, *Jefe.*"

Montoya turned and walked over to stand in front of the camera. He straightened his white coat and brushed off his white pants. Stroking his manicured goatee, he nodded to the man. "I'm ready."

The man leaned over the camera, pressed a button and nodded back.

Montoya cleared his throat and started to speak. "My name is Juan Montoya, and I have a message for the *imperialistas* north of our border."

———

THE PENTAGON, WASHINGTON, D.C.

The door to General Hank Jones' office opened, and a young first lieutenant entered. "Sorry for the intrusion, sir, but you need to see this. It's being streamed live onto the internet."

Jones, Thurston, and Peters glanced at each other while the young man brought it up on a flat screen hanging on the wall.

"*...your prison could not hold me, and your government is useless against me. My reach from my beloved Mexico is beyond what your leaders even realize.*"

"Son of a bitch," Jones growled. "I'd like to put a bullet in that prick's brain. Where is this coming from?"

"We're not sure, sir. But we figure it has to be somewhere in Mexico."

"*...my country is for my people, not for imperialist gringos who think they can come down here without permis-*"

sion and do as they wish. This will stop. If not, then you will see more of what happened to the puta you call your ambassador."

Montoya paused thoughtfully and then smiled. *"Maybe you should come. Yes, why not? I would welcome all of you who do, with bullets and bombs. And to the dictators in the big house who think they are the gods of all, you cannot touch me. This is Mexico, it is my country, not yours. Stay the fuck out!"*

The picture disappeared, and the screen went black. Thurston stared at Jones. "You want me to put my team on alert?"

"No. I'll get onto Alex Joseph. He can have one of his SEAL teams put on standby. Once the intelligence guys nail this bastard down, we'll send them across the border. When the president sees, this he'll start breathing fire. That Mex bastard just stood there and fed us a big old shit sandwich. Surely he realizes we won't let this stand."

"Sir, request permission to be put on that team," Brick said.

"No. You're now a member of Team Reaper, son. Mary's your boss now."

CHAPTER 15

THE GATES OF HELL , ISLA DEL VOLCÁN, PERU

THE GATES OF HELL! It was aptly named. A large stone-built prison seemed to rise out of the thick green jungle surrounding it. Serving as a backdrop to the seemingly ancient structure was a towering slab of rock; the long-extinct volcano from which the island got its name.

Edging alongside a rundown dock, the boat stopped but didn't tie up. Instead, one of the armed guards stepped forward and said, "*Final de la línea.*"

Kane frowned. "What?"

"He wants us to get off," Spencer said.

"I know what he said. I want to know why they aren't coming with us?"

"You really don't know, do you?"

"You're the spook. How about you tell me."

"There are no guards here," Spencer explained. "The prisoners roam free on the island."

"You're shitting me. How do they keep them here?"

"We're a hundred fucking miles from anywhere," Spencer hissed. "What are they going to do? Swim?"

"What's to stop anyone coming to get them? The cartels?"

"Peruvian navy."

"I thought this was some kind of secret place."

"They have a rapid deployment force which is sent out whenever someone breaches the ten-mile exclusion zone."

"*Rápido! Rápido!*" the guard said animatedly.

They stepped ashore and almost immediately the boat drew back from the dock. Kane said, "They didn't even say goodbye."

"That's because they are scared."

"What are we meant to eat?"

"There are food drops once a week. If we last that long."

Kane stared at him. "How do you know all this shit, and no one else has ever heard of this place?"

"Like you said, I'm the spook."

"I can't believe something like this exists."

"That's not the worst of it."

"Really?"

"Reports are that most of them are split into factions. Like the cartels, Mexican, Colombian, FARC, Dominicans, Haitians, gangs out of Brazil. It's a veritable fucking melting-pot of hardcore criminals. If any of the countries in Central or South America want to get rid of their worst cases, they hand them over to Peru. The Peruvian government just dump them here and let them sort themselves out."

"Could be worse," Kane pointed out. "They could have guns. Come on, let's get out of here. That boat was bound to have drawn attention."

Indeed it had, for no sooner had the words escaped Kane's lips, when the first signs of life appeared from near the prison. Reaper nudged Spencer. "Let's get into the jungle."

They began a slow jog towards the end of the dock and then veered left. Their track had them on an oblique angle away from the prisoners. A shout drew their attention, and they saw that their observers were now moving in their direction at a good clip. They were armed with what appeared to be spears and clubs.

"Shit!" Spencer exclaimed. "Look!"

Ahead of them, another group of prisoners materialized. These ones were different. They were dressed in mottled green fatigues. "I'd say they're FARC!" Kane said to Spencer as they skidded to a stop.

Like the others, the FARC prisoners were armed with spears. Their leader looked to be a tall, solidly-built man with a full beard. Beside him, a slimmer man pointed in the direction of the island's latest arrivals.

With a wave of his arm, the leader sent his men forward. Kane figured that there were probably twenty of them. With shouts and yells of excitement, they surged towards Reaper and Spencer.

Then a shout drew their attention once more, and they saw a lone figure standing on a low rise at the edge of the jungle, waving to them. He signaled them to run his way with urgency.

"Could be a trap," Spencer said.

"I guess we'll find out. Move!"

They started running again, this time towards the man. The closer they got to him, the narrower the gap became between the FARC and the others, whoever they were. The ground was uneven and damp, which made it all the more difficult to keep up a fast pace. Spencer slipped and almost fell. He would've if Kane hadn't steadied him with an arm.

"We're not going to make it!" Spencer exclaimed.

He was right. The gap had narrowed exponentially, and the last part of their passage was about to shut.

Slamming a shoulder into the first snarling recidivist, Kane used such force that he heard ribs snap. A cry of pain confirmed his suspicions as the man reeled away.

He'd been armed with a blade of some descript, more than likely manufactured on the island, and Reaper felt the sting of its bite.

Gritting his teeth, Kane turned to meet another assailant. This one had a spear made of a branch with a sharpened piece of metal at its tip. The Latino drove it at Kane's face, but he leaned back, and it slid harmlessly past his nose, missing by only a few inches.

Reaper took it in a firm grip and twisted the weapon free. He then reversed it and drove the point into the would-be killer's throat.

Wrenching it free in a spray of blood, Kane twisted to meet the next assault. Out of the corner of his eye, he saw Spencer break the neck of a man with a heavily-tattooed face, then watched on as his friend was struck from behind by a large man with a bald head. The glint of sunlight on steel preceded a spray of blood as a wicked homemade blade exploded from Spencer's chest.

The CIA man's mouth dropped open and more blood poured forth. Kane cursed and threw the spear at Spencer's killer. The tip ripped through his throat, and the man gagged as he tried to stem the flood from the ghastly wound.

Then something strange happened. A gunshot sounded. A head exploded, and then everything stopped dead. Kane whirled to meet the new threat and was stunned to see Anatoli Petrov, one of the most wanted men in the world, standing there with an MP-443 Grach in a rock-steady fist. Even with the gray beard, he was recognizable.

"Are you just going to stand there with hand on cock, or fucking move?" he growled in heavily-accented English.

Kane didn't wait for a second invitation. He moved to stand behind the notorious Russian arms dealer. "I'm kind of glad to see you."

"You are American?"

"Yes."

Petrov snorted. "Should have fucking left you."

"You have gone too far this time, Anatoli!" snarled a Latino with tattoos and a thick beard. "Manuel will surely kill you this time for shooting his brother."

A mirthless chuckle escaped from Petrov's throat. "Tell him if he asks nicely, I might let him suck my dick."

A surge of anger rippled through the group.

Then Petrov turned to the FARC group who, for some reason hadn't engaged in the melee. "What about you? You want some too?"

With a few muttered words they turned away and walked off.

"Now it is your turn," Petrov said to Thick Beard.

"This is not over," he hissed. "Your days are numbered, *Cabrón*."

With that, they also turned and walked away.

Kane hurried over to Spencer and crouched beside him. Mercifully the CIA man was dead. With the wound he had, if he'd survived, his death would have been slow and agonizing. "I'm sorry."

Kane stood back up to be confronted by Petrov. His face was a mask of anger as he spat, "I can't believe that I fucked up everything because of a son of a bitch American."

Kane said, "I can't say I'm unhappy."

The Grach came up, and Petrov growled, "Maybe that will change when I shoot you in the face."

———

ISLA DEL VOLCÁN, PERU

"This is where I live," Petrov said with a hint of pride.

Kane stared at the wreckage of the Antonov An-124 transport aircraft. It was a strategic airlift jet which could transport up to five hundred thousand pounds of cargo. One of its wings had been sheared off, and it had three holes in the fuselage. The tail was broken off also. Already the jungle had begun to envelop it with its tangled tentacles.

Kane said, "Looks like it came down hard?"

"You would too with full load," Petrov said.

"A full load of what?"

"Jelly Beans," he said with a voice laced with sarcasm. "What the fuck you think? You know who I am."

Nodding at the gun in Petrov's waistband, Kane said, "Weapons."

"Of course."

"What happened?"

The Russian shrugged. "I was taking a load of arms to customer. Dumbshit pilot flew into fucking storm. Lightning hit wing, and next, we are going down. This is where we crash."

"What happened to all the weapons?"

"Well, after first contact with prisoners, we hide them."

"Before they fell into the wrong hands?"

Petrov nodded.

"How?"

The Russian's face contorted and he snarled, "What is this? Fucking twenty questions?"

"I was just curious is all. How long have you been here?"

"What year is it?"

"Twenty-eighteen."

"Three years."

Kane was surprised. "You've been here that long?"

"Yes. No more questions, or this time I do shoot you in face. We go inside before it rain."

As if on cue, a crash of distant thunder sounded. "All right, lead the way."

Inside, the Antonov was pretty much stripped bare. Petrov had divided what remained of the fuselage into sections as one would a house with walls. "Where is everyone else?" Kane asked.

"They are dead."

"What happened? Did they die in the crash?"

"I kill them."

Kane stared at the Russian. "Why?"

"They know secret."

"What secret?"

"If I tell you, then I have to kill you too," Petrov explained. "And I may need your help."

"What for?"

Petrov grew angry. "Do you think that our friends will leave us alone? Not Manuel Ortega. I kill his brother. Because of you. He will come with his *soldados*. To kill me and to kill you. To stay alive, I need your help. What is your name?"

"Kane."

"Get some rest, Kane. You will need it."

———

ISLA DEL VOLCÁN, PERU— THE PRISON

The old prison was damp and cold, especially without sunlight. A large fire blazed in the center of the open room, and around it sat four men, one man each from the four most powerful factions on the island.

Manuel Ortega represented the cartel faction, Carlos Andreas was from the FARC syndicate, Janjak, the Haitians, and Jasiel, Dominicans.

The prison itself had last been fully guarded in 2010. In June of that year, there had been a riot in which eight guards had lost their lives. The Peruvian army was brought in to retake control of the island with bloody ferocity. When they were finished, fifty prisoners were dead. Then a bright politician suggested that they let the prisoners have the island to themselves. The army withdrew, and The Gates of Hell was born.

"I want to hear what you all have to say," Ortega said to the others.

"You are suggesting that we form a truce for the time being, all because of one man?" Jasiel asked.

Ortega nodded. "That one man killed my brother. Besides, he is hiding something. I know it."

"How do you know it?" Janjak asked. "What secret could he possibly have?"

"What about his guns?"

"Rumors," Carlos Andreas mocked. "Nothing but rumors. All he has is that handgun that we see."

"Do you not want to find out?" Jasiel asked thoughtfully.

"I don't care about him finding out," Ortega snapped. "I just want him dead."

"Well go up there and kill him," Janjak said matter of factly.

"So none of you will help me?"

"I want to see what you are scared of," Jasiel said. "We will help you, but we want half of what you find."

Half of what? Ortega thought. It could be something, or it could be nothing. "*Sí.* Half."

"Then we will go with you tomorrow, kill Petrov, and divide whatever it is we find."

Jasiel started to stand when Janjak snapped, "Wait! We will all go."

Ortega eyed them with suspicion but nodded anyway. "*Sí.* We will all go."

CHAPTER 16

EL PASO, TEXAS

THE FOLLOWING MORNING, on her return to El Paso, Thurston called Swift into her office. He looked tired. His hair was unkempt, and there were dark circles around his eyes. She studied him for a moment and said, "You look like shit. Sit down before you fall down."

He gave a muttered, "Yes, ma'am," and fell into the chair across from her.

"Have you had any sleep at all?"

He shook his head. "Not since we got back. Not a full night anyway."

Thurston gave a frustrated sigh and stabbed a finger at him. "Damn it, Sam. You're no good to me if you go toes up in the middle of something. Get some rest. And that's an order."

"Yes, ma'am."

He started to rise and stopped, let himself slump back in the chair and asked, "Do you want to know what I've found?"

Sitting forward in her seat, Thurston said, "What have you found?"

An expulsion of air came from his lips, and Swift told her about his activities over the past few days, searching for their lost men. "I've been digging into anything I can connect to. Satellites, security feeds, anything with a damned camera on it, and all I got was nothing. They disappeared. So then I went back to the warehouse feed, and I managed to get a plate number from one of the vehicles. The one they left behind and burned because it was all shot up."

"How did you manage that?"

"The fire from the warehouse had a huge glow, and before the SUV completely disappeared in flames, I got the number."

"And?"

"It was registered to a company called Incursion Global."

"Who are they?"

"No one. A shell company. So, I tried to track the owner from there and came up with three more. Whoever owns them really didn't want anyone to find them."

Thurston frowned. "Didn't?"

Swift raised his eyebrows in a tired daze. "Hmm?"

"You said didn't."

"Oh, yes. I found out who the registered owner is."

The general felt frustration start to build inside her but remembered her man was operating on virtually no sleep. "Come on, Slick, speak to me. Stay with it. Who owns the company?"

"Captain Ward Collins."

"Son of a bitch."

"Uh huh. He's got himself quite a setup."

Thurston thought for a moment about the information just delivered by Swift. "He's obviously working for someone. If we find out who, we might be able to figure out what happened to Kane and Spencer."

"Or if they're alive," the computer tech said. "Can I suggest something, ma'am?"

"Go ahead."

"Pete Traynor has contacts over the border, from when he worked undercover. Maybe you could send him and Carlos across the river. It may be quicker than me digging through computer files."

"OK. Call the team back in. If we're sending people across the river, I want everyone on it."

"Yes, ma'am."

―――――

ISLA DEL VOLCÁN, PERU

When Petrov entered the Antonov, there was a look of worry on his face. Kane looked up at him and asked what was wrong.

"They are coming," he said. "All of them."

"What do you mean, all of them?"

"The FARC, the Haitians, Ortega, all of them. They will be here soon."

"Then we'd best not be," Kane answered matter of factly. He nodded at the gun tucked inside Petrov's pants. "If you have any more of those floating around, now's the time to get them out."

The Russian grunted in agreement and walked part way along the fuselage of the plane and stopped. He ripped aside a crate which was sitting on the floor, to reveal a hole. He reached down inside and pulled out an AK-74M. Tossing it to Kane, he then fossicked about some more in his stash. By the time Petrov was finished, he'd extracted magazines and boxes of 5.45 caliber ammunition, F1 grenades, a Dragunov sniper rifle, ammunition for it, and another Grach.

Kane asked in a dry tone, "You got any RPGs down there?"

"Hidden somewhere else."

"You're shitting me."

"You load magazines," Petrov ordered.

Kane did so with practiced ease. Before long he had eight magazines loaded. Petrov looked at him and said, "You have done this before?"

"Once or twice."

"You were in American army?"

"Yes."

The Russian snorted. "Great. I am here with fucking cowboy."

"And I'm here with the world's most fucking wanted arms dealer," Kane retorted. "Get used to it. If you want to stay alive, we'll have to work together."

Reaper scooped up some magazines and stuffed them in his pockets. Then the Grach and placed it in his waistband. Meanwhile, Petrov found a cloth bag and stuffed more loaded magazines in it and slung it over his shoulder. He handed the Dragunov to Kane. "You can use this?"

"Yeah," Reaper answered as he slung it across his back.

"Now we will make our stand," the Russian stated, a look of determination on his face. "Kill many before they kill us."

Kane shook his head. "No. We're going into the jungle."

Petrov was about to protest when Kane said, "Trust me, it's what I do."

"OK. But wait." The Russian pulled the crate back

over the hole. "There are things in there we don't want them to find."

"Are we good now?"

"Yes."

"Then let's get the hell out of Dodge."

Petrov shook his head. "Fucking cowboy."

———

"They are gone," Ortega growled angrily.

Andreas stepped forward and glanced about. He said, "I will have my men look around."

He disappeared outside while the other scanned the fuselage, looking for anything they could confiscate for themselves.

Janjak found a watch, picked it up, shook it, then threw it away with a curse. They turned over things, lifted others up, then out of frustration, Jasiel kicked the crate which was concealing the hole, moving it far enough to reveal what was beneath it.

With renewed vigor, he thrust it aside. A hiss of pleasure escaped his lips as he stared down into the excavation. His smile grew broad as he realized what he'd found. "Guns!"

The other whirled to see Jasiel already on his knees, retrieving the weapons which Petrov had left behind. There were three AK-74Ms, two Graches, and a second Dragunov. Fortunately, the Russian had extracted all of the F1 grenades. But not all of the ammunition.

The four leaders split the find between themselves, with the Dragunov going to the FARC faction. They exited the Antonov's fuselage and gathered their men around them. Ortega pointed towards the dense green jungle to his left and said in a loud voice, "They are in there somewhere. Whoever kills them will get this."

The cartel leader held up a Grach. A murmur rippled through the crowd. To have a weapon on the island would elevate the status of the owner. Ortega continued, "With it will come the bullets it fires. Now, find them. Kill them!"

The first anyone knew that a shot had been fired, was the wet sound made by the impact of a 7.62 round, having traveled from almost a thousand meters out. It was a lucky shot, for the sights hadn't been zeroed, but allowing for that, Kane took aim at center-mass.

The target, a broad-shouldered Haitian, shuddered under the violent impact and dropped to the damp jungle grass. Just over two seconds after the bullet's impact, the shot sounded. By the time it reached the island's inhabitants, another was already on its deadly journey.

It almost took the arm off a FARC soldier, in a spray of bright red. He was spun around under the impact and stood there staring down at the shredded mass of flesh that barely kept his arm attached. Then came the pain. Burning, stomach-churning pain. Followed by a noise that you would hear at the real gates of Hell.

Men scattered, looking for cover, hoping to minimize the chances of becoming the sniper's next target. Unbeknown to them, they needn't have worried. Kane's objective was to issue a message. He was creating a certain level of nervous tension about what they could expect should they choose to follow.

Kane climbed to his feet and raised the scoped rifle, observing the carnage of his handiwork below. Two from two. Not bad going for an unfamiliar setup. The prisoners had scattered or dropped to the ground. The leaders, brave in every sense of the word, had done the same.

"They found the gun stash," Kane told Petrov.

"I thought they might."

Reaper turned to look at the Russian. "I don't suppose you have any food hidden around the island anywhere?"

Petrov shook his head. "No."

"What day are the food drops?"

There was a pause while Petrov lapsed into deep thought, then he said, "Tomorrow."

"Where?"

"Where ever they land."

"OK. That just means we'll have to get there before the others. Come on, let's keep moving."

After a quick look back towards the Antonov, they were swallowed by a thick wall of undergrowth.

———

By the end of the day, the pair had covered a lot of ground, then circled back to a position that Petrov said was the best place to shelter against a coming storm. The humidity had built throughout the day and was now thick and cloying. Then, in the late afternoon, the steel-gray clouds overhead opened, loosing great sheets of rain. Both men were soon soaked through, but at least the rain was cool and refreshing.

The cave was beside a small spring where they could get fresh water. Thick brush surrounded it and had to be pushed aside to enter. Once through, they ensured that there was no trace of their passing. Inside, Kane saw a small opening in the ceiling, great for letting in light, but it also admitted the water. Lots of water.

"I guess we'll be sleeping in the wet tonight," Kane surmised.

"You? Yes. Me? No," Petrov informed him. He walked towards the back of the cave and pulled away a large tarpaulin which blended in with its surroundings. Beneath it was a pile of crates.

Petrov dragged the tarp across the cave to an area as yet untouched by the rain. Curious, Kane walked over to the crates to examine them. Aware that he was under close scrutiny by the Russian arms dealer, he ignored it and looked over the stamps on the boxes. They said: *Bazalt*.

Kane knew *Bazalt*. They were the manufacturer of Russian RPGs. Another crate was stamped: *KB Mashinostroyeniya*. Reaper turned and asked, "SA-18 or SA-25?"

Petrov said, "Eighteen."

Other crates held semi-automatic weapons, handguns, and ammunition. Another crate made Kane frown. "You have a fucking MATADOR?"

"Yes."

The MATADOR was a shoulder-launched anti-armor weapons system. It could destroy armored vehicles and was useful for blowing holes through walls in urban situations. The next few crates were unmarked. Kane reached out to look when Petrov said, "Please do not touch those."

Kane turned to face the Russian, who, to emphasize his point, had the Grach in his fist aimed at the American. "Please."

"All right," Reaper said, not wanting to push it. "I won't."

He stepped away from the crates. "Tomorrow when

the food drop comes in, we'll need to get there before anyone else does. How many prisoners are on the island altogether?"

Petrov lowered the gun and shrugged. "One-hundred and fifty. Maybe more."

"Are they all like these that are chasing us?"

"Yes."

"Should make it interesting then."

CHAPTER 17

TEAM REAPER WAS GATHERED by the following day. The last person to arrive was Cara, after her turn-around flight on a C-130 had been delayed by bad weather. Now, however, they were all together in their briefing room, waiting for Thurston to appear.

The new Reaper element commander felt tired. She had hardly slept the previous night, and now she was in a briefing for God only knew what. She knew that they'd been ordered back to duty for a reason and for a fleeting moment she thought of Reaper and had a flicker of hope. She looked across at Ferrero who was talking to Pete Traynor. Climbing wearily to her feet, she walked over to him. Looking up at her, he smiled. "You look like shit, Cara."

"Midnight flights will do that to you," she said. "Any news?"

He thought about waiting for Thurston to brief them, but it was different for Cara. She'd been with him from the start. He looked at Traynor and said, "I'll be back in a moment, Pete."

Traynor nodded. "Sure, boss."

Ferrero ushered Cara away from the others, and she felt her blood run cold. Was he about to tell her that Kane was dead? She didn't think she was equipped to hear that right now. Through her fog of exhaustion, she realized that there was a possibility that she might have feelings for him. *Might!* But if Reaper was dead, she'd never get the chance to find out.

Looking Ferrero in the eyes, she said, "He's dead, isn't he?"

He reached out and gently touched her arm.

Oh God, it's true.

"We don't know. Slick was able to trace the vehicles used back to Ward Collins. Mary wants to send Pete and Carlos over the river to see if there are any whispers we can follow up."

There was a questioning look on Cara's face. "Whispers?"

"Relax. It's better than sitting waiting for Slick to dig something up. Besides, he was the one who suggested it. OK?"

Cara remained silent but ran her hands over her face and hair.

"OK?" Ferrero said again.

"Fine, but I'm going with them."

The operations commander was taken aback for a moment and shook his head. "I don't..."

"My team, Luis. My choice. I'm going with them."

"Give me a minute, and I'll run it past Mary. You look like you need a week of sleep, so if she says no, then you stay. Agreed?"

"Agreed."

"One other thing you should know. You're getting a new team man today. He's not here yet, but I figure he's not far away."

"Who?"

"Brick Peters."

"The guy from the ambassador's detail?"

"Yes. You're a man short at the moment, so he's it. He's also a medic which could prove invaluable."

"What about when Kane comes back?"

"*If* he comes back, Brick will stay on."

"Fine."

Ferrero disappeared from the room, and Cara went back to sit down. Axe made his way over to her and asked, "What was all that about? News of Reaper?"

"It was about the briefing." Then she deflected by saying, "Did you see Montoya on the television?"

Axe gave her a smile and shook his head. "No. I was kinda busy. He's a crazy motherfucker though. The sooner someone puts a slug in his head the better."

"What were you doing that had you so busy?" Cara asked.

"Not what, who?"

Cara thought and stared across the room at Reynolds who was smiling while talking to Teller about something. She laughed and glanced at Axe. Cara grinned knowingly and turned her gaze back on the ex-recon marine. "Son of a bitch, you were screwing Reynolds."

"What? No...nooo. Not me. OK, I was, but keep it to yourself. All right?"

"I wouldn't have to if you could," Cara pointed out. "You wait until I talk to her."

"No, Cara. Don't!" Panic was etched on Axe's face. "You can't...no, don't...please...fuck!"

Cara got up and walked towards Reynolds, leaving an

ashen-faced Axe behind her. There was too much fun in this not to drag it out. She'd never seen the big guy squirm before.

"Hey, Brooke, how was your downtime?" she asked.

Reynolds' gaze was immediately directed over Cara's shoulder, and she sensed Axe there trying to convince her not to say anything. Then came the realization. "Son of a bitch, you frigging told her. Christ!"

"Told her what?" Teller asked.

"Nothing," Axe blurted out. "I told her nothing."

"Bullshit! How else would she know that you and I were screwing on our downtime?"

Teller guffawed. "You and him?"

"What's wrong with me?" Axe snapped. "I'll have you know that beneath this rugged exterior lies a smooth loving machine."

"Oh, please," Reynolds moaned.

"Hey," Arenas called across to join in the fun. "I heard he was the regular Casanova. The *Chicas* talk about him all the time."

"Shut up, Carlos. There's enough going on here without you adding to it," Axe snapped.

Arenas chuckled but said no more.

Suddenly, Thurston and Ferrero appeared in the room with a third man. The general walked to the front and turned to face them. "All right, listen up. Everyone, take a seat." Her eyes shifted to Axe. "You too, Casanova."

Axe opened his mouth to protest but saw the look on Reynolds' face and clamped it shut. He glared at Cara who smiled innocently back at him. Mumbling something under his breath, he sat down.

"OK, first things first. The new guy is Brick Peters. He'll be joining Reaper Team as a combat medic. Play nice with him."

Axe turned to look at Brick and said with an exaggerated wave, "Hi, Brick, leave now before it's too late."

Brick gave an uncertain smile and nodded.

"We also have a non-fraternization rule too," Axe added.

"Shut up, Axe," Reynolds snapped.

Cara threw an empty plastic coffee cup at him.

Axe ducked. "What did I say?"

"OK, that's enough," Thurston said over the growing noise.

Things quietened down, and the general began their briefing.

"Over the past few days, Slick has been trying to run down our two MIAs. His search has led us to believe that Ward Collins and his mercenaries were involved. What it also does is give us a link to Montoya since he was the one Collins broke out of federal prison. What's going to happen is this. Cara, Pete, and Carlos are going over the river. Pete has a contact or two over there he can talk to. If we're lucky, we might even get a lead on either Collins, Montoya, or hopefully, Reaper and Spencer."

"I thought there was only going to be two of us," Traynor said.

"There was. But it's Cara's team now, and she insisted she go. Problem?"

"No, ma'am."

"The rest of the team, Axe and Brick, will stay on alert just in case. All of Bravo will provide their usual support."

"UAV, ma'am?" asked Teller.

"Not this time. But there'll be one on standby in the event that it's needed."

"Ma'am, if me and Brick are to provide any kind of effective support, we'll need to be on the other side of the river too," Axe pointed out.

"When I was in Washington, I asked for more assets," Thurston explained. "We now have two Black Hawks at our disposal, an HC-130, two UAVs, and we should also be receiving new armored Humvees and Tahoes. You'll be out at Biggs Airfield on standby."

"Yes, ma'am."

"All right, gear up and let's get out there."

The cell in Thurston's pocket rang, and she dragged it free. While the team dispersed, she listened intently and then said, "Thank you, sir," before hanging up.

"They've found the house where Montoya made the broadcast from," she said out loud. "SEALs are about to kick the doors in now."

Everyone stopped and stared at her.

"Slick, find it and get it on the screen. The Whitehouse has a live feed going into it."

Swift's fingers danced across his tablet, and the screen lit up with an aerial view. Sound followed with the SEALs' comms being fed back too.

After fast-roping to the street from a pair of Black Hawks, two six-operator teams were now moving on the house where Montoya was supposed to be. Separating, the second team moved to take the rear.

More voices over the comms and they breached.

"Something's not right," Cara said. "There are no guards. There should be guards."

Thurston nodded. "You're ri—" she never got the word out before a bright flash turned the screen white then receded.

"Son of a bitch," Axe gasped. "The fucker blew the house."

The group stood transfixed in a drawn-out silence, shocked by what they'd just witnessed. Over the feed, they could hear radio chatter and a voice calling for the leader of the insertion team to respond. Each transmission was met with static.

After a while, Thurston said to Swift, "Shut it down."

The screen went black.

"You've all got jobs to do," Thurston continued. "Get it done and we might just be closer to finding that bastard and bringing our people home."

———

CANNON AIRFORCE BASE, CLOVIS, NEW MEXICO

Captain Sean Richards was in his office when the call came through. He was writing up reports for his commanding officer in the 33rd Special Operations Squadron, which specialized in the General Atomics MQ-9 Reaper UAV when the phone on his polished desktop screeched at him.

He muttered under his breath and dropped the pen on the uncompleted form. Picking up the handset, annoyed at the interruption, he spoke gruffly, "Richards?"

"Is that Captain Sean Richards?" a male voice asked.

"It is."

"I'm sorry to bother you, sir, but I'm Doctor Michael Sweet from Plains Regional Medical Center in Clovis."

Richards felt his heart lurch. "Yes, what can I do for you?"

"Sir, I have to inform you that your wife and daughter were involved in an accident earlier today. And..."

"Oh, God. Tell me they're OK."

"I'm afraid, sir, that they were both badly injured and we need you to come in to make some decisions before we proceed."

"I'll leave right now," Richards blurted out, his thoughts only of Megan and Rachel. "I'll be there soon."

Richards hung up and ran from his office.

Five minutes later, the captain hit the 84 and headed towards Clovis.

Reaching the outskirts of the town, he turned left onto North Wheaton, blew past Madison Road and made it as far as Coyote before a stolen truck T-boned him and put his SUV on its side.

Within moments, a dark-blue van arrived, and four men climbed out, armed with M4A1s. The larger pair dragged a stunned Richards from his vehicle, piled him into the back of the van and followed him in. Climbing into the front seats, the remaining two quickly scanned the scene, and then the van drove away. The whole thing was achieved with military precision and had elapsed no more than two minutes.

Richards began to gather his wits after a short time and then realized he couldn't move. His hands and feet were bound, but worse still was the fact that he couldn't see due to a hood having been placed over his head.

"What – What is going on?" he managed to get out.

"Shut up," a voice snapped.

"My wife and child," he continued. "They've been hurt. I need to get to them."

"They'll be fine as long as you do what we say."

"You don't understand."

The hood was ripped from his head, and he blinked to clear his vision. Two men were in the back with him. Both wore masks over their faces. One thrust a cell in front of Richards' face and showed him a live-stream feed of his wife and daughter sitting on the sofa at their home. Beside them was an armed man.

Richards looked up. "Please don't hurt them."

"That depends on you."

———

ISLA DEL VOLCÁN, PERU

A branch lashed Kane's face, and he felt the sting as sweat flooded the nick on his cheek. The next one he managed to duck before he broke out into a small clearing. Slung across his back was the Dragunov, while in his hands was the AK-74. He looked up and saw the last of the parachutes coming down, figuring there to be still at least a mile to go before they would come across the first of the food crates.

The crashing sound behind him signaled the arrival of Petrov. Dropping his AK at his feet, the Russian bent over with his hands on his knees and drew in great gulps of air. He straightened and said, "This is *chush' sobach'ya*."

Kane looked at him and raised an eyebrow. "Huh?"

"Bullshit!"

"It may be, but we have to keep going if we want to get to that food," Kane said and started to run across the clearing.

"Fucking cowboy," Petrov hissed, scooped up his weapon and followed.

When the plane had first passed over the island, it had been low enough for Kane to recognize it as an Alenia C-27J Spartan. It had then circled and come back for its cargo run. Now all Kane and Petrov had to do was get there before the others.

When Reaper topped the low ridge, he broke out of the thick foliage and stopped. Below him, perhaps five-hundred meters away, were three crates with parachutes attached. The open piece of ground was perhaps a thousand square meters. Good ground.

Petrov reached him and collapsed with exhaustion. He threw up onto the grass and moaned. "I not hungry anymore."

"You will be," Kane assured him. "Now stand up and get down there and find us something to eat."

The Russian gave him a cold stare. He wiped a hand across his mouth and grated, "Who make you boss?"

"I could go, but I don't think you can hit shit at five-hundred meters. That leaves me. Now get down there."

Petrov came to his feet and started forward. He mumbled something under his breath, and Kane asked, "What?"

"I said, don't miss."

"I'm sure I'll hit something."

When Petrov reached the crates, he found one of them busted open, and some of the contents had spilled onto the ground. Tins, shiny and silver. He stuffed some in an empty bag and moved onto the next crate. For a few minutes, he worked, grabbing all he could. He was about finished when Ortega and the other faction leaders showed with their followers.

A shout alerted Petrov to their presence, and he whirled about to see them at the edge of the clearing. They were between him and the ridge, cutting off his direct escape route to where Kane waited. The Russian guessed that if he was going to trust the American, now was the time. Instead of running away from them, he started to jog back the way he'd come.

That was when the first shots erupted from one of the captured AK74s.

———

Kane expelled a slow breath and squeezed the trigger on the Dragunov. The weapon slammed back into his shoulder. A 7.62 round erupted from the barrel and flew straight and true. An unlucky Haitian who'd stepped in beside his boss, who had been the original target, lost the side of his head a second after the shot was fired.

Blood and brains splashed across Janjak's face and made him flinch. The involuntary movement made Kane's next shot miss, albeit, not by much. The Haitian faction leader felt the heat of the round streak past and knew the bullet had been intended for him.

He dropped to the ground just as a third bullet from the hidden shooter smashed into the side of a FARC member, tearing up the man's insides.

"Get down!" someone shouted. "He is killing us!"

Kane's fourth shot kicked the right leg out from under a Dominican who fell in a heap, screaming and clutching at his leg.

Reaper's work was cold and methodical. If the shoe had been on the other foot, they would have killed him without compunction. He paused for a moment to glance at Petrov. The Russian was lumbering under the weight of his load, but he seemed to be managing.

The Dragunov pivoted back towards the factions, and through the scope, Kane could see them gathering themselves under the instruction of a tall man armed with an AK74. He dropped the crosshairs onto the target's head and had just taken up the pressure of the trigger when a bullet slammed into the ground not far from his head. Dirt spewed upward in a violent eruption, spraying his face and making him flinch.

"Fuck!" Kane exclaimed as he jerked the trigger on the Dragunov. The slug flew wide, missing its intended target. Immediately, Reaper rolled to his left, taking the rifle with him. Just in time as another bullet scorched the air where he'd been laying. If he'd remained there for even two more seconds, he was sure it would have blown a fair-sized hole in his head.

Then it dawned on him. There was another fucking Dragunov out there somewhere, and the shooter knew where he was.

Using the ridge for cover, Kane moved further to his left and then bellied back up to the edge through some long grass and eased the Dragunov forward. Below him, Petrov was laboring heavily under the load he carried. Kane had to give it to the man who refused to drop it even though he was in dire straits.

The factions had reorganized and were once more closing on him. The problem was that if Kane went back to work on them, the sniper would see where he was and target him again. His first priority had to be finding the shooter before he could even think of helping the Russian.

Kane used the sights to sweep the tree line behind the factions as they advanced. The thick green brush revealed nothing, not even the flash of sunlight on the glass of a scope.

Suddenly he heard the loud bark of the enemy Dragunov. He braced for the impact of the 7.62 round but then castigated himself. Such was the firepower of the sniper weapon that the slug would have killed him before he'd heard the shot.

That meant they were now targeting Petrov. It wouldn't take long before a bullet found a home in the Russian, so Kane had to find the shooter now more than ever.

Scanning the tree line slowly, he failed to see anything but lush green vegetation. He started a sweep back the other way when the shooter fired again. A burst of flame was followed by the sound of the weapon. Kane dropped the crosshairs on the position and squeezed the trigger.

He didn't have to wait to see if he'd hit his target. He'd been shooting guns long enough to just know. And even if the sniper wasn't dead, with a 7.62 round in him, he wasn't long for this world.

The Dragunov moved, and Kane placed the crosshairs on the lead prisoner and fired again. Arms and legs flailed, and the target went down in a heap. The rest hesitated, and it gave Petrov a chance to get further away. A minute went by, and Kane held his fire. He figured he'd killed enough of them to make them think twice. And they did, then slowly backed away, retreating towards the tree line.

The Russian reached the ridge, and Kane stood up. He was blowing hard and out of breath. Reaper said, "Enjoy your run?"

"Fuck you," Petrov hissed. "You think this is funny? They not shoot at you?"

Kane just smiled at him as he remembered the shooter with the Dragunov. "Come on, Ivan. Let's get out of here. I'll buy you dinner."

CHAPTER 18

CIUDAD JUÁREZ, MEXICO

CARA HESITATED THEN SAID, "Reaper One, comms check."

"Reaper Two, comms check."

"Bravo Two, comms check."

"This is Zero, read you loud and clear. Out."

It felt weird to Cara. This was Kane's job, not hers.

"Are you OK?" Arenas asked her in a soft voice.

Cara nodded. "Yes."

"You will get used to it. Have confidence in your decisions. I do."

She smiled at him in the orange illumination of the street light. The sun had been down for a good two hours. They'd crossed the border under the cover of darkness and made their way to the west of the city. All three had changed their clothes before crossing the river. Traynor wore jeans and a shirt with the sleeves ripped from it, exposing his tattooed arms. Arenas wore jeans and a T-shirt. Cara also wore jeans, but she wore a navy-blue singlet crop which exposed the tops of her breasts and part of her flat midriff.

Both men had their M17s stuffed down the back of their pants, while Cara had hers hidden away in a black handbag that was slung over her shoulder. She looked at Traynor and asked, "How do you want to do this?"

"Roberto was a soldier in the Mexican Army," Traynor explained. "He bought this place after he got out. Most of the people who come here are military people."

"Most?" said Cara. "What about the rest?"

"Occasionally he has cartel come in to collect their protection money. Just how it works. That way they leave him alone."

"How long since you've seen him?"

"About a year."

"Let's hope he's still friendly. Lead the way."

When they entered the premises, all three stopped. The club should have been jumping; after all, it was a club. Instead, the place was dark and dingy. Standing pride of place in the center of the main room was a chrome pole extending all the way to the ceiling. Slowly and sensually, a young woman with long black hair and small, rose-tipped breasts, wearing nothing but a lacy red thong, wrapped herself around it. The music from the speakers was meant to be sexy, but it was far from it.

What had once been an energetic, vibrant club, was now nothing but a gutter-class strip joint.

Cara said out of the corner of her mouth, "This looks interesting."

"I have a bad feeling, *amigo*," Arenas said warily.

"Yeah, me too."

"All right, let's see if your guy is here."

They started across the room towards the bar when a waitress appeared in front of them. She looked to be in her early twenties. Like the dancer, she wore nothing but a thong, but hers was black. She ran a finger over Traynor's muscular arm and asked, "*Puedo ayudarte con algo, señor?*"

"I'm fine, thank you," Traynor told her in English.

Her eyes lit up at the prospect of making extra money from the border-hopping gringo. "American? I can give you house special if you wish? Just for you." She looked at Cara. "The *dama* can join us too if you want?"

Cara caught a whiff of her nauseatingly cheap perfume and screwed up her face. She stared at her and said, "Thanks for the offer, but I think I'll pass."

The waitress pouted. "Shame."

Traynor looked around the room through the haze of cigarette smoke. Without looking back at the stripper, he said, "I'm looking for Roberto. Is he here?"

"He is in his office."

"Is that still where it used to be?"

"*Sí.*"

Traynor reached into his pocket and took out a fifty. He handed it to her, and she tucked it into her panties. "Thanks for your help."

"*El gusto es mio.*"

As she walked away, he said, "Not tonight it wasn't."

Carlos said, "This is bad. I count four guys on security, and they aren't the type you would hire for the job."

"I counted six," Cara said. "Every one of them has the look of cartel about them."

"This way," Traynor said and started to walk towards the far corner of the room.

As she followed, Cara said, "Zero, can you still hear everything we say?"

"Copy, Reaper One. Loud and clear."

"It looks like we've walked into the lion's den here, Zero. Proceeding on mission."

"Copy. Anything you want me to do, Cara?"

"Notify the local morgue that they're about to get busy."

They reached the door to the office and ran into a six-foot-four roadblock. The man had cartel stamped all over him by the way of ink. Not to mention the two dirty great .44 caliber Desert Eagle handguns tucked in holsters on either side of his body.

"I'm here to see Roberto. Tell him it's Pete. He'll know who I am."

The security guard pressed the talk button on a radio and said, "*Hay un gringo aquí para verte. Dice que su nombre es Pete.*"

A voice came back, "*Voy a estar fuera.*"

"He says he will be right out."

The door suddenly jerked open, and a tall man appeared. Seeing the smile on his whiskered face, one would assume that he was happy to see them. The MAC-11 in his right hand pointed at Traynor's face said otherwise.

"Tell me why I should not kill you right now, asshole," Roberto growled and for the first time in a long while Traynor had nothing.

———

"What's happening, Reaper One?" Ferrero's voice filled her ear.

"You pull that trigger, and you'll have American Special Forces crawling up your ass so fast you'll think you got lucky," Cara snapped.

"Talk to me, Reaper One."

Roberto smiled coldly and said to Traynor, "Who is the *puta*?"

Before Traynor could answer, Cara snarled, "I'm the bitch who'll put a bullet in your fucking head if you don't lower the gun."

"Oh shit."

While she'd been talking, her hand had slipped into her bag and was wrapped around her M17. Arenas had seen it and was poised for what came next.

In a flurry of movement, things happened which could have ended very badly. Roberto started to shift his aim, but a glint in his eyes telegraphed the move. Cara's hand came free of her bag, bringing with it her handgun. Behind her, Arenas had seen the muscles in her arm tense and started his own draw. Traynor relied on the pure instinct of a man used to doing undercover work for years and was moving too.

Cara's M17 settled on Roberto's face before the MAC-11 had completed its traverse. Arenas had his weapon stuck in the crotch of the big guy with the Desert Eagles, while Traynor had his handgun rammed into Roberto's guts.

Behind them, the sound of scraping chairs and stools could be heard. A few muffled yelps from the girls were accompanied by mixed curses. The noise of weapons being cocked and ready to fire rattled loudly across the room.

A smile touched Cara's lips, and she winked at Roberto. "This is a little awkward."

"Why don't you lower your weapons and we can talk this over?" Roberto suggested.

"Not frigging likely," Traynor hissed.

"Reaper One, report."

"We're all good, Zero. Just saying our hellos before we settle down to business."

"Copy."

"What's it going to be, Roberto?" Cara asked. "We could be all nice and civil about this. Or we could do it the other way, in which case, I'll put a bullet through your head."

Roberto lowered the MAC-11 and stood aside. "You best come into my office then." Roberto looked at his security guard. "Espera aquí."

The man with the Desert Eagles took up his post again beside the door. Once it had closed, one of the cartel men in the bar, took out his cell and punched in a number.

———

The office was small, cramped. It had a pungent odor about it which made Cara wrinkle her nose. "Did someone take a shit in here?"

Roberto shook his head and chuckled. "You come into my place looking for help, point a gun at my head, and then insult me. Great way to go about it."

"What happened to your club, Roberto?" Traynor asked.

"The cartels. They run everything now. You do as they say, or they kill you."

Traynor nodded, remembering his last trip below the border when he'd seen a similar story. "We need your help, Roberto."

"Why should I help you? I should be killing you. You're DEA. You're worth money to me. Ten thousand dollars."

Cara reached into her handbag and pulled out a wad

of notes. She tossed it on the cluttered desk. "There, three thousand dollars. All you have to do is answer a few questions, that's it."

The club owner reached out and picked the money up. He flicked through it and then said, "What do you want to know?"

Cara said, "American mercenaries have been working with the cartels below the border."

"*Sí.*"

"Which ones?"

"I don't know. It could be any of them."

"These ones are professionals. We think they're working with Juan Montoya. They're the ones who broke him out of prison."

Roberto went quiet and tossed the money on the desk. "I know nothing."

"Come on, Roberto," Traynor said. "That's bullshit, and you know it. Is it Montoya who owns this place?"

"I own this place!" he snarled.

"Fair enough. Look, we're missing a couple of friends. We're pretty sure that Montoya and the mercs are in this up to their balls. All we need to know is what happened to them after Montoya got hold of them."

"They're dead."

The answer was too quick, and Cara knew it. "Cut the crap, Roberto. Carlos, our friend here needs a little persuasion."

Arenas moved around behind the now nervous club owner and whispered in his ear. "You better answer the *señora*. She is lacking *paciencia*."

"I told you, I know nothing."

Arenas grabbed a handful of hair and slammed Roberto's head into the desk. There was an audible crunch and blood squirted. The club owner's knees buckled, but the strength of Arenas stopped him from falling to the floor.

The ex-special forces commander dragged Roberto erect and pointed his face towards Cara. Again, she tried. "Tell us about Montoya. Does he have our friends?"

"Fuck you," he snarled, a spray of bright red blood escaping his lips.

"Carlos."

Arenas reached around with his M17 and pressed the barrel hard against the back of Roberto's right hand which was on his desk, supporting him. "Last chance, *amigo*."

"Wait!" Roberto blurted out. "Word is Montoya took them. But he doesn't have them now."

"Where are they?"

Suddenly the door and wall behind them exploded in a spray of razor-sharp wooden splinters. Bullets punched through the flimsy material in a deadly hail of lead stingers. Cara and the others dived to the floor as the office seemed to disintegrate around them. A lamp on the desk shattered in a small explosion of ceramic shards. Papers took on a life of their own and were ripped into confetti from multiple bullet strikes.

Roberto's chest was decimated into a mass of red mush from several slugs. His was a macabre dance as each round punched into him until he fell to the floor. Hugging the floor, the three team members waited for the firing to stop before they came to their feet, M17s extended and ready to fire.

"Reaper One, copy?"

Cara spoke quietly. "Can't talk, Zero, they're trying to kill us."

She nodded to Arenas who crossed to the door. Debris crunched under his boots with each step. The others followed him, expecting another round of devastating gunfire to erupt through the perforated walls and door.

Nothing happened.

Arenas reached out and let his hand rest on the doorknob. He looked back at Cara, and she nodded.

The former special forces officer flung the door back and walked through the opening. On the other side, an armed Mexican had the same idea. His hand was extended, about to grasp the knob himself. Instead, Arenas grabbed the outstretched hand and dragged the killer close. He rammed the handgun into the man's belly and pulled the trigger three times on the M17. The slugs ripped through the soft tissue of his guts, and he fell away to the floor.

Cara followed him through and immediately her M17 settled on a shooter armed with an AK-47. Her first shot blew a hole in the man's chest, knocking him back. The second punched into his skull, killing him.

Once Traynor was through the congested opening, a flurry of shots ensued, and more cartel men fell. In all, the three team members put down seven shooters, every one of them armed with AKs.

The echoes of the gunfire died away as Cara swept the room with the M17, looking for any further targets. There were none. All that remained were a few patrons and strippers who'd ducked for cover when the shooting broke out.

Behind her, she heard the crunch of boots on scattered debris. She turned and saw Traynor disappear back into the office. She said, "Carlos, are you OK?"

"*Sí.*"

"Sweep the room. See what you can find and keep an eye out just in case."

"Copy."

"Reaper One, copy? Over."

"Copy, Zero."

"What happened?"

Cara turned and started to walk back into the office. "We had a small altercation with some of the natives. We'll be out of here in a moment."

"Is everyone OK?"

"Yes. All except for our informant. He took multiple rounds in the exchange."

"Keep me posted."

"Copy. Out."

Traynor leaned over Roberto. By some miracle, he was still alive and conscious. Although not for much longer judging by the state he was in.

"Come on, Roberto," Traynor said to him. "Don't die just yet. Where are they?"

The dying man coughed, and blood spilled from his mouth. His chest rose and fell with frequent shallow breaths. He tried to say something, but it was only a soft whisper.

"What? What did you say? Don't die, you son of a bitch. Tell me again."

The former DEA agent leaned in close as the dying club owner's lips moved one last time. He rocked back onto his knees and stared up at Cara. "He gave us a name."

"What?" she asked.

"*Las Puertas del Infierno.*"

"You're shitting me?"

"Nope. That's what he said. The gates of Hell."

CHAPTER 19

"ARE you sure that's what he said?" Thurston asked Traynor again.

"Yes, ma'am. Those were his exact words."

It had been three hours since the shootout across the river, and the team was gathered once more in their briefing room. This time, however, it was early morning hours. As they'd been driving away, the first police cars were starting to arrive on the scene.

Thurston shook her head. "I've heard of it but thought it was just bullshit. What about you, Luis?"

Ferrero nodded grimly. "It exists. Off the coast of Peru, about a hundred miles out. They keep the worst of the worst there. If we're going to mount some kind of rescue mission, we should do it now."

Thurston stared at Cara. "This is your mission. Start planning for it. I'll get in touch with General Jones and get approval. Make me a list of what you need when you're done. It'll be you, Carlos, Axe, and Brick as the insertion team."

Cara glanced at Brick and nodded. "Yes, ma'am."

Thurston eyed her recruit. "Make sure you have everything you need in your Unit One Pack."

The Unit One Pack was a backpack full of medical supplies. From IV fluids and catheters to tourniquets, a catheter for chest decompression, bandages, and morphine. Plus, anything else that might be required.

"Yes, ma'am."

"Slick, find Reaper Team a photo of the island they can work with," Thurston snapped. "And somebody get a fresh pot of coffee on. It's going to be a long night."

———

"The question is, where do we find Reaper?" Cara asked out loud as she looked at the color satellite picture that Swift had acquired.

The team agreed that the best way onto the island was by parachute. They'd picked out a drop zone on the north side of the island, which would allow them to enter under the cover of darkness with relative safety. From there they would work their way south. Hence the question, where would they find Reaper?

Axe said, "If I were Reaper and I was still alive, I'd take to the jungle and stay far away from anyone else."

"That's ninety percent of the island," Brick pointed out.

Cara frowned. "How old is this photo?"

"Hot off the press," Swift told her.

"Is there any way you can put this on the big screen and blow it up?"

"Sure, give me a minute."

"What have you seen?" Arenas asked.

"I'm not sure yet," she said. While she waited for Swift, she looked at Axe. "You'll be packing the M110 this time out."

"Yes, ma'am."

"Brick, you'll be Reaper Four for this op. Take only what you need in the medical kit. I know this is our first time out together, but I'm sure it'll be all fine."

Brick nodded. "I may be speaking out of turn, but we seem to be going to an awful lot of trouble for two men. Not that I'm complaining, because there's no way I'd like to leave a man down range. If it were me, I'd like to know you guys were doing everything to get me back. It would be good to know who these guys are."

There was pride in Axe's voice when he spoke. "John Kane. He is the original Reaper. He's served in Africa, the Philippines, Colombia, and any other small shithole you can think of. He and Cara are the backbone of the team. When it was first formed, Ferrero chose Reaper to head it up."

Cara continued. "It all started in a small Arizona town called Retribution. Montoya killed my boss. I was a local deputy sheriff. Kane was just passing through, but I knew him from my time in the Corps."

A light went on in Brick's head. "There was something on the news a while back about a blowup on the border. That was you guys?"

"Yes. We stole Montoya's money, and he didn't take it so well. He got lucky and killed the DEA administrator. After that went down, Carlos joined us and so did Axe. We all went into Guatemala together after Montoya. Although we got him, we lost one of our own. But Axe is right. Reaper is the backbone of this team. And every one of us would do whatever it takes to get him back."

"When you guys are done with the history lesson, I have that picture you want," Swift interrupted.

They turned and looked at the screen. Cara's eyes danced across it, and she saw it again. A lot clearer this time. "There."

She walked closer to the screen and poked it with her finger. "Does that look like what I think it does?"

They all stared at it, and it was Brick who broke the silence. "Antonov. Russian."

"Exactly."

Axe said, "I suppose if Reaper is going to be anywhere then that would be it. Spencer too. It'll give us a place to start anyhow."

"Who's Spencer, again?" Brick asked.

"CIA guy," Axe answered. "We don't talk about him much because we don't like him."

"I see."

In the background, Swift had been researching something on his tablet. His eyes widened, and he gasped, "Fuck me!"

They all turned to look at him, and Cara said, "Something you want to say?"

"I managed to pick out a number on the fuselage of the plane," he said excitedly. "This particular Antonov belonged to one Anatoli Petrov."

"The arms smuggler?"

"The same. He disappeared from the radar a few years ago. Looks like we now know why."

"Can you capture us some live feed from across the island between now and when we jump? I'd like to know what the hell is going on down there."

"Consider it done. I'm sure the NSA or CIA won't mind if I borrow one of their birds."

"Just don't get caught. Now, all we have to do is convince Thurston and Luis that this is how we do it."

————

Thurston and Ferrero listened patiently as Cara laid out the team plan. It was simple. They parachute in, find Reaper and Spencer, and get out.

Thurston nodded. "I can get you in, and I can get you out. *But* I don't want to be sending you into harm's way for no reason. We need to somehow confirm that Reaper and Spencer are there."

Cara said, "Swift is rigging up a live-feed so he can keep a watch and see if anyone there might be Reaper, ma'am. He can do that right up until jump time."

The general's eyes narrowed. "Have you parachuted before?"

"Yes, ma'am. A while back."

"How far back."

"Ten years."

"Shit. Don't break your damned neck."

"No, ma'am."

Thurston sighed. "All right. It's a long haul so I'll see if I can get you a C-17 for the trip down. Also, if we can get a destroyer down there to pick you up, they'll have an RHIB to be able to take you off the beach. However, if we can't confirm that Kane is there before you jump, I'll pull the pin."

Cara looked across at Ferrero. He said, "That's the plan. No need to be sending you into a hot zone if there's no need."

"He could be anywhere down there, and we not see him," Axe protested.

"That's right."

The team knew there was no winning this one. There was a moment of silence which Thurston took to mean acceptance of her ultimatum. She asked, "Anything else that you might need?"

The team stared at each other like they were holding something back. Their commander picked it up straight away. "Out with it."

Cara said, "Any chance of a Spectre?"

Thurston chuckled. "You want an AC-130 gunship?"

"Yes, ma'am."

The general stared hard at her. "You're serious?"

"Yes, ma'am. I figure that with Petrov's plane crashed down there, he could have been smuggling arms. If so, then we have to assume that there are a lot of unfriendlies on the ground with guns."

"Are you sure you wouldn't like the First Marine Division too?"

"Spectre will do just fine, ma'am."

"I'll see what I can do."

"There's something you need to be aware of," Ferrero said.

"There is a ten-mile exclusion zone around the island, enforced by a special branch of the Peruvian navy. Their ships have special detachments of marines on them. They are dispatched from the mainland at the first sign of trouble."

Cara smiled. "I guess we'd best not hang around then."

ISLA DEL VOLCÁN, PERU

Kane walked outside of the cave and stretched his muscles. Rubbing his full stomach, he looked about for Petrov. He found him sitting on a rock, picking his toenails. Kane grimaced and said, "Get yourself some chow, Anatoli. I'll take overwatch."

The Russian pulled a worn-out shoe onto his foot and stared at him. "I'm not hungry."

"It wasn't my fault you grabbed tins of sardines."

"They taste like shit."

"There's tinned peaches as well."

"Fruit. Pah," he snorted in disgust.

Kane unslung the AK-74 and checked to see that there was a round in the chamber. "At least go and get some rest."

"Maybe later."

"Your loss."

Suddenly Kane felt the overwhelming urge to look up. It was almost like a sixth sense telling him someone was watching him. So that's what he did. And two things happened.

The first was that over ten thousand kilometers away, a guy behind a computer screen got excited. The second was closer to home.

Anatoli Petrov's head seemed to blow apart when a 7.62 mm round from the second Dragunov smashed into it.

"Shit!" Kane exclaimed and dived to the ground. Then the jungle all around him came to life with gunfire.

———

TEAM REAPER HQ, EL PASO, TEXAS

The door to Thurston's office flew open as Swift burst in. "Ma'am, I found him! I found Reaper! But he's in trouble."

"You're sure?"

"Yes, ma'am. Have a look."

Swift brought the feed up on the large screen in Thurston's office. She could make out what seemed to be a gunfight going on in the jungle. The computer tech used his finger and said, "This is him. I know because he looked up. This dead guy, I think is Petrov. The ones who're shooting at him, I have no idea. But I'd say they're the bad guys."

"How many?"

"Thirty, forty. Maybe more."

"Damn it. All right. Get everyone together. We'll run everything from here. Tell Cara they leave now. There's a seven-hour flight ahead of them. By the time they get on the ground, it'll be dark. Let's hope Kane can hang on until then."

———

ISLA DEL VOLCÁN, PERU

Kane crawled up behind a rotted tree trunk and waited while bullets chewed great chunks of bark and timber from it with every impact. He cursed under his breath and rose up high enough to fire two quick shots at a man who was creeping up on him. This one was armed with a spear. It seemed that the men with the weapons were trying to keep his head down while the others were sent forward to kill him.

And there was still the shooter with the Dragunov. They must have found someone else who was proficient with a long gun. Slipping away from the tree trunk, he made his way back into the cave.

He found a box with the Russian word for grenades stenciled on it. Cracking it open, he pulled three F1s from it, then hurried back to the cave mouth. Pulling the pin on the first one, he threw it out in the direction of the attackers. Even before the first one went off, the second was on its way. Then the third.

As they exploded, Kane moved back into the cave. That would give them something to think about and give him time to get organized.

He slung the Dragunov over his shoulder and grabbed extra ammunition. Also, he picked up some more F1 grenades and some of the tins of food. He wished he could take an RPG, but that wasn't going to happen. Then his gaze settled on the crates that Petrov had warned him about. Kane shrugged. "What the hell."

The first crate he opened was filled with money. US dollars. A quick estimate came to one million dollars. Three more crates and Kane figured out why the others in Petrov's crew had wound up dead.

Reaper shrugged again. "Shame." He pulled the pin from one of the grenades and dropped it into the crate it had come from.

Then he ran. As fast as he could. He'd only just got past the mouth of the cave when the grenade exploded and blew everything to Hell.

CHAPTER 20

TEAM REAPER LZ—ISLA DEL VOLCÁN, PERU

"REAPER ONE, RADIO CHECK. OVER."

"Reaper One? Zero. Read you loud and clear."

The flight, although just over seven hours, had seemed longer. The team took the time to go over last-minute details before departing their aerial taxi. Swift had been giving Cara updates every hour, and as far as he could tell, Kane was still alive.

"Zero, everyone is down and accounted for. We're preparing to move out. Bravo Four, do you have an update?"

Swift's voice came over their comms. "Copy, Reaper one. The last time I had a fix on Reaper, was just on dark. He was three klicks southeast of your current position."

"And the tangos?"

"They've formed themselves a perimeter around his position. If you want to reach him, then you'll have to go through them."

"Roger, Bravo Four."

"Zero, any news on that Spectre?"

"I've been reliably informed that it should be on station just before dawn, Reaper One. Callsign, Striker One-One."

"Copy, Striker One-One. Reaper One, out."

Cara gathered her team around her. "Carlos, you're on point. No further than fifty meters from me at any time. Axe, you're bringing up the rear. It should be quiet, but you never can tell. Is everybody good to go? Brick?"

They all answered in the affirmative.

"Move out then."

Cara dropped her night vision goggles down, and the darkened jungle turned green, the laser sight on her suppressed HK416 reaching out and piercing it like an endless thin needle. To her front, she saw Carlos disappear into a wall of foliage. She pressed her talk button. "Reaper Two, One. Keep to a southeasterly heading. Keep a check on your compass."

"Copy, One."

Cara cursed herself under her breath. It was pointless her saying that to Arenas. The guy was a professional. They were just useless words. She kicked herself again.

For the next four hours, they moved silently through the black of the jungle. On the map, it was only three klicks, but on the ground, it was better to be careful than sorry. Every thirty minutes Cara checked in with Bravo. Every hour they took a short break. They were about five-hundred meters from their target when Arenas broke squelch.

Quickly, Cara took a knee and whispered into her mic, "Everyone hold." Then she said, "Bravo Four, do you still have us on your screen?"

"Negative, Reaper One. The bird we were using

doesn't come back into range for another ninety minutes."

"Shit," she said softly and slapped at a bug on her neck. "Carlos, I'm coming to you."

He broke squelch once. "No."

"Do you have a tango close?"

Twice. "Yes."

"We'll hold and wait for you."

Ten minutes ticked by before Arenas appeared from the dense jungle to Cara's front. He crouched next to her and said, "There are three tangos to our front. I think we've hit their perimeter. What do you want me to do?"

"We'll hold here until we get our bird back. It'll be ninety minutes until the next flyover. That way we'll know what we're up against. Get some rest."

"*Sí*."

Cara pressed her talk button and said, "Zero, this is Reaper One. Copy?"

"Copy, Reaper One."

"Reaper Team is holding until we get our bird back, over."

"Roger, Reaper One. We'll let you know when we have visual. Zero, out."

"Listen up," Cara said into her mic. "We're here for a while. Get some rest. Axe, you're on first watch."

Kane's head dropped forward for the fifth, or was it the sixth time? He was tired after being on edge for God knew how long. He was running low on energy and knew that if he didn't get some sleep soon, he was screwed. But while he was surrounded by those who sought to kill him, it was dangerous to even contemplate closing his eyes.

He knew they would come for him when the sun came up. All he could hope to do was be able to kill enough of them so that they would lose heart and back off.

Then there was the shooter with the second Dragunov. Every time he exposed himself to take a shot, he was putting himself in the shooter's sights.

As if on cue, the wound to his upper arm burned slightly. It wasn't much, just a graze, but in a place like this, it could turn bad in a heartbeat.

Kane knew he should be using the dark to slip through their net. However, his exhaustion would make him careless. Tiredness...

His eyes closed once more.

———

"Reaper One? Bravo Four, over."

"Read you, Bravo Four."

"Just a heads up," Swift said. "That was a good call to wait for the bird. The tango headcount has increased to around seventy. They're as thick as fleas on a hound dog's ass, between you and where we think Reaper is."

Cara thought for a moment. Then, "Wait one, Bravo."

Brick was on watch, so she shook Axe and Carlos awake. Once Brick returned from his stint, she filled them all in as to what was going on.

Axe said, "It won't be impossible, but with the help of Swift and his eye in the sky, we should be able to sneak through them, yeah?"

"If we screw it up, we'll be in the middle of a shit sandwich in the dark," Cara pointed out.

"Could be worse," Brick commented.

"I have another idea," Cara told them. "But if we go ahead with it, it'll be in the daylight."

"The dark is an operator's best friend, ma'am," Brick said.

"I know, but not at this time."

"What then?" Arenas asked.

"Once Striker One-One gets overhead, I intend on using him to open a door for us to walk through."

"Ma'am?" Axe said.

"We'll get him to kick the fucking door in. Plain enough?"

Even though it was dark, Cara could tell that Axe had his usual big, shit-eating grin on his face. "Yes, ma'am."

———

It seemed to come out of nowhere. One moment the early morning jungle was quiet, next, the booming sound of four Allison T56-A-15 turboprops on an AC-130 shattered the stillness. The sun had already been up for half an hour. So much for it arriving just before dawn.

"Striker One-One to Reaper One. We're on station and ready to help out in any way we can. Over," the female pilot's voice came over the net.

"Good to hear from you, Striker One-One. If you're not too busy up there, we might just have a small job for you. What are you packing? Over."

"We have a Gatling gun, a forty mil Bofors, and a one-o-five Howitzer. Take your pick, Reaper One."

"I'd like you to kick a hole in a wall for me, Striker. If you set up for a gun run from the northeast to the southwest, we'd be mighty thankful."

"Copy, Reaper One. We'd be glad to kick the door down for you."

"As soon as you make your pass, Striker, we'll be threading the needle. We'd appreciate you keeping any unfriendlies off our backs."

"Just so we're clear, Reaper One, are you asking for a danger close fire mission, over?"

"Yes, ma'am. As close as you can get it. The package is one of ours."

"Copy, Reaper One, Striker One-One is inbound. Good luck. Out."

Cara turned to her team. "Listen up. As soon as the fireworks start, we're moving in. We'll form up in a diamond shape. I'll lead. Brick, you'll be on our six. Weapons free."

Slowly the distant drone of the Spooky II Gunship grew louder, steadily building in pitch. Then the ground beneath their feet started to tremble as the jungle in front of them exploded with fire.

———

Kane was jolted awake by the first pass of the AC-130. He'd been deep in sleep, and the roar seemed to be almost on top of him. Looking up, he saw what had made the sound, and smiled.

As he moved, stiffness caused him to grimace. The noise of the plane's engines slowly dissipated but didn't completely disappear. Kane scooped up the AK-74 and checked its loaded magazine. Climbing to his feet, he moved silently through the brush, relieved himself against a tree, then continued until he was sure that he'd reached the furthest possible point. Beyond that, he was in Indian country. He found cover behind a rock big enough to conceal him, and then waited for the assault he was sure would come.

When it did, it wasn't quite what he expected.

———

Ortega clambered to his feet with the overhead roar of the plane. He grasped at his AK and shouted at the men who were nearest to him to get up. *"¡Levántate! ¡Levántate!"*

Gathering the men around, he snarled, "Something is happening. I want to know what it is."

A couple of his men disappeared into the jungle, and Ortega could still hear the plane in the distance. He looked at the others. "Did any of you see what it was?"

"It was big," said one man dumbly.

Another, a FARC soldier, said, "It was a *gringo* C-130."

There was a crashing sound from the jungle and Andreas appeared with a couple of his men. "What are Americans doing here?"

Ortega gave him a 'How the hell do I know?' look and asked, "Are you sure?"

"Who else would it be? But the question is why are they here?"

More noise and Janjak and Jasiel appeared. "They are after the American," Janjak stated.

It made sense. Ortega nodded. "We must get him before they can. Dead or alive, I do not care. Go now."

The cartel faction leader held Andreas back. "Put your man with the long gun somewhere where he can see everything. If he can shoot the American, then so be it."

"I will see to it."

The roar of plane engines grew louder as it returned, steadily growing in rhythm as it got closer. Then something else shattered the steamy morning air.

WHUMP! Then, CRUMP!

The latter sound was joined by an earth-shaking tremor and the sudden uprising of dirt and debris laced with bits of jungle flora. The second explosion was closer than the first. Then as if that wasn't enough, a tearing sound ripped through the air, and the jungle seemed to lay over as a hail of 25mm rounds from the Gatling gun rained down with ultimate ferocity.

Ortega was amazed at the bizarre sight before him. So much so, that he stood transfixed. Then a man, no more than twenty feet away from where he stood, seemed to disintegrate in a spray of red.

"Get down!" Ortega shrieked. "Get down!"

Some were too slow in following the shouted directions and suffered the same fate as their comrade. Another toppled like a tree when his right leg was severed halfway up his thigh. The spray from the Gatling gun was brutal and efficient.

But from where Cara and the rest of the team were, it looked marvelous.

Cara's suppressed HK416 spat a single round, and the spear-wielding killer reeled away with a slug through the fleshy part of his throat. Violent explosions erupted close to them in a mix of dirt and metal shards. The Gatling gun sound tore through the air over the team's heads with the latest pass of Striker One-One.

Off to her left, Cara saw a man with an AK in his hands. He raised it and cut loose with a burst of automatic fire. It was short-lived, however, because a burst from Arenas stitched across his chest and he collapsed in the grass.

"These crazy pricks just keep coming," Axe growled as he dispatched another spear-toting killer.

"Just make sure they don't stick one of those things in your ass, Axe," Cara snapped. "Reynolds might not be forgiving if I got her favorite man killed."

"Shut up," Axe mumbled.

"Shit!" Brick snarled. "Sniper! Get down."

As one, the team dived into the grass patch they were traversing. Cara felt a surge of adrenaline course through her. They were caught out in the open with stuff all over.

"Bastard almost got me," Brick continued. "The round thumped into the Unit One pack I'm carrying."

"Where is he?" Cara asked.

"Somewhere to the east."

"Axe," Cara snapped.

"On it."

Beneath her, Cara could feel the vibrations ripple through the ground when another 105mm round from the HC-130's Howitzer came in. All around them Cara could hear shouts from their attackers. She found herself wondering if this was how it felt for the veterans of Vietnam or Guadalcanal when the enemy came out of the jungle.

Behind her, she heard the slap and mechanism of Brick's HK 416 as he fired.

"Reaper One? Zero, over."

"Copy, Zero."

"What's going on? You haven't moved in over a minute."

"We have a sniper, Zero. Our boy here is just trying to get a fix on him."

"Roger."

"How's it looking, Axe?"

"I can't see shit, boss," Axe growled. "I figure he's in

the trees about five-hundred meters to the east, but he's dug in so tight I can't lay my sights on him."

"You need to find him, Axe. We can't lay around here all day."

"No shit."

"Try this," Cara offered and leaped to her feet.

She counted to three and dropped back down. The shot from the Dragunov whistled overhead a fraction of a second later, followed by the report.

"You're one crazy bitch, boss lady," Axe chuckled. "But I got the bastard. All I have to do now is shoot him."

"Maybe not," Cara said. "Give me a location."

"The shooter is about six-hundred meters to our east."

"Copy." Then, "Striker One-One, this is Reaper One, how copy?"

"Good copy, Reaper One."

"Striker, I have a fire mission for you, over."

"Copy, Reaper One. Send, over."

"We're pinned down by a sniper approximately six-hundred meters to our east. We'd be obliged if you could dig him out of there."

"Copy, Reaper One. We'll light him up on the next pass. Keep your heads down. Striker One-One, out."

"Get ready, team," Cara said over her comms. "Once Striker opens fire on that sniper nest, we're moving again."

A few moments later the WHUMP! WHUMP! of the Howitzer reached their ears. Then the hide to their east exploded with the detonations of the shells.

Cara came to her feet. "All right, let's move."

The 416 came to her shoulder, and she started forward. Two men to her front appeared suddenly. One was armed with an AK, the other a home-made spear. She dropped her sights on the immediate threat first. The AK bearer jerked abruptly as two 5.56 rounds slammed into his chest. She shifted aim to the second threat and squeezed the trigger again.

Nothing happened. "Shit!" she cursed out loud and dropped the carbine to dangle by its strap. The M17 came clear of Cara's thigh holster in a sweeping movement. As soon as it leveled on her target, she squeezed the trigger three times. BLAM! BLAM! BLAM!

The spear-wielder spasmed wildly with the impact of each bullet punching into his chest. The tip of the weapon flicked up and across Cara's cheek, slicing a shallow groove in the flesh. Blood ran instantly and mixed with perspiration, the salt in the wound stinging. She wiped it away and holstered her M17.

Cara then reached for the 416 and said, "Changing mag."

She slammed a fresh magazine home and kept moving.

The team pushed forward, meeting all resistance head-on. Then all of a sudden it stopped. There was no one else to fight. They'd pushed through the perimeter. Cara said, "Watch the perimeter. I'll see if I can find our packages."

A voice came from some thick brush beside her, "You won't have to look too far, but it is just one package. Spencer didn't make it."

The bushes seemed to part, and there was Kane, dirty, smiling, the Dragunov slung over his shoulder, and an AK-74 in his hands.

Cara smiled and said into her mic, "Zero, we have the package. I say again, we have the package."

"Copy, Reaper One. Now get the hell out of there. The Peruvian navy has just despatched their QRF."

"Copy. Out."

With Striker One-One flying cover, the team was able to make it back to the pickup point without further incident. Along the way, Kane filled them in on what had happened since his arrival on the island. He'd raised the prospect of searching for Spencer's body, but Thurston had quashed it.

They were shadowed all the way. Ortega stood and watched them climb onto the RHIB and pull away from the shore.

"What do we do now?" one of the prisoners asked Ortega.

The cartel man shook his head. "Nothing. Nothing at all."

――――――

RICHMOND, VIRGINIA

Frank Styles, behind the wheel of his red Ferrari, pulled into his driveway, and the streetlight flickered across his vanity plate which read, STYLIN'. He switched off the 6.5 L F140 GA V12 engine and climbed out of the car.

The lights inside the house were on which indicated that his wife, Marge, was home. He wondered if she'd been out all afternoon spending his money again. The bitch was a shop-a-holic. Just as well lawyering paid so well. Especially his last case representing Montoya. Even though the cartel boss had escaped, Styles still received some hefty payments. The last of which was to make sure he kept quiet. Styles assured Montoya that he was bound by confidentiality and could say nothing. Montoya, on the other hand, didn't believe that it would be enough, so he paid him an extra million to keep his mouth shut.

In the shadows across the street, lurked a thin man dressed in black. He wore a long coat which reached his knees. As soon as Styles climbed from his car, the man stepped out into the light and began to cross the pavement.

Styles dropped his keys and cursed. Normally he would have put the Ferrari in the garage with his wife's Dodge, but he had to go back out for a client meeting. Styles leaned down and picked the keys up. He locked the car and then stuffed them in his pocket.

Footsteps sounded behind him. Someone was coming across the street and Styles rolled his eyes. Maybe it was Bert Cross coming to complain about his dog shitting on the lawn again. The fucking animal was more trouble than it was worth.

Styles turned around to head off any abuse that would be forthcoming from his irate neighbor. Instead, he stopped cold, and his jaw dropped.

The killer swept back the right side of his coat to reveal a MAC-11. Styles' blood ran cold, and his bladder let go. The stench of his own urine filled his nostrils. He was about to die, and there was nothing he could do about it.

With his mind reeling in those final few moments, Styles opened his mouth and said, "No, don't!"

The killer depressed the trigger, and the 32-round box magazine emptied at a rate of twelve hundred rounds per minute. At that rate of fire, the magazine ran dry in just over a second. Styles' chest was a bloody pulp of flesh and shredded material.

The lawyer dropped to the concrete beside the Ferrari and blood began to run down into the gutter. Lowering the MAC-11, the killer turned away from the scene. His shoes sounded loud on the pavement as he began to walk away.

He reached into his pocket and pressed speed dial. A few seconds later a voice answered. "Yes?"

"It is done."

"Good."

CHAPTER 21

"WHAT ARE you doing back here, Reaper?" Thurston growled when Kane walked through her office door. "You were given a week off. It's been four days."

Reaper shrugged. "That's what Cara said."

"Well, you should listen to her. The team is in good hands with her."

Kane nodded. "I know that. I just hate sitting around. Any news on Montoya?"

Thurston shook her head. "Slick has been trying to run down all the information he can, but so far, nothing. If Montoya's up to something, we haven't been able to nail it down yet. Every damned agency with letters of the alphabet in its name is concentrating everything they have across the border."

"Maybe that's what he wants," Kane proposed.

Thurston was curious at his comment. "What do you mean?"

"Everybody is looking at Mexico. A major rule when

you want to surprise someone, make sure they're looking the other way. Everybody is doing that as we speak. You said so yourself. Couple that with the fact he has trained American mercenaries working for him, and what does that tell you? If you ask me, I'd say diversion."

"Going by your theory, I'd say he has something planned on American soil. Who better to blend in than US citizens?"

There was a knock at the door, and Ferrero entered. He saw Kane and opened his mouth to speak when Reaper cut him short. "Don't you start."

"Start what?"

"You know."

Thurston stared at Ferrero and said, "Kane has an interesting theory about our Mexican friend, Luis. I actually think it holds more water than what we're following now."

Ferrero eyed him and asked, "What is it, Reaper?"

"Everything that's happened so far is a diversion," Kane offered.

"Uh huh. I agree. But for what? Slick can't find anything that stands out. That's what I came to see Mary about. I think we need to change our search."

Thurston climbed from her chair and walked over to her window to stare out through the grime-smeared glass. "I take it by change you mean to concentrate on home soil?"

"Makes sense," Ferrero said.

"Where would be a better place to hide than right under the nose of your enemy?" Kane surmised.

The general turned around and faced both men. "All right. Put Slick onto it, Luis. Kane, you help him with anything he needs."

Kane raised an eyebrow. "I don't know shit about what he does."

"Then it's about time you learned," Thurston told him. "Either that or go and get some rest. Cara still has command of your team until I have Brick clear you to become operational again."

"And when might that be, ma'am?"

"In three days."

———

OUTSIDE CHARLOTTESVILLE, VIRGINIA

The Agusta Westland AW169 helicopter lifted from the field and disappeared into the pitch black of the Virginia night. Two black SUVs remained in the lush green pasture, headlights ablaze from where they had lit the landing zone for the midnight touchdown.

Juan Montoya, dressed in his usual resplendent white suit, stopped before Ward Collins and asked, "Is it all ready?"

Collins nodded. "I've been here for two days overseeing a few things. It should be good to go when we need it."

"I want to see it before I leave for Charlottesville."

Collins opened the door on the SUV and said, "Jump in, and I'll take you there right now."

The cartel boss climbed into the vehicle and closed the door. Behind him, another door opened, and Hall got in. The SUV rocked with the big man's size as he settled into the rear bucket seat.

The driver's door opened, illuminating the interior light. Collins climbed in and was about to close the door when Montoya said firmly, "Tell your man behind me to change sides. I don't want him sitting there."

The former ranger stared at Hall through the rearview mirror. Hall mouthed, "What the fuck?" and shrugged his heavy shoulders. Collins kept staring at him until the big man shook his head and opened the door. He got out and swapped sides. Once in, he couldn't help himself and the sarcastic tone as he said, "Is that better, *Señor*?"

"Hall!" Collins cautioned.

Montoya ignored the jibe and said, "Shall we go?"

The SUVs bounced across the field until they passed through a gate and out onto a gravel road. Turning left, they headed west until they reached another road which led off into a large and dense pocket of forest. They followed that for five or so minutes before turning right into a drive. This took them another mile or so before they reached a farmhouse with a large barn off to the right side. The yard held a semi-trailer rig.

The SUVs pulled up on the drive, and the support team climbed from the vehicle. Apart from Hall, Collins had four other men in the second SUV. Inside the farmhouse were an additional four, and on the perimeter were four more.

From habit, the four, who had climbed out, set up a small perimeter around the vehicles. Montoya, Hall, and Collins followed them out, and the former ranger captain directed his employer towards the barn.

"It's in there," he said to Montoya. "Follow me."

Collins opened one of the large double-doors and moved around to the left and flicked on a light. It wasn't the brightest globe, but it did what it was designed to do. Montoya stopped and stared at the sight before him. He nodded. "It is *magnifico*. The pilot?"

"He's secure in the house."

The cartel boss' eyes never left the MQ-1 Predator UAV. A smile split his lips when he saw the Hellfire missile beside it. "He will fly it for us – the pilot?"

"While we have his wife and kid prisoner, he'll do anything we want. Normally it would take two or three to fly it, but for what we want, one will manage. And there is a cleared area behind the house long enough for it to take off."

"Good," Montoya said, his voice distant as he took a step forward. He paused and then walked over to the UAV and ran a hand over its glossy exterior.

"When we jacked it, it was all disassembled. My guys on the ground here were able to reassemble it satisfactorily. We also have a satellite dish big enough to accommodate our needs. So, when the target arrives at the specified location the day after tomorrow, we'll be ready."

"And the team I requested?" Montoya asked.

Collins hesitated. This was the part of the plan he figured went too far. Holding the family hostage, the UAV strike, that was fine. But the raid on the DEA evidence facility made him nervous. Not for himself, but if it all went to shit, it would cost him four men. That was the number he was sending with Montoya to do the job. They would be led by Hall, and only because the loss of Hall wouldn't be a big deal.

"Are you sure you want to do it this way?" Collins asked.

"Of course. It is one of the main reasons. They took my money. I want it back. Twenty-million dollars they have, and it all belongs to me."

"Hall will lead the team. It has been planned to coincide with the UAV strike. The team will follow your orders. I have chosen a place for you all to stay until it is time."

"Excellent. We will leave tonight."

———

EL PASO, TEXAS

"We have to stop doing this," Cara said to Kane as she lay there listening to the clunk and hum of the ceiling fan above their bed.

"Why?"

"You know why."

"Am I doing it wrong?"

A chuckle escaped Cara's lips, and she elbowed him in the ribs. Kane grunted and stiffened as pain shot through him. "Christ!"

"Be serious," Cara growled.

"I was. I didn't think I was that bad."

There was a flurry of blankets as Cara swiftly rolled on top of Kane and sat up. The sheet fell away from her naked torso, and light filtered through the gauzy curtains to highlight her lithe form. She leaned down and kissed him and then left her nose resting on his, the gesture hinting at their level of intimacy. "I thought I'd lost you, you know that. Which is why we can't keep doing this. We work together in dangerous situations. We can't be worried about each other in the middle of a shit storm. It'll get people killed."

Kane knew she was right, as he reached out with his thumb and grazed it across the now healing wound from the spear tip. To start a serious relationship was wrong. This wasn't the time. And if they kept sleeping together, it would inevitably become just that. "You're right."

Cara sat back up. She twisted his right nipple between her thumb and forefinger. "I'm always right."

"Ouch! Bitch."

Suddenly, their cells began to buzz on the nightstand. Cara reached across and picked her's up. "Billings."

She listened for a moment while Kane's cell kept jumping. She hung up, and Kane's stopped. Cara stared at him and said, "Get your clothes on. Slick has something. The team's been recalled."

———

The hot Texan sun had been up an hour by the time the team gathered in their briefing room. Everyone was huddled around to listen to the news of Slick's discovery.

Standing before them, he looked tired, as he'd been working hours on end to find something which the team could use. But his persistence had paid off. On the big screen, he had three pictures. The first was of an MQ-1 Predator. The two others were of an air force captain and a man dressed in a suit.

"I've been looking and combing through more shit in the past few days than I care to think about. When we turned one-eighty to concentrate on home soil, this is what I came up with."

He paused and then spoke again. "A few nights after we got back from that nightmare in Juarez, outside of Embargo Tennessee, someone stopped a transport and stole an MQ-1 Predator UAV. Killed the transport drivers and stole the 'coffin' it was in. Not only that, they stole a Hellfire missile which was being transported with it."

"WTF," Axe growled. "Didn't it have an escort or something?"

"Sometimes the air force sees fit to transport them in

the middle of the night without one. I don't know why. OK?"

There was more than a hint of sarcasm in his voice brought on by lack of sleep. Reaper said, "Easy, Slick, we're all on the same team."

Swift swallowed and went on. "The air force captain is Sean Richards. He specializes in UAVs. Used to be a pilot, now is part of the chain of command at the 33rd Special Operations Squadron. He disappeared the other day. So did his wife and child."

"That brings us to our next guy. This, ladies and gentlemen, is Frank Styles. The defense lawyer of Juan Montoya. He was shot and killed outside of his home four nights ago. Actually, he was shot up close with a MAC-11. Pretty much turned him into dog food."

Kane said, "OK. I can see the connection of the captain to the UAV. But what is it with the lawyer?"

"Nothing on its own. But I managed to track down some footage of who I believe to be the killer."

A picture of a man appeared on the screen. He had a thin face and a tough look about him. "This is Mark Alvarez. He's an ex-marine. Discharged three years ago. He is the one who I think killed the lawyer. And if you can find him, he might be able to give you something about Montoya. Rumor is that he may be attached to Collins' mercenaries."

Axe asked, "Do we know where he is?"

Swift smiled. "Glad you asked that. We do. He's in New York. Been there for a month living under an assumed name."

"But why?"

"Maybe you can ask him when you pick him up," Thurston said. "Wheels up in an hour. We're going to New York."

CHAPTER 22

NEW YORK

"YOU DO KNOW this is bullshit, right?" Axe complained. "Crap like this only happens in the movies. Yet here I am dressed up like a fucking pizza delivery guy."

"I think you look cute," Cara teased.

"Really?"

"No."

It was an hour after dark, and the bright New York street-, shop- and neon-lights dazzled in the night. The team had been watching and planning since they'd touched down. The consensus was that it should happen in the evening. That way there would be less pedestrian traffic on the streets.

Alverez's apartment was directly above a pizza joint; hence Axe's getup. There would only be three of them to breach the apartment. The other two, Brick and Arenas, would be backup.

Having left all their tactical gear at their base, so they

didn't stand out too much, they carried only their M17s and a couple of spare clips.

"All right," said Kane. "Let's do this. Bravo, comms check."

"Read you loud and clear, Reaper One."

"We're going in now."

"Roger."

They crossed the street and moved swiftly towards the apartment block's doorway. Parked at the curb was the second SUV where Arenas and Brick Peters waited.

Once inside the foyer, Kane and Cara drew their M17s. Axe had his stashed in the pizza box he carried. Starting to climb the stairs, the stairwell brightly lit with harsh fluorescent lights, they moved quickly and silently until they got to the level they needed.

"Zero, we've reached the third floor."

"Copy."

Entering the passageway without a sound, they moved cautiously along the communal space until reaching apartment thirty-two. Cara and Kane took up position on either side of the doorway, while Axe readied himself with the pizza box.

From beyond the closed door, they could hear a television but couldn't quite make out what was on. Kane nodded at Axe who knocked on the door. "Pizza!"

There was no sound of movement from within. Even the television stayed at the same volume. Axe glanced at Kane and shrugged. He made to raise his fist to knock again when the door seemed to explode outwards.

Axe reeled away as sharp splinters assailed his body. "Motherfucker!" he shouted, grabbing for the gun in the pizza box.

Cara leaned over and pumped four shots from the M17 through the door. Kane kicked the shattered obstacle open with his foot and blew off six shots through the opening. He was forced to duck back when their target appeared holding a shotgun and fired back at them.

Small steel balls ripped through the air. Kane leaned back around the opening and fired again. Meanwhile, Cara helped Axe to his feet. She took one look at the blood on his face and said into her mic, "Brick, I need you now. Bring your medical kit."

"Motherfucker," Axe hissed again.

"Just take it easy, big man. You've been hit worse. Just sit down there. Brick will be right here to patch you up."

"Is he OK, Cara?" Kane called across to her between bursts of gunfire.

"He'll live."

Another shotgun blast rocked the night and blew more plaster off the passage wall. Kane ducked reflexively. He called across to Cara, "We've gotta dig him out of here pronto."

She nodded and then sat on the debris-strewn carpet. Kane stared at her for a moment and then realized what she was doing. "You ready?"

She nodded.

Reaper leaned around the doorway and fired off three more shots before he withdrew. While he was firing, Cara lay down across the doorway. As soon as Kane ducked back, Alverez showed himself, and she put two slugs in his chest.

"Target down!" she called out, and Kane swung around the doorway and stepped over her to enter.

Now on her feet, Cara followed him inside. They cleared all the rooms before coming back to check on the fallen man. He was dead.

"Zero? Reaper One. Target is down, and we're secure. Reaper Four took some shrapnel but is ambulatory.

Reaper Five is checking him out now. We're also expecting local law enforcement anytime soon."

"Copy, Reaper One. Target's condition, over?"

"He's dead."

"Copy. Secure what you can before the LEOs get there. Mary is on her way to you."

"Roger. Reaper One, out."

Kane put his head outside the door and saw Arenas and Cara watching Brick work on Axe. "How is he?"

"He's lucky. Few cuts," Brick told him. "Face bleeds like a bitch when you cut it."

"Always knew you were a big baby," Kane said, relieved. "I need you two inside. We have to turn this place over before the cops get here. Thurston is on her way."

Arenas and Cara followed him back in, and they began searching all the usual places. They found nothing at all they could use. That was until Arenas lifted the mattress and found the laptop.

Kane said, "Hide it in Brick's medical pack. Swift can have a look at it when we get back."

Arenas did as ordered, and while he was gone, Kane checked Alverez's pockets. Finding a cell with a locked screen in the man's shirt, he stuffed it into his own pocket. Turning to Cara to see how she was faring, he saw her going through a food cupboard where she found a cereal box. Upending it onto the table, the contents spilled and bounced across the surface, revealing a USB stick.

Hurriedly she picked it up and tucked it inside her bra. Just in time as shouting began to filter in from outside. The NYPD had arrived.

————

"Get in your vehicles and let's get out of here before they change their minds," Thurston said hurriedly. She'd been engaged in conversations with the NYPD, and the FBI for the past two hours. The FBI because Alverez had been on a federal watch list. But phone calls behind the scenes had secured the team's release.

Her gaze drifted to Axe. "You look like shit."

Apart from a couple of bruises, scratches, and sticky bandages to cover two more deeper cuts, the ex-recon marine was fine. "A shotgun blast through a door will do that to you, ma'am."

"He was lucky," Brick said.

Thurston nodded. "Let's go."

———

SUNSET PALACE, CNR 9TH AVE AND 55TH ST, NEW YORK

The team had booked out seven rooms in the Sunset Palace; the most central of which was set up as a control center with all their equipment. The other six were utilized as sleeping quarters. Thurston and Ferrero each had their own, one of the privileges of rank. Cara shared with Reynolds, Kane with Axe, Arenas with Brick, and Teller with Traynor and Swift, however, the computer tech was busy working on the laptop and cell found in Alverez's apartment.

Kane relaxed in a chair, drinking a bottle of Bud Light. Condensation was running in little rivulets down the side of the glass and dripping onto his lap. He looked across at Axe who was perched on the edge of his bed, cleaning his M17. Kane asked, "What's this I hear about you and Reynolds?"

Axe stopped what he was doing and stared at his friend. "Don't you start."

Kane feigned shock. "Start what?"

"You know. Especially when you and Billings are doing the horizontal dance between the sheets."

"I didn't mention me. I'm asking about you."

"It was a damned one-time thing, OK? Besides, since it's made world headlines thanks to your lovely friend, she's hardly talking to me."

"Not the way I heard it. I heard that you told Cara. Couldn't help yourself."

"Shit. It kinda slipped out."

"Uh huh."

"What about you and her? Screwing a team member is one thing, screwing one that you operate within intense situations in the field is another. You know that, Reaper."

Kane nodded. "That's why we've decided to dial it back. Keep it professional."

"Same with me and Reynolds."

Kane chuckled. "Lying son of a bitch."

"Hey, I'm offended, my friend. Are you doubting my word?"

"Get some sleep. I've a feeling we're about to get busy."

Kane never knew how prophetic those words were.

———

Soon after dawn, the team was dragged from their beds to bad news. Swift had managed to crack the computer and cell of Alverez, and they were in the central room being briefed on the findings. There had been a big screen set up, and General Hank Jones was dialed in on the meeting.

Thurston said, "Slick managed to find some troubling

things on the Alverez laptop." A picture of a park flashed up on the screen. "This is McIntire Park in Charlottesville. Over the past twelve months, it has gone through extensive renovations and is due to be opened today by the president. After all, it's his hometown."

Everyone in the room made the connection before they were told. Kane said, "That's why the UAV was stolen. Montoya is going to hit it."

Thurston nodded. "That's our assumption."

"It seems our resident drug lord has grown himself some big balls," Jones growled.

"What's being done about it?" Cara asked.

"Nothing," Jones told her. "They're opening it at two pm today."

"Which means we need to stop it before it happens," Thurston added.

"Why us?" Reynolds asked. "Why not FBI? Or Secret Service?"

"It'll take too long to get them organized," Jones said. "Besides, I want this done right."

"By right you mean KIA every one of them?" Kane asked.

"Exactly, Gunny. Send all of them to Hell."

Teller joined the conversation. "They'll need somewhere out of the way to launch the Pred, yet still be within range."

Another picture flashed up on the screen. Thurston continued, "We think this is it. A farm outside of Charlottesville. It's secluded, and there is an area out the back for the UAV to be able to take off."

"You think?" Kane said.

"We're pretty sure. This will be the target of team two."

"Hold up," Kane interjected. "Team two?"

Ferrero said, "You heard right, Reaper. We're running two ops in conjunction with each other."

Kane was concerned. "Why?"

Another picture flashed up. "I know that place," Traynor said. "It's the DEA offsite evidence store."

"That's right," Thurston agreed. "It currently holds twenty million of Montoya's money. I wonder where that came from?"

"So, you're saying that he intends to take his money back? From there?"

"Yes."

"Why not just have a shitload of guards posted to it?" Kane asked.

"Because we want to nail their asses, not scare them off. We scare off whoever does it, then they pop up somewhere else. Besides. Montoya could be at either one of the target sites."

"Or none of them," Kane pointed out.

"I guess we'll find out, won't we, Gunny?"

"Yes, sir."

Thurston continued. "Like I said, there will be two teams. Kane will lead team one and Billings team two." Her eyes drifted over to Kane. "You want to tell me who you want on each team?"

Kane thought briefly. "Axe and Brick can go with Cara. I'll take Carlos. I want Traynor too."

The ex-DEA agent snorted. "Just what I need. To get shot at again."

Reaper smiled. "I'll look after you, Pete. Besides, you know your way around the place, yes?"

Traynor nodded.

"How much time do we have to prep?"

Thurston's face was grim. "You don't. As soon as we've finished here, team two will be transported to a waiting Black Hawk which will insert them about two clicks from target one. Understand this, the UAV must be stopped. Captain Sean Richards will be on site, and if you can't stop the UAV, then you stop him."

Thurston's eyes lingered on Cara to make sure she understood what was being implied. Cara nodded but remained silent. Then she said, "Ma'am, I'd like to take Teller with my team. If something happens and the UAV gets airborne, and the captain is KIA, we'll need someone to bring the bird down."

Nodding, Thurston said, "Do it."

"What about our target?" Kane asked. "Do we have blueprints or anything?"

Ferrero said, "You've got what's in Traynor's head to start with. I'll see if I can dig something else up for you. The good part about your mission is that your target building is only three blocks away."

"I don't like it," Reaper growled. "If we don't intercept the assault team before they get inside, there's going to be hell to pay."

"A good thing it's Sunday then, isn't it?"

"What's that got to do with it?"

"There's no one in that building on a Sunday. It is all under security camera feed. That's why we figure they'll hit it today."

"Let's hope so."

"All right," Thurston snapped. "Gear up. Cara, by the time you reach your target, we'll have satellite link. That should help you out some."

"Yes, ma'am."

"Good luck."

———

In the parking garage beneath the hotel, Cara and the rest of her team readied their tactical gear which had been stored in the SUVs. Everything apart from their weapons, of course, which they'd kept in their rooms. Kane gathered them around to make sure they were good to go.

"Everybody watch your asses out there. Collins and his men aren't your average gun nuts. They've nearly all had training courtesy of Uncle Sam."

Cara said, "The bit I don't like is having no prep."

"Hopefully a bird overhead will help with that."

"Brick, strip your kit to a bare minimum."

"Copy that."

Axe thumbed fresh loads into a magazine for the M110 he was going to be using. "I'll keep an eye on them, Reaper. I'll be their fairy godmother."

Kane smiled. "Shit, that conjures images of you in a tutu. I think I might just throw up."

Once they were finished, Cara said, "Time to go. Teller, you drive."

"Yes, ma'am."

The team climbed into the SUV, but Cara hung back. She stared at Kane and said, "I'll see you when we return."

"You got this?"

"I'm good."

"Don't second guess yourself, OK? You've already proved yourself to these guys. They'll follow you anywhere."

Cara nodded. "Don't forget to duck."

CHAPTER 23

"BRAVO, COMMS CHECK, OVER."

Thurston's voice came back over the radio. "Read you loud and clear, Reaper Two."

"Team two is on the ground and moving towards the target, over."

"Copy. Bravo, out."

The sound of the retreating Black Hawk was long gone. The pilot was under instructions to fly to a holding position three clicks to the east and put down in a field there to await further orders, or to offer air support to Cara's team.

"Axe, you're point. Brick, watch our six. Let's move."

Apart from Axe, each team member was armed with their usual HK416. Once they reached their target, Axe would break off and provide overwatch with the SASS. Provided that there was a spot for him to do so.

They made their way through the trees towards the farm, careful as they went because Collins was sure to have some kind of early warning system up. When they were five-hundred meters from the farmhouse, the trees stopped. To continue, they had to cross open ground.

Plus, there was another problem. The UAV was on the makeshift runway. And it was moving.

Cara hissed. "Axe, find yourself a hide."

"Copy."

"Bravo Four, are you seeing this? Over."

"Just looking at it now, Reaper Two. Our satellite feed had just come online."

"You need to stop that thing, Reaper Two," Thurston snapped. "Whatever it takes."

"Copy. Four, do you have any thermals from the buildings?"

"Roger, Reaper Two. In the barn and the house. A bigger heat signature is coming from the barn."

"That's where the console will be," Teller said. "If you can get me to it, even if it takes off, I can stop it."

"Bravo, can you tell how many people are in the house? Over."

"Three. That could be the wife and child with one guard."

"Copy."

"Axe, are you in position?"

"Yes, ma'am."

"Ok. We're moving in. Weapons hot. Brick, you think you can clear that house?"

"Yes, ma'am."

"Follow me."

As soon as Cara stepped out into the open, the Predator's Rotax 914F turbocharged four-cylinder engine, with one hundred fifteen horsepower of thrust, sent it rumbling along the grassy runway.

———

NEW YORK CITY—SAME TIME

Kane, Arenas, and Traynor sat in the SUV and patiently waited for things to happen. Each man was dressed in a tactical vest and armed with suppressed HK416s. The street where they were parked was busy, but Kane figured that had it been a weekday, it would have been a lot busier.

Cars passed with regular monotony as commuters went about Sunday business. They called New York the city that never sleeps. His guess was that Sundays were the same as every other day.

"I don't like this, Zero," Kane said. "Even though there's no one in the building, there's still plenty of pedestrians and vehicular traffic."

"Just take the intercept off the street, Reaper. Try and keep it that way. Once they enter the building, then move."

"Have we got any movement yet."

"Nothing suspicious."

"Pete, where is the money stored?"

"Downstairs in the first basement."

"What's in the second basement?"

"That's where they keep all the firearms."

"Shit. This keeps getting better."

Ten minutes later, a van appeared along the street. It was plain white, unmarked, and traveling at speed. Just as it approached the DEA evidence store, it swung wide and turned towards the building itself. Right before it plowed into the front of the building, the driver jumped out.

The van crashed through the brick façade of the building and came to a sudden stop. As they watched from their SUV, the driver came to his feet and ran off. Then realization hit Kane right between the eyes.

"Get down! It's a bomb!"

Then the van blew up in a blinding orange flash.

————

OUTSIDE CHARLOTTESVILLE, VIRGINIA

The Predator drone lifted from the makeshift runway and Cara cursed their predicament. She let loose with a burst of fire from her 416 and saw her target fall. Off to her right, she caught sight of Brick firing his own burst as he advanced on the house.

"Be aware, Bravo, the Pred has just taken off. It's armed with a missile. Copy?"

"Copy, Reaper Two."

To her front, Cara saw three men emerge from the barn. One of them jerked and fell to the ground. Axe's voice filled her head. "Scratch one tango."

Collins' men returned heavy fire and bullets split the air all around Cara. She saw one man running towards the house and reacted instantly. Her sights dropped onto him and she let loose with another burst.

Thurston's voice came over the comms. "Reaper One, you've got exactly three minutes before that UAV is in position to fire that Hellfire. If they launch it, the president is toast."

"Nothing like a bit of pressure, Bravo," she breathed into her mic. Then, "Step it up, people. We've got three minutes. After that, we're screwed."

In an instant, things changed. Someone on the other side fired an M203 Grenade Launcher. In a spray of metal splinters and debris, Cara was knocked flat on her back.

Then she heard the cry come through her comms from Axe. "Man down! I say again, man down! Reaper Two is hit!"

NEW YORK CITY—SAME TIME

The explosion rocked the SUV so much that Kane thought it might tip over. Every window facing the blast was punched in, spraying glass all over those within. They were stunned by the impact for a moment, but then Kane's training kicked in.

"Is everyone OK?"

A few low groans of yes told him all he needed to know. "Zero? Reaper One. They just drove a fucking bomb into the building. Over."

"Say again your last, Reaper One."

"I said it was a bomb, Zero. In a van. Send EMTs and fire department. We're going to take a look."

"Copy. We felt it from here. Is everyone OK?"

"We're still alive."

"It doesn't make sense, Reaper. Why would they blow up the building?"

Kane turned in his seat and stared at Traynor. He still looked stunned. "Hey, Pete, why would they blow up the building like this?"

"Huh?"

"Concentrate, man. Why would Montoya blow up the fucking building?"

"How should I know?"

They were about to climb from the SUV when the first NYPD cruiser screeched to a stop with its siren wailing and lights flashing. The officer leaped from it and stood, scratching his head as he took in the scene before him.

Where the van had blown, it had taken out most of the front of the building. The upper levels that were left hung precariously over the charred and debris-strewn chasm, threatening to come crashing down at any moment. Two more cruisers pulled up, and their drivers gathered and began a three-way conversation. One indicated the gaping hole while another pointed at the upper floors. Then they turned around and looked up and down the street, working out where to set the perimeter.

Thick dust hung in the air, and now smoke could be seen rising into the pale blue sky above. Sirens blared, and yet more cruisers pulled up. The first paramedics arrived on scene and then a fire truck.

"Reaper One, copy?"

"Copy, Zero."

"What's happening? Over."

"Things are starting to get busy here, Luis."

"Do you want to stand down?"

"Wait one."

While Kane watched, the first responders sprang into action, going about their business. Except for the firemen who stood back. One of them started towards the building but was called back, and Kane assumed, was told to stand down.

Then a thought hit him. "Traynor, is there another way into this place?"

"What?"

"Another way in that I don't know about?"

Traynor thought for a moment and shook his head. "I'm not sure."

"Zero? I need to know if there's another way into the store. Over."

"Give me a minute."

Carlos said, "Those policemen will be over here checking on us shortly. We need to work out what we're going to do next."

Kane nodded. "Pete, go and show them your creds. Fill them in on what we know. I'll be with you in a moment. And don't let some trigger-happy cop shoot you."

The ex-DEA man climbed out and walked towards a tall officer who was giving directions to a fireman. For a moment he seemed taken aback at the sight of a man dressed in tactical gear walking towards him. But Traynor already had his identification out which seemed to set the officer's mind at ease.

"Reaper One, this is Zero, over."

"Copy, Zero."

"Reaper, we've managed to track down old blueprints, and apparently an abandoned subway station is situated alongside the first basement level of the DEA store. At some stage, the line was meant to go under the river to link up at Hoboken. But someone screwed up, and it couldn't be done. Anyhow the station is still down there."

"Christ!" Reaper swore. "That's it. This is a decoy. They're coming in from below."

Climbing from the SUV with his 416, Kane said, "Carlos, grab your NVGs."

Kane opened the back door of the vehicle and took out Traynor's carbine. Then he went to the back where Arenas was. The Mexican handed him his helmet and attached NVGs. Then Kane took Traynor's.

The rear door closed, and both men started towards Traynor and the cop with purposeful strides. When they sensed what was happening, both men looked in their direction. The cop's jaw dropped, and the former DEA agent knew what was coming. "Does this mean what I think it does?"

"They're coming in through the basement level," Kane snapped and tossed him his 416. His helmet followed.

"What's going on?" asked the bewildered cop.

"We're going inside," Kane told him.

"I – I can't let you do that. It's too dangerous."

The three men pushed past him and kept walking. Kane said, "You can come along if you want."

———

OUTSIDE CHARLOTTESVILLE, VIRGINIA

Cara drew in deep breaths, and her ears rang with a high-pitched squeal. She rolled onto her side and was aware of bullets sending up small eruptions all around her. In her ear, she heard Brick say, "Stay down, Two. I'll be right there."

"No," Cara hissed. "Get to the family. I'm fine. Axe get that fucker with the two-oh-three before he kills one of us."

"On it."

Teller moved to her position and helped her to her feet. "Can't hang around here all day, ma'am."

Suddenly he grunted and twisted violently. He dropped to the ground and immediately Cara could see the bright red blood on his upper left arm.

"Christ! Man down!" Cara swore and grabbed him by the collar with her left hand. She started to drag him along with her, the 416 in her right hand spitting out lead.

"Cara, leave him!" Axe snapped in her ear.

"Reaper Two, you have one minute to stop the launch," Thurston said. "What are you doing?"

"Damn it, ma'am. You have to leave me. You have to get to the barn to stop the launch."

"It's too fucking late!" she hissed. "I can't make it."

"Reaper Two, this is Viper One-Three. We're a flight of two AH-64s tasked as air support. Over."

Tasked? I never asked for air support.

"Say again, Viper One-Three."

"Just tell us what to shoot, ma'am," the pilot said as the two Apaches swept overhead.

"Forty-five seconds, Reaper One," Thurston said in her ear.

"Call the shot, Cara," Axe growled.

More bullets snapped close to her head, and she dropped to her knee. Through gritted teeth, Teller said, "If you destroy the control system and the UAV loses signal, it will RTB, ma'am. It's all we have."

"Thirty seconds."

"Shit! The barn, Viper One-Three. Hit the barn. Cleared hot."

"Copy, ma'am. Missile away."

"Reaper Team, get down!"

Cara dived across Teller and covered her head with her arms. She could hear the inbound Hellfire above her. Suddenly the barn erupted in a huge ball of flame. The heat from the explosion washed over the two prone team members, followed by the concussive blast.

Debris started to rain down in large clumps. The mushroom cloud had been replaced by flames spewing black smoke into the air.

Cara barked into her mic, "All elements, report."

"Four, OK."

"Five, OK."

Teller groaned, "You're a solid unit, ma'am."

She rolled off him and sat up. "Brick, save the family."

"Ma'am."

Cara stared at the blazing pyre that had been the barn. A pang of guilt tugged at her heart, but she quickly pushed it aside. There would be time for that after. She came to her feet. "Pete, are you OK?"

"I'll be fine."

"Reaper Two, report."

"Target destroyed, Bravo Three is wounded, but ambulatory. Moving on the house."

"Copy, Reaper Two."

"Go, I'll be fine," Teller told her.

Cara raised her 416 and swept the scene before her as she moved. "Axe, you got anything?"

"Negative."

That was when a smoldering figure staggered from behind the blazing barn, holding a Bullpup assault rifle. An FN FS2000. And it was pointed straight at Cara.

NEW YORK CITY—SAME TIME

Kane led them down the stairs towards the first basement level. Directly behind him was Teller, then the cop whose name was Miller. Lastly came Arenas. Their footsteps seemed to echo loudly as they descended the concrete thoroughfare. The stairwell had been their only option with the lifts being rendered unusable due to the power outage from the explosion. The store, however, had its own backup power system for lighting which had engaged immediately after the other had cut out.

Kane called a halt when the four of them reached the

door with a large B1 stenciled on it in bold black letters. He said to Arenas in a hoarse whisper, "When we breach, you follow me. Pete, you follow Carlos. Miller, you wait out here."

"I ain't afraid," Miller hissed with a hint of indignance in his voice.

"I didn't say you were," Kane assured him. "But on the other side of this door are trained killers with automatic weapons. And all you've got is that Glock. Watch our backs."

Miller nodded. "OK."

The three assaulters moved into position and waited for Kane's signal. Traynor stepped to the right of the door and reached out to try the door handle. Twisting it, he found it open. Looking back to Reaper, he nodded. Kane raised his 416 to his shoulder and nodded back.

This time Traynor turned the handle all the way then pushed the door open. Without any hesitation, Kane strode through into a dimly-lit room lined with metal cages.

He swept the room and found it empty, then walked further in. With the cages lined against the walls, it resembled a long, steel-lined passage.

Heading towards a doorway at the far end of the thoroughfare, perhaps sixty feet away, his breathing was loud in his ears, and his heart was pounding. He kept his sights on the opening ahead of him, prepared should one of Montoya's hired guns appear.

It surprised him, however, when a man appeared less than fifteen feet in front of him, not from the doorway itself. The black-clad figure emerged from an open cage, carrying two canvas bags Kane could only assume held bricks of money.

He caught a glimpse of the armed men advancing on

his position and released the bags in his hands. Next, he reached for his slung M4 and desperately tried to bring it around to fire. Kane was too quick for him, even though he'd been caught a little off guard himself.

Reaper squeezed the trigger on the 416 twice. The flat cracks of the suppressed fire bounced off the concrete surrounds. The man in front of him jerked as both slugs struck home. The first hit his tactical vest, the second, slightly higher, in the throat. The mercenary dropped to the floor, slumped over the money-filled bags.

Kane moved quickly forward and stepped over the corpse. He glanced into the cage as he went past and saw that it still held money. The others followed him to the end of the passage then paused as Kane peered around the jamb. The next space was far more open with larger cages. On the other side of the room were two large doors to what Kane guessed was a huge elevator. That would have been how they got the four vehicles down there. One was a Humvee, another a Shelby Cobra, and the last two were a pair of matching Mustangs, one complete with bullet holes.

"Moving," he whispered into his mic and eased around the corner...

...into a hail of automatic gunfire from a MAC-11 held by Juan Montoya.

Bullets gouged chips of painted concrete from the walls in a diagonal pattern. Kane went down on one knee and fired reflexively. His burst went wide, although it had the desired effect.

Montoya sought cover behind one of the Mustangs. The one without the bullet holes in it. However, that was rectified with the squeeze of the trigger on Arenas' 416. The suppressed carbine rattled off two bursts, smashing the car's front window and grill.

The cartel boss rose and emptied another magazine with one squeeze of the trigger. Then, through a jagged hole in the wall, another shooter emerged. He held an M4 and started to fire shots with more efficiency. It forced the three team members to seek cover. The Humvee provided the best they could hope for. Bullets slammed into the solid vehicle like large hailstones from a fierce storm. Traynor rose and fired a single shot. More by luck than design, the 5.56 round took the shooter in the face, killing him when the misshapen slug ricocheted off bone and up into his brain.

"Fucking asshole," Traynor hissed. "Ever since joining this team, people are always trying to fucking kill me."

Something hard hit the floor and Kane heard it roll closer. It sounded like it stopped under the Humvee, so he bent down to have a look. His eyes widened when he saw what it was. At the top of his voice, he shouted, *"Grenade!"*

CHAPTER 24

WHEN THE ATTACK STARTED, Captain Ward Collins was at the console, watching over the launch of the Predator. His headset came to life with warnings of intruders. Issuing orders to his men to stop whoever it was, he then said to Richards, "Get that thing within range or I'll kill your family myself."

"I'm doing it, I'm doing it. Please don't hurt them."

Outside, the sound of battle echoed across the farm. Calls came over the comms as he lost two of his men. Then more, and finally the Apache thundered overhead. He hesitated for a moment. "How long before we launch?"

"Thirty seconds."

"Just make sure it happens," he demanded and picked up the FN FS2000 and walked towards the back door of the barn. Collins had only just walked through it when the missile struck.

The explosion was deafening, the searing white heat

intense. But somehow through it all, Ward Collins remained conscious. His clothes felt as though they were on fire, the left side of his face seemed as though it had melted away. Blind in his left eye where the heat had seared it, he staggered to his feet. His weapon was still in his right hand; his left was nothing but scorched meat.

With pain ripping through his body, Collins limped around the barn until he saw the person dressed in tactical gear to his front. With a groaning snarl, he raised his FS 2000. "Fug yah!" he managed to mumble and started to squeeze the trigger.

———

Cara saw the man's head snap back and the brains explode from it as the 7.62 round from Axe's M110 punched through it. Collins dropped to the ground like a marionette with its strings cut.

"Tango down," Axe breathed into his mic.

Cara heaved a sigh of relief. "Thanks, Axe."

"My pleasure."

Now Cara moved towards the house. As she did, she said, "Keep an eye out for any more."

"Copy."

By the time she reached the building, Brick had already breached. Cara had started to move along the sparsely-decorated hall when she heard the flat slap of the suppressed 416 and then the cries of alarm from a woman and child. Then came the voice of the former SEAL as he tried to calm them.

Cara shouted, "Friendly!"

Brick appeared from a room ten feet in front to her left. "In here, ma'am."

"How are they, Brick?"

"They seem fine, all things considered."

"You got this?"

"Yes, ma'am."

Cara said into her mic, "Bravo, packages secured."

"Copy, Reaper Two."

She emerged from the house and scanned the scene before her. The barn was still blazing, there were bodies strewn in the grass, and Teller was walking towards her, holding his wounded arm. She said, "Axe, anything?"

"No, ma'am. I think we got them all."

"Come on down."

"Copy."

Behind her, Brick escorted the two hostages from the house. The mother, a thin woman with dark hair, came up to her. "My husband. Where's my husband?"

Cara stared at her for a moment, the solemnity of the situation evident in her eyes. She gave her head a slight shake and said, "I'm sorry, Mrs. Richards. Your husband didn't make it."

The woman sank slowly to her knees, a high-pitched sound emanating from the back of her throat. The little girl ran across to her mother and wrapped her arms around her. Not fully comprehending the gravity of the situation, she said innocently, "It'll be OK, mommy. I'll help you."

Feeling the tears start to well in her eyes, Cara turned away. She went to speak, and her voice caught in her throat. Then she tried again. "Bravo? Reaper Two. Target secure."

"Copy, Reaper Two. Good job."

———

NEW YORK CITY—SAME TIME

When the grenade blew, it lifted the heavy, armored Humvee off the floor at least six inches. Flames and metal shards shot out from under it across the floor in all directions. Kane and the others hugged the floor, praying that none would find any vulnerable spots on their person.

The BOOM! of the explosion bounced off the thick walls and threatened to burst eardrums. Kane winced as his ears rang from the blast and for a moment his vision blurred. Through the dust of the disturbance, he saw Montoya stumble out of the hole in the wall. Reaper came to his feet, staggered, then brought up his 416 and fired a sustained burst. More from frustration than anything.

"Shit! Zero, Montoya is squirting out through the old subway, over."

"Copy, Reaper. If you lose him in there, he could emerge anywhere within two city blocks."

"I'd best not lose him then."

Kane lurched across to Arenas who was trying to regain his feet. Grabbing him by the arm, he helped him up. Arenas smiled, or rather grimaced, at him. "Thank you, *amigo*," he shouted above the ringing in his ears.

Behind them, Traynor limped across. "Are you OK?" Kane asked.

"Hit my fucking knee when I dived on the floor."

"Will you be all right?"

"I'll manage."

"Bring up Miller. Carlos and I'll go after Montoya."

Kane and Arenas started towards the hole in the wall. The room was filling up with thick, choking smoke from the Humvee. A shooter leaned around the jagged edge of the opening and fired a burst. Instead of diving for cover,

Kane had had enough. He fired a shot from the 416, and the shooter disappeared.

"I wish I had a flashbang about now," Reaper said to Arenas.

"Fuck it, *amigo*. Let's do this."

Arenas led the way. He dived through the opening, spraying rounds as he went. He figured if there was anyone on the other side, they would be one of the bad guys. Safe bet.

But there was no one. The open space of the platform was empty. "Reaper One to Zero. Copy?"

The radio crackled, and Kane said, "Say again, Zero."

Then, "Copy, Reaper."

"This place is lit up like a Christmas tree, Luis. Any idea where we can cut the power to it?"

"Are you sure?"

"Of course I'm damned sure. It's almost damned well blinding me."

"Sorry, Reaper. I wasn't talking to you. Wait one."

"While you're at it, might pay to try and divert some assets to cover some of the exits."

"Already done. About that power, I'm surprised it's on, that place has been shut up for years."

Kane ignored him and waved to Arenas. He'd seen the boot prints in the years of built-up dust and grime on the floor. They lead along the platform straight ahead.

"Reaper, you copy?"

Kane signaled Arenas to follow him. He raised his 416 to shoulder height, and they started along the platform. They passed two large columns and then an old garbage bin sitting on a short pole base.

"Reaper...? Zero...you..."

Kane turned his comms off.

The trail continued along the edge of the drop off that

led down to the tracks. Thirty meters further along, they disappeared where Montoya and his man had jumped onto the tracks below.

Kane and Arenas climbed down, the gravel crunching under their boots. The ex-special forces commander walked across to the platform on the other side. He checked to see if anyone had climbed out there but found nothing. Crossing back over to Kane, he said, "There is nothing. They must have kept going along the tracks."

Staring along the darkened tunnel, there was no sound nor sign that anyone had gone that way. Kane said, "They can't have gone too far, not carrying bags of money."

"They could be waiting to see if we follow," Arenas pointed out.

"Well, shit," Kane snorted, lowering his NVGs into position. "Let's not keep them waiting."

Arenas followed suit, and together they walked into the luminous green tunnel. As they did so, both men turned on their laser sights, the red lines reaching out through the space and into oblivion.

Kane worked his way across to the right side of the tunnel, while Arenas worked the left. As the pair moved further in, the smell of damp earth and mildew became stronger. Ahead on their left was a maintenance door, and it was open.

"There," Kane said, lighting it with his laser sight. "They went that way."

The two team men climbed from the tracks and passed through the doorway. Ahead of them was a narrow, concrete tunnel, graffitied on both sides with numerous tags. At the end of the passage was a set of stairs going up.

Kane and Arenas made their way to the top and

stopped at the narrow twin doors. They lifted their NVGs and Kane tried the left side door. It swung open. There was no one on the other side. The entrance to the system had been well camouflaged down the end of a debris-strewn alley...

...and disappearing from the mouth and onto the street was a white van.

"That's them!" Kane snapped. "Come on."

The two men started to jog along the alley. Kane switched his comms on and said, "Zero, copy?"

"Where the hell have you been, Reaper?" Ferrero growled.

"No time. We're back above ground and Montoya is getting away in a white van. He's just turned left onto... shit, I don't know. Don't even have a damn idea where we are. We're in pursuit."

"That's OK. I'll see if we can pick you up."

Reaching the end of the alley, Kane searched for a signpost. He found what he wanted and said, "Hudson Street! He turned left onto Hudson."

Suddenly both men became aware of the pedestrian traffic on the sidewalk. Or the lack of it. Many of the people had stopped completely and were staring at the two men in their tactical gear. Some had started to back off, while others, a sign of the times, started filming with cell phones.

"There!" Arenas cried out, pointing at the van stopped at lights in the distance.

"We've got the van you're after, Reaper," Ferrero said over the comms. "We think so, anyway. It's currently stopped at lights on West Houston."

"Copy, Zero. That's the one. We currently have eyes on. Shit, he's turning left."

Kane and Arenas jogged along the sidewalk. The

pedestrians in front of them seemed to peel to either side at the sight of the armed men running towards them.

"This way," Arenas said when they reached King Street. "I think I know where he's going."

"What do you mean?"

"He'll need to get out of the city fast before they shut it down, right? They'll do that because of the bomb?"

"Yeah."

"The only way to do that is by air."

"Yes."

"So, he'll need somewhere big enough to put a helicopter down. It's the only option."

"Pier Forty."

"Exactly."

"Zero, we think he's headed for Pier Forty. Check the area for any inbound air traffic."

"Copy."

They ran along the pavement to the end of King Street, then took their lives into their own hands and ran out onto Greenwich Street without hesitation. Car tires screeched, and horns honked as drivers jammed on their brakes. One vehicle stopped an inch short of Kane, and the driver cursed at him as he disappeared behind a truck.

"Reaper, Slick has just informed me that..."

The rest was lost in the noise of a helicopter flying overhead.

"Got it, Zero," Kane snapped as he turned right to run along Washington Street. "Looks like you were right, Carlos."

"Let's hope we can get there before he takes off."

Once the pair reached West Houston, they were starting to labor from running so far under the weight of their tactical gear. Their hearts were pounding, and their lungs seemed like they were about to burst. But still, they pushed on. Turning left, they reached the six-lane carriageway which consisted of West Street and Westside Highway. On the far side, the helicopter was now visible as it came to a hover above the green football field encapsulated by the Pier 40 structure. It was an Agusta Westland AW169.

Digging deep once more, Kane and Arenas continued running. Amid the blare of car horns, they traversed the last paved obstacle before reaching the white van parked outside the entrance.

Kane brought up the 416 and checked the van. The back was empty as was the front. "Zero, we've found the van empty. Proceeding inside."

"Copy, Reaper One. Backup is on the way. DEA has agents *enroute*."

When they broke out onto the football field, the helicopter had almost touched down. Waiting impatiently for it were two men. One was tall, with a shaved head, and the other was Montoya, gesticulating wildly with his left hand.

The big man seemed to sense their presence and whirled about. On seeing them, he brought up his M4 and let loose with a sustained burst.

Angry lead hornets filled the air surrounding Kane and Arenas. Both men dropped to their knees and returned fire. They scored hits to the shooter's chest, but his vest took the full force of the bullets.

Any day of the week, such impacts would floor a normal man. But Hall was far from normal. Instead of dropping, he staggered, shook the blows off, and fired more rounds from the M4.

"Headshot," Kane snapped.

He and Arenas squeezed their triggers at the same time. Two 5.56 rounds slammed into Hall's head. One just above the bridge of his nose, the second high on his forehead. Blood sprayed from the back of his bald pate and was whipped away in the downdraft from the chopper.

Montoya was now on his own. He was about to climb aboard the helicopter when Kane sprayed it with gunfire. The pilot reflexively yanked on the cyclic, and the helicopter pitched up and across to the right. It careened out of control across the field and slammed into the side near the top carpark. A great fireball erupted as the fuel tank ruptured on impact and the highly-volatile Avgas ignited. Black smoke billowed up into the sky above.

The cartel boss was flung from his feet, his not so white suit now with grass-stains.

Kane and Arenas never even flinched. They walked forward, 416s raised to cover their target. Montoya recovered himself and fought to bring the MAC-11 around. A bullet from Reaper punched into his gun arm, and the MAC fell from nerveless fingers.

Montoya's snarl was filled with pain and rage. "Come on, you fucking *puta*. Do your best."

Both Kane and Arenas closed in on the cartel boss. "Looks like we got us our fish, *amigo*," Kane said.

"He doesn't look like the big fishy in the pond anymore," Arenas said. "More like the little one that gets thrown back."

"What now?" Montoya sneered. "Prison? Your jails cannot hold me. And when I get out this time, I will kill you, your families. *Follaré a tus esposas y les cortaré la garganta!*"

Kane glanced at Arenas. "Did he just say something about having sex with our wives and murdering them?"

Arenas nodded. "*Sí*. In his own special way."

"Uh huh," Kane nodded and shot Montoya in the head.

"Zero? Reaper One. Target is down, I say again, the target is down."

He stared at Arenas. "You got a problem with that?"

The former Mexican special forces commander shrugged his shoulders. "It saved me from doing it."

EPILOGUE

THURSTON STARED hard at the team gathered before her in the briefing room. "The president has asked me to pass on his gratitude for neutralizing the Montoya threat and for taking out Collins and his mercenaries. He wants all of you to go to Washington so he can parade you in front of the nation's media."

"You're shitting me," Axe growled.

Thurston shook her head. "No, it's what he wants. However, I told General Jones that it wouldn't be possible. Doing something like that would have you all compromised. Yes, it is inevitable that one day your faces will all hit the television screens or front pages of newspapers. But until then, I would like to do everything I can to not have you all exposed."

The general paused before continuing. "I have to say, for our first time out together, I am impressed at the way you all operate. Now we'll find out how good you all are at paperwork. I want reports on my desk by the end of the week."

Teller held up his sling and smiled. "I may have a problem."

"Did you get shot in the tongue?"

"No, ma'am."

"Then tell someone else your report, and they can type it for you."

"Ha!" Axe guffawed loudly.

Thurston shifted her gaze to him. "And Axe just volunteered."

"What?"

"Reaper, Cara, my office," Thurston snapped.

They followed the general out of the briefing room and into her office. She sat behind her desk and stared at them both. "I'm impressed by the way you both lead your team."

"Ma'am," they both said together. Then Kane added, "We're glad to have you on board too. Don't get me wrong, Luis is a great operational leader, but he doesn't have your clout."

"Thank you. I also wanted to ask if you would like your family moved closer? Maine is a long way away. I thought closer would be more convenient."

Kane shook his head. "No thank you, ma'am. The further my sister is away from me, the better. Even with what happened, I still think she's better off."

"My thoughts too, ma'am," Cara said.

"OK. It was just a thought. One last thing. The new man, Brick Peters. How did he go all up?"

"I've no problem, ma'am," Cara said. "He's more than capable."

"And if you keep on giving us these tough assignments, a medic is bound to come in handy," Kane added.

"All right. Dismiss."

They left the office and stopped outside the door. Kane turned to Cara and asked her, "What do you think?"

"Beer?"

"Why not? Get the team together, and we'll find a bar we can haunt."

"What about the reports?"

Kane smiled. "They'll wait."

A LOOK AT: TERMINATION ORDER
A TEAM REAPER THRILLER

IT IS A FIGHT THAT THE TEAM CANNOT LOSE, FOR TO DO SO MEANS DEATH...

Strap yourself in while Brent Towns takes you for an action-packed thrill ride in book three of the Team Reaper series.

It started with two cataclysmic events: the cold-blooded killing of a Pakistani journalist by a CIA special ops team, and the murder of a young woman in Los Angeles.

From the Mojave Desert to the mean streets of L.A., then on to Europe. Team Reaper finds themselves in a bloody battle with an elite special forces team while trying to save one of their own, who is on a personal crusade of vengeance and has been marked with a termination order.

The bad news for the other side, they're about to find out that the "Reaper" is real!

Can they outmaneuver a lethal special forces unit to save their own, or will the Reaper claim another soul?

AVAILABLE FEBRUARY 2025

ABOUT THE AUTHOR

A relative newcomer to the world of writing, Brent Towns self-published his first book in 2015. Last Stand in Sanctuary took him two years to write. His first hardcover book, a Black Horse Western, was published the following year.

Since then, he has written twenty-six western stories, including some in collaboration with British western author, Ben Bridges; several action adventure novels, such as his bestselling Team Reaper series; the novelization to the 2019 movie, Bill Tilghman and the Outlaws; as well as scripted a handful of Commando Comics. Not bad for an Australian author, he thinks.

Often up until the small hours of the night, bashing away at his tortured keyboard in Queensland, Australia, Brent loves to lose himself in the world of fiction. If you're interested in sharing your thoughts in more detail, scan the QR code below! Your feedback is invaluable to him—and often helps shape his future writing endeavors.